In the Name
of the
Otherworld

HERMIONE LEE

This is a work of fiction. Names, characters, places, and incidents are products of the author's imagination or are used fictitiously and are not to be construed as real. Any resemblance to actual events, locations, organizations, or persons, living or dead, is entirely coincidental.

World Castle Publishing, LLC
Pensacola, Florida
Copyright © Hermione Lee 2021
Paperback ISBN: 9781955086363
eBook ISBN: 9781955086370
First Edition World Castle Publishing, LLC, September 21, 2021
http://www.worldcastlepublishing.com
Licensing Notes
Cover: Hermione Lee & Karen Fuller
Editor: Maxine Bringenberg

TABLE OF CONTENTS

Dedication

For my incredible parents. Mom and Dad, you nurtured me with tales of classic and modern, of fantasy and science fiction, of romance and mystery, fostering a profound love for reading in me. You made me who I am today.

Acknowledgements

For every writer, a fiery flame of passion for writing flares within. Because of the firewood each and every one of you has kindly provided, the blazing fire in me continues to burn more vigorously than ever....

Dear Mom and Dad: When I was young, you satisfied my insatiable curiosity with stories. I, the avid reader, am now an author, and I pay it forward, contributing to the marvelous world of literature, a book I myself have penned, as a salute to all the stories that broadened my horizons. Mom and Dad, I hope you know how big an influence you had on me and how much you deserve to be on this list.

Dear Aunt Rebecca: I remember the day you called and offered your honest critique on my first manuscript. Every word of yours enlightened me, eventually leading me to the recognition of my flaws. Because of you, my craft of writing has skyrocketed during the past years, and I attribute my growth—both in skill and in character—to you.

Dear Grandma or Ama: Pure ecstasy reigned me every time I wrote at your cozy home, a veritable paradise for writers. You pampered me with delicious home-cooked meals and a comfortable armchair to nestle in while I worked my magic on paper. Thank you for all the seemingly insignificant yet heartwarming little things you did for me.

Dear Maxine: Words fail to express my gratitude and appreciation for all the effort and time you spent on perfecting my story, every sentence, every word, and even every comma and period. You never pressured me with deadlines or urged me to hurry up. Instead, you always told me to take my time and make my changes. I am touched by everything you did and all the long nights you devoted to my book. You are a remarkable lady, and I am incredibly lucky to have you as my editor.

Dear Karen: I had never known the true meaning of euphoria until the day you informed me of your decision to publish my book. It was you who granted me the ticket to the Pearly Gates of publication, exposing me to a whole new world of endless possibilities. You saw the potential behind a messy manuscript and bestowed upon me an invaluable opportunity to share my words with the world. You changed my life, and I have committed to my permanent memory, that sensational moment when I realized my dream was no longer merely a dream.

Dear friends and relatives: Thank you for your support and encouragement. Thanks to my two grandfathers, my other grandmother who is in Heaven, my uncles Henry and Bryan, my aunt Rose, my cousins, and all my teachers and neighbors. Also, a special thanks to my good friend, Abby, whose infectious positivity strengthened my confidence in my book.

Dear everyone who made this list: I thank you for everything you have done to make my dream a reality. I owe my success to each and every one of you.

Chapter One

MONOLOGUE OF A DREAMER
(ALEXANDRIA)

The golden medallion shaped like a unibird gleamed under the iridescent sunlight, a souvenir from the most unforgettable event in my life. Back then, before that miraculous adventure took place, I had not even the slightest inkling that everything about me, from my whimsical dreams to my relationships with others, was never a coincidence.

A few days before that life-changing event, I remember gazing into a full-length mirror that belonged to my foster sister, Daphne. In it, I saw a teenager staring back at me. I knew her past and present, just as she knew mine. Her long red hair, like a flow of sizzling lava, didn't match her features—asymmetrical eyes and a wide mouth. She looked plain, unattractive, and obviously lacked confidence.

That was me—Alexandria Richardson.

I lived in an orphanage for the first ten years of my life until a couple decided to foster me. The caretaker of the orphanage, Mr. Jones, told me that my parents abandoned me after I was born and sent me there. Three years later, leukemia claimed their lives.

The ten years in the orphanage was the worst experience

of my life. Every day, we got up at five to have breakfast—bags of off-brand cereals, which was never enough for so many of us. That left us with an empty feeling in our stomachs for the rest of the day. Lunch was even worse since the little pot of stew was always wolfed down by the older kids, leaving the rest of us with nothing to eat. We always had bread and margarine with a large pot of pea soup for dinner. Although the bread had a stale, musty taste, we had no choice but to eat it.

The orphanage treated us terribly. Our rooms were humid in summer and freezing in winter. Mr. Jones, a man with severe mysophobia, made us scrub the ten floors of the building every week, even when it was snowing outside and our fingers were numb and icy. Because of this, many little kids froze to death every year, but I, fortunately, wasn't one of them.

The older kids often threatened the younger ones to make them do their chores. I had the sense to not argue back since those who refused to comply always ended up in the infirmary. Many younger orphans, including me, were very used to getting hurt. The older ones were into a game which involved injuring us. We were forced to stand in a line, and they would throw bricks at our arms and legs. Every time their pointless game ended, there were bruises, cuts, and blood all over our limbs. Mr. Jones took no notice of the scars—or perhaps pretended not to—so the older kids were never punished.

Four years ago, a ray of light slanted into the abyss of my misery—a couple, Mr. and Mrs. Wilson, fostered me. They took in two orphans—me and Daphne, a bully my age who took delight in spreading rumors about my parentage. Despite the misfortune of having Daphne as my foster sister, I was overjoyed that I had found a family since I had always craved a real home. Unfortunately, Mr. Wilson was always busy at work, and when he left his office, he would drink with his friends until midnight. As for Mrs. Wilson, she spent every day attending galas, shopping at department stores, and having meals with wealthy socialites at deluxe restaurants. I was left home alone with Daphne every day.

Daphne, unlike me, was attractive yet vain. She spent almost every minute checking her reflection in the mirror, and her vanity had worsened since Mr. and Mrs. Wilson took us under their wing. She dyed her hair blue and wore black lip gloss. Pretty and popular, she was the queen bee of our school, always teasing the shy kids and pranking the teachers. However, that did not stop her from bullying me at home. She was always looking for reasons to start a quarrel or pick a fight with me by accusing me of things I'd never done. This was why I kept myself locked up in my room at all times, where I was safe from her fists. With my foster parents gone in the daytime, my days were filled with loneliness and isolation. The ray of light that had once smiled upon me had died, and the darkness of the abyss closed around me once again, leaving me stranded, wretched, and miserable. My hope of being accepted in a family that truly loved me was gone.

Countless nights I slept with nothing but tears to keep me company. Many times, I pondered to myself, *Maybe my birth was a mistake. Maybe it was a cruel joke fate played on me. Entering a world, being abandoned by my parents before I even had a memory, being mistreated and bullied.* I wanted to be anybody except for myself. I did not belong anywhere. I was a nuisance. An outsider. My existence was a disturbance to the world.

School was even worse. Even though my academic performance was acceptable, most teachers treated me like an outcast. Every time I got annoyed, sparks of fire would emit from my fingertips and zap at the others. Sometimes I could even make things blow up without meaning to. One moment I felt my anger mounting, fire licking my insides and flames burning in my eyes, and then the next—*boom*. Something beside me would explode.

I wasn't always hot-tempered. Years of dismissal, rejection and the traumatic experiences of being bullied had shaped me into an irritable person with accumulated hatred and darkness deep down. Despite this, I never really meant to hurt anyone and couldn't explain why the accidents would always occur in my presence. Unfortunately, that didn't stop the other kids from isolating me and depicting me as a witch who attacked people with sorcery. One time, when I accidentally started an explosion by glaring at the wooden podium in the auditorium, I discovered something appalling—I was immune to fire. But even though I kept this to myself, everyone pinned the accident on me because they claimed to have seen flames blazing in my pupils and sparks of fire dancing on my fingers before the podium exploded.

The podium incident nearly got me expelled. A week later, the school scheduled a meeting with Mr. and Mrs. Wilson, who then had a huge quarrel with the principal and the teachers. My foster parents insisted that magic and sorcery didn't exist and that the school was responsible for the explosions. That left the principal and teachers speechless, and they finally decided to resolve the matter by leaving it unresolved. After all, my foster parents had been right—magic did *not* exist. Since there was no logical explanation for the explosions, nobody could do anything about it. The news of how I had seemingly caused an explosion and escaped punishment spread through the school like wildfire, and that made me more alone than ever. Nobody paid me the slightest attention. Nobody even wanted to bully me. Instead, almost everyone steered clear of me, as if afraid I might attack them with my strange powers. I was a freak, a monster, a witch, a threat to their safety. Even Daphne, though constantly sending me reminders of her hatred of me, shunned me in the hallways.

Fortunately, not everyone kept their distance from me. I managed to befriend two girls—Clarissa and Eileen—after a few months of being a loner.

A tanned complexion had Clarissa, with curly, dirty-blonde hair parted neatly in the middle, large round eyes that often glistened with curiosity, and a wide mouth always curved into a pleasant smile. As an extrovert, she was sanguine and enthusiastic about almost everything, especially skydiving. She was also energetic, outgoing, and had a broad mind, as well as a naïve heart.

Eileen, the prettiest and smartest girl in our grade, had silky brown hair that she always wore in a sleek ponytail, green eyes that sparkled like two emeralds, and sweet, heart-shaped lips. Eileen was introverted and always spoke timidly. However, she had such an adorable manner that her shyness made her seem twice as precious. Both Clarissa and Eileen believed the school was being unfair about the explosions and were always there to support me whenever I needed them.

Apart from my peers, I also received some support from the teachers. I had been very fond of our previous language arts teacher, Evonne Fitzgerald. Ms. Fitzgerald was demure and seldom spoke. She had a mild temper and was always patient with us, encouraging us rather than raising her voice. Sadly, she had resigned from her job six months ago for some unknown reason.

Ms. Fitzgerald's successor was a brunette by the name of Helen Edmunds, whose fair complexion and cascading waist-length hair exemplified her beauty. Clarissa and Eileen disliked her for her strict character and prim manner, but I adored her wisdom and elegance. Ms. Edmunds had told me that she knew how it felt to be an outcast, having been one in her youth. She was the one who smoothed the wrinkles in my heart and brought me joy and hope, filling the empty void in me that my foster parents had failed to. I looked upon Ms. Edmunds as a family member I could confide in.

Always genuine and straightforward, our geography teacher Lilith Jackson earned my permanent respect by standing up to the principal and protesting against my expulsion. She insisted that he was absurd and that expelling students for something they never did would damage the school's reputation. She was never afraid to speak her mind, and I liked her boldness and outspokenness. Unlike many others, she was easy to be around.

Zachary Valentino—or Zack—was my English teacher. He was charismatic and cheerful, which made him popular with us students. Among the girls in my grade, many were infatuated with and worshipped him for his handsome appearance, light blond hair, and cerulean-blue eyes. I, on the other hand, admired him for a different reason—his amiable temperament and easygoing personality. The two of us shared some wonderful afternoons chatting in his classroom after school.

Nevertheless, the happiest times I had were the ones I spent alone, fantasizing about the impossible. I found great delight in the times when I was all by myself, roaming wild in my imagination, which was based on eccentric dreams I had at night.

In my dreams, whimsical beasts that did not exist in reality visited my mind — bearnixes, bears with bodies like phoenixes; unibirds, unicorns with great, feathery wings; kittenpillars, caterpillars with catlike heads; and dogfishes, dogs with scaly fish-bodies. The four creatures belonged in the Otherworld, a magical world home to people and animals with magical blood. I'd been there in my dreams countless times.

However, back then, I had no idea that everything about me, from my bizarre dreams to my relationships with others, was never a coincidence.

Little did I know what awaited me in the future.

Chapter Two

THE FOUNTAIN PORTAL
(EILEEN)

So many days and weeks have passed, and yet I still remember that wondrous adventure as though it were yesterday. Every now and then, I indulge myself in memories of that mission, reviewing and savoring every little detail of it.

***

It all happened one school day.

I arrived at school on a mundane Friday and immediately registered that something was wrong. The principal was not standing in front of the gates. Even though the school building looked the same as before, it was pervaded by an eerie atmosphere. Strangely enough, the campus was devoid of students.

Regardless, I walked into the school courtyard, only to discover that it was enveloped in strange swirls of purple mist. It was a peculiar sight since the sun had been shining earlier that morning, and I had awoken to the cacophony of cicadas humming in the late summer. The large white-bricked fountain was perched in the middle of the courtyard as usual. The waters glimmered, even though there was no sunlight; I shuddered and intuitively backed away. There were rumors about this fountain — terrifying rumors that would make children cry and shout for their mothers.

At that thought, I turned away from the fountain and glanced down at my green watch. *September thirteenth, Friday, 8:14 a.m.* It wasn't a weekend, but not a living soul was visible on the campus.

I was born with the uncanny ability to communicate with nature. Also, I knew the scientific names of all the flora and fauna, their habitats, and even the countries they originated from.

Since the age of five, I had been a nature lover. I enjoyed long strolls in the forest every day. Somehow, I had a strong emotional bond with nature, as if my life was linked to it. Having the ability to interact with flora and fauna, I conversed with the trees and animals in the forest whenever I paid them visits. They were my confidants, always listening attentively to what I had to say, and I provided assistance in return whenever they needed it. The skinny bare trees used to complain that the tall, strong ones hogged the sunshine and rainwater all to themselves, leaving them starving and thirsty. I encouraged the smaller trees to speak up for themselves and fight for their rights, and because of this, the once undernourished trees had now become stout and healthy. I felt at home whenever surrounded by nature, a place where I could find my true self and freely express my emotions.

On the other hand, my parents were everything but pleased at the fact that I spent hours out in the forest instead of devoting myself to math, English, and science. They pressured me to get top grades in every subject. As professors at a prestigious university, they wanted me to follow in their footsteps in the future. However, the more they pressured me, the more I wanted to escape, and the more I did, the more I missed my true home — nature. I would sneak into the forest whenever my parents were stuck at boring seminars, and my bosom friends would be standing there, arms outstretched and welcoming me home. The gentle rustling of their leaves was like the soft laughter of the occasional breezes that swept through the forest. I loved everything there with all my heart.

"Hoot."

I turned around and saw Michael, the eagle owl flying in

my direction.

"Hi there," hooted Michael. He perched himself on my shoulder, and I caressed his feathers.

Michael had always been a close friend of mine. One day, while I was minding my own business in the forest, I heard an owl crying in agony. I followed the source of his voice and came upon an injured eagle owl that had accidentally gotten himself stuck among some branches. He had bent his tail feathers in a painful angle. I smuggled him home and nursed him back to health. Although Michael preferred living in the forest rather than the cage in my room, he promised to pay me weekly visits and be my confidant and helper.

"What's up, Mike?"

"Not much. The school looks quite spooky today, doesn't it? Oh, it's the perfect time for horror stories! Do tell me one!"

"Michael, you mind if we go somewhere else to chat? This fountain gives me the shivers."

"Oh, yes it does! Tell me the legend of the two lovers and the fountain again!"

"What? Haven't you heard it more than ten times?"

But that naughty rascal hooted and chirped and badgered me so much I had no choice but to give in. Reluctantly, I retold the tragic story of the two lovers.

"Once upon a time, there was a twelfth-grade couple in our school, Ricardo and Geraldine. Ricardo was a gifted straight-A student, yet his girlfriend Geraldine failed every subject. Regardless of this, they fell in love and began dating. They'd smooch in the hallways and go for romantic walks on campus, which made the other students jealous. As a result, everyone started dating. Nobody would focus on their studies. An important examination was around the corner, but none of the students cared about their academic performance because they were too centered on dating. So, of course, everyone did awfully on their exam. Our school was ranked last place in the nation, and it thoroughly destroyed our school's reputation. Ricardo was a clever boy who used to get top grades, so he decided to repeat the twelfth grade, start fresh, and be a good student this time. Because of her boyfriend, Geraldine followed suit. However, Ricardo didn't want himself to get carried away by romance for a second time, so he broke up with Geraldine."

Michael's eyes became as round as coins as he heard the tragic climax. "What happened next? What did poor Geraldine do? Tell me, I must hear the ending!"

"You already know what happened next, don't you?" I sighed. "I told you before, this is a poignant love story. Geraldine was heartbroken after the breakup. You see, she was a person of sensitivity, so she took it very seriously. Some even say she went insane. One day, while Geraldine was in this very courtyard, sobbing and thinking of Ricardo, she saw an illusion of him falling into the fountain. To save him, she plunged into the fountain herself and drowned." I cast a glance at the fountain and shivered. "Ricardo found out the news after a few hours and was overwhelmed with sorrow. He followed his lover's footsteps and drowned himself in this fountain, too. The two lovers became aquazombies — water zombies — and haunt this fountain forever. Ricardo and Geraldine died on September thirteenth. Every year on that date, the two aquazombies emerge from the fountain and drown bystanders by tossing them into—" I gasped. "Oh no! Today's September thirteenth! I shouldn't have told—"

"No, the tale's fascinating! How did their—?"

"Michael, stop joking. This is serious. Something's wrong today. Our school's chilly and misty even though the sun was shining earlier. It was as if the school was under a curse. What's wrong? Where's everyone?"

"I only wish I could tell you."

My heart almost stopped. "What…what do you mean?

"I can't believe Mrs. Wilson gave me a sour carton of milk for breakfast for the third time this week!" moaned a familiar voice. "She cares about nothing except that gathering with her stupid friends."

"Hang on," said another voice. "What's wrong with our school? And who's that girl over there?"

"Eileen?" the first speaker called out to me. "Is that you?"

I turned around and saw Alexandria and Clarissa at the school gates.

"What's wrong with our school?" said Alexandria, surveying the empty campus. Confusion creased her forehead.

"The campus is filled with purple mist." Clarissa shot an unnerved look at the fountain. "The school looks haunted."

"Tell me about it. Nobody's here, but it's a Friday!"

"I know, I know. Calm down. You're not the only ones who are confused." I turned to Michael. "Why? What's wrong?" I had told nobody about my ability to communicate with flora and fauna, including Alexandria and Clarissa, but now I had no choice.

"I'm not supposed to tell you."

Clarissa shuddered. "Is it...the owl that's talking?"

"Owls can't talk, silly," replied Alexandria.

Michael hooted in indignation.

"But he can," I said, stroking Michael on the head. "Where's Daphne, by the way?"

"Gossiping with her lot at the sports field, I guess." Alexandria combed her bushy red hair with her fingers absentmindedly, then paused. "Hold on for a moment — did you just tell us that it *can* talk?" she pointed her finger at Michael, who flapped his wings menacingly at her.

"Show some respect," I scolded. "He's Michael."

"Yeah, right, and I'm a unicorn," said Clarissa, grinning.

"No, I mean it. He told me his name was Mic —"

"He *told* you? You...you can talk with animals?"

The two of them exchanged looks of incredulity.

"Why have you never told us?"

"I...well, the weird thing is, I don't even know why —"

"Long time no see," an icy voice sounded from behind us. It was Daphne.

Clarissa and I both nodded politely while Alexandria displayed no sign of acknowledgement of her arrival.

Daphne sneered at her indifference. "Well, I thought you were expelled yesterday," she said, wrinkling her nose as if she'd caught a whiff of a funky odor. "Such a pity I'm wrong."

"I'm *not* expelled," retorted Alexandria, turning to face her. Flames burned and sizzled in her eyes.

"Ah yes, my apologies. What a bad memory I have. I forgot you bribed Ms. Jackson, who went directly to the principal to beg him not to expel you."

"That's not true." Alexandria's hair quivered in cold fury.

Daphne sniggered and turned to Clarissa and me. "I witnessed everything yesterday before leaving school. I passed the principal's office and heard our geography teacher, Lilith Jackson, begging the principal not to kick her out of school. Apparently, she set her workbook on fire in history class and almost got another kid killed. Say, Alexandria, how come Lilith Jackson's always sticking up for you? I thought you would've been expelled last time because of the podium incident, but Jackson went up to the principal and made a big fuss about it. How much money did you give her that time?"

Alexandria looked as though she could spout fire.

"Well, at least I'm not as pathetic as you are, Alexandria Richardson. I don't need anyone to *beg* for me." Daphne batted her eyebrows innocently at an infuriated Alexandria.

I sensed a bitter tang of animosity as an unpleasant atmosphere formed, bit by bit.

"Daphne, that's enough," warned Clarissa. "Ms. Jackson was just doing justice to Alexandria. After all, we know for a fact that she didn't cause the explosion."

"Oh yeah? Is that so?" Daphne shot Alexandria a spiteful look. "That's interesting. You know, you are a threat to us." With an amused expression on her face, she calculated with her fingers. "Let me see…you made the podium in the auditorium explode once during an assembly. Then, you almost got a few kids killed by zapping sparks of fire at them. Plus, you set your workbook on fire in history class. Wow, are you planning to murder our history teacher, poor Mr. Carson?"

"Enough!" shouted Clarissa. "Stop joking about getting anyone killed!"

But Alexandria and Daphne were deaf to everything

except the continuous insults the other hurled. "So what if I did it on purpose?" said Alexandria relentlessly, her hands balled into fists. "What if I lose control the next second and burn down the whole school? What are you going to do? Run to Mommy?"

Daphne ran her fingers through her hair and yawned. "Nope. You don't scare me, Alexandria Richardson, because I know you're nothing but a freak. Hey, what about this? Let's have a fight, right here, right now. The winner gets to push the loser into the fountain."

Clarissa gasped. "No, you can't do that! It's against the rules!"

"Plus, it's September thirteenth, the day you-know-what happened!" I added. I felt my stomach churning as if an ominous premonition were brewing.

"What?" Daphne sneered. "Oh, the legend the eleventh graders told us? Don't be daft. There's no such thing as an aquazombie. Tell me the ridiculous story again after I win this fight."

Alexandria, struggling to preserve her composure, did her best to conceal her uneasiness.

"What's wrong?" said Daphne. "Are you scared? Or are you going to chicken out?"

"I'll fight you," said Alexandria, edging closer to Daphne. "On my count, three, two—"

"No, on mine!" protested Daphne.

"No! Don't!" Clarissa and I made an attempt to break the two of them apart, but right at that second—

"Nasty students, fighting by our resting place?" a disembodied voice snarled from nowhere.

I gulped. Alexandria and Daphne broke apart. Clarissa clapped her hand to her mouth. The waters in the fountain shimmered and rippled.

"It's Ricardo and Geraldine's ghosts!" squeaked Clarissa. "We're all going to die!"

"Michael? Michael! Where are you?" I looked around frantically, but clever Michael must have fled from the terrifying fountain, for he was nowhere to be seen.

"NOBODY HAS EVER DARED TO DISTURB OUR RESTING PLACE!" another voice thundered.

Alexandria, Clarissa, and I exchanged looks of shock. Daphne, on the other hand, turned towards the fountain.

"Are you the aquazombies the eleventh graders told us about? Why don't you show your ugly faces?"

"Daphne, no!" squealed Clarissa, her body shaking like a leaf.

"YOU WILL PAY FOR THIS RUDENESS! WE WILL TEACH YOU A LESSON AND DROWN YOU, THE SAME WAY WE DROWNED OURSELVES!"

Before we knew it, two giant beasts with pointy yellow fangs, scaly skin, and green hair rose from the fountain.

Alexandria, Clarissa, and I clutched each other's hands for support. Seized by terror, the three of us cowered as the aquazombies towered over us.

"Wow," said Daphne, her voice thick with sarcasm. "So you are the two aquazombies from the legend, huh? Perhaps I should take a picture of you two and send it to my —"

"YOUR DOOM HAS COME!" one of the aquazombies snarled at her.

Helpless and terrified, we watched the monster snatch Daphne off the ground and toss her into the fountain. Daphne's screams shattered the air, but there was nothing we could do.

"YOU! YOU THREE FOOLISH BYSTANDERS! I'LL HAVE YOUR LIVES AS WELL!" the other monster clutched Alexandria with his right arm, grabbed Clarissa with another, and almost strangled me with his third arm.

"No! Let us go! Please!"

"DON'T TELL ME WHAT I SHOULD OR SHOULDN'T DO!"

Then, we felt ourselves lifted off the ground. Screaming and kicking, we were hurled into the fountain. I held my breath and wrapped my arms around my head, bracing myself for a painful death. However, I didn't drown, nor were my clothes wet. Instead, I felt myself plummeting through a bottomless pit, descending into a void and engulfed by blackness.

Chapter Three

THE OTHERWORLD
(DAPHNE)

Splash!

One moment I was flying through an endless darkness, and the next, a pool of water caught me. I popped my head out and saw Alexandria waving her arms and kicking her legs to get herself out of the water. A savage surge of pleasure bubbled in me at that sight.

"We aren't drowned yet?" Clarissa flexed her fingers in amazement. "Where are the aquazombies?"

"I'll...kill you...Daphne!" Alexandria coughed, tumbling out of the fountain. "How...How...dare you get...us all involved!"

All of us were drenched and shivering with coldness.

"Listen, stop arguing and let's focus on getting out of here," Clarissa said, silencing the two of us.

"You mean—this darn fountain," Eileen gasped for air.

"So, big geniuses, where are we?" I hurled a question at them.

"No idea, but it's definitely not our school," Clarissa said, observing the landscape around us.

"Some gone-wrong wonderland, isn't it?"

The trees around us were veiled by thin mist, gloomy and

dark in the distance. The overcast sky, crammed with dark gray clouds, seemed to foreshadow the arrival of a storm. There was a village, but it looked deserted as if no one had been there in a decade. However, the silhouette of a person was visible to us.

I was terrified, but there was no way I would show it. "This place reminds me of the setting of a fairytale in bad weather."

Alexandria, who usually loved to give a piece of her mind, remained silent.

"Scared, aren't you?" I sneered at her.

She shook her head vaguely. Her eyes, as though glassy orbs, were staring straight ahead. "I...I've been here before in my dreams. I think...I know where we are."

"Where?" I felt the hair on my back rising.

Instead of answering immediately, Alexandria closed her eyes. Just when I thought she was going to ignore my question, she spoke again, her voice a whisper. "The Otherworld."

Clarissa blinked as if having trouble comprehending her words. Eileen uttered a little scream.

"Look," I explained, trying to talk some sense into the three of them. "There is *no* Otherworld. Eileen, aren't you an expert on geography? Surely you know that—"

"I'm telling you, there *is* an Otherworld!" Alexandria cut across me.

"You must have hit your head on the floor of the fountain. It doesn't exist."

"But—"

Eileen gasped. "Daphne, look out! Behind you!"

A sense of foreboding crept over me. With my hands clenched into fists, I turned around to fight whatever was there.

Only to see a gorgeously appareled woman who seemed to be in her thirties. She was tall in stature and had an oval face. A cordial smile played on her lips. Her wild chestnut curls were in a braided updo, a few stray curls hanging on either side of her face. A lavender satin gown with a plunging illusion neckline and straps that sat off her shoulders hugged her slender waist. Below her ruched waistband bloomed a skirt with countless layers of cascading ruffles. She looked somewhat familiar, yet because of her changed hairstyle, I failed to recognize her. But those brown eyes...I felt a pang of déjà vu as I noticed them.

Eileen clutched Clarissa's arm so tightly that her knuckles went white. Clarissa, on the other hand, gazed at the woman with her large shining eyes, not betraying even the slightest hint of fear.

I'd read enough stories to know that encountering a strange woman in the middle of nowhere could only mean one thing: *danger.* I was ready to fight her when—

"Hello there, Ms. Jackson!" Clarissa called out to the woman cheerfully.

"Yes, Clarissa, it's me," the woman said. Her low, calming voice confirmed the fact that she was indeed our geography teacher, Lilith Jackson.

"Oh, you again. I thought you should be at school teaching geography. Or did you get here by accident, like us? Help us back to the school, won't you? Please?"

Ms. Jackson chose not to answer me, or perhaps, didn't bother to. Her gaze fell on the other three.

"Where...where is this...this...place? " Eileen asked, trembling from head to toe.

"Let me answer Daphne's question first, dear. No, I'm sorry, but I can't help you back to the mortal world because I belong here."

"What? But—"

"As for Eileen's question, welcome to the Otherworld." A wide grin spread across Ms. Jackson's face.

Dead silence.

"There is no such place," I replied flatly.

Ms. Jackson raised her eyebrows, affronted by my words of defiance. "I wouldn't be so sure if I were you."

Clarissa looked puzzled. "Isn't the Otherworld supposed to be a world of the afterlife? For people who have passed away in the real world? Are we...dead?"

Eileen wailed and tightened her grip on Clarissa's arm.

"You are *not* dead. The Otherworld is simply another

world, a magical world home to people and animals with magical blood. You were transported here by the fountain. I assure you'll all be safe now that you're with me."

"Liar," I muttered.

Alexandria snapped her fingers. Sparks of fire emitted from her fingertips and burnt a hole in my sleeve.

"Get a grip on yourself and watch your manners," Ms. Jackson said to me, her voice softening with implied danger. "As for you, Alexandria, you must learn to control those magic powers of yours."

"Magic?" I echoed. "You li—"

"I could turn you into a porcupine if I wanted to," said Ms. Jackson nonchalantly.

"Excuse me? I could report you to the principal and have you fired right away if I wanted to!"

"Whatever you need to tell yourself. Anyway, let's get down to business. The reason I'm here is to take all of you to the palace of the Otherworld on the king and queen's orders."

"Why would they be interested in us?" said Alexandria, tilting her head. "We're just four ordinary teenagers, aren't we?"

"Come with me, then, if you're so curious," Ms. Jackson answered, beckoning mysteriously at the four of us. She glided away, her feet hidden under the ruffles of her gown.

Without hesitation, Alexandria tagged along with her. Clarissa motioned for us to follow them.

"What, you trust Ms. Jackson?" I looked at her incredulously.

"Wouldn't hurt to try," replied Clarissa, shrugging. She hurried over to Ms. Jackson and Alexandria.

I glanced at Eileen, the only one left who had some sense. "So, what next?"

Ignoring my question, she sprinted towards the three of them.

I heaved a sigh of frustration and walked over to them, fuming. "Why are you doing this?"

"It's the safest thing to do," explained Clarissa. "We can't trust anyone if we don't trust Ms. Jackson. She's our teacher."

"A teacher who appeared suddenly in this deserted world. You must admit it's odd. Especially when the teacher's a batty old crackpot."

"Listen, I know you don't like Ms. Jackson. But what if she *is* a real witch? Keep insulting her like that, and she'll probably turn you into a porcupine for real."

"We've been transported to another world by a fountain," said Eileen. "And in times like this, we have no choice but to trust anyone we already know."

As we set foot on a purple-bricked path that formed by itself, four statues of the strangest creatures I had ever seen came into view. One was of a bear with the body of a phoenix; the second one a unicorn that had sprouted great, feathery wings; the third one a cat with a caterpillar's body; and the fourth—

"Is this a dog or a fish?" Eileen, who had been scrutinizing it carefully, questioned.

"A dogfish, Eileen," said Ms. Jackson. "It's half-dog, half-fish."

"What nonsense is this?" I couldn't help laughing at the absurdity.

Ms. Jackson sighed. When she spoke, her tone was surprisingly soft. "Daphne, I know this is a lot to take in, but like I said, this is the Otherworld. There are only four animals in the Otherworld—bearnixes, unibirds, kittenpillars, and dogfishes. No rabbits, lions, dogs, cats, or any common animals, as in the mortal world, exist here. The four magical creatures each have their respective brand of elemental magic: fire, air, nature, and water. All four creatures have their own language, too. There are also some human residents here with magical blood. They are known as Otherworldians."

I had the sense not to argue back, for there was way too much proof that magic existed in this whimsical world. "So...the four creatures you mentioned, they're all over the Otherworld?"

"Of course. We've got about five hundred of them working in our palace. Some are chefs, guards, doctors, nurses, or servants, while others are designers." She fluffed her gown to make her point. "There are—"

"Could you tell us more about the four creatures?" interrupted Clarissa.

"Sure. Bearnixes are bears with bodies like phoenixes. They spout fire when they're angry and are the most aggressive animals among the four creatures. Although they have wings, they, like chickens, can only glide for a few feet. Unibirds are winged unicorns. They neigh like horses when they talk and squawk like birds when they shout. They can fly, as they have bigger wings and lighter flight muscles compared to bearnixes. In fact, unibirds are mostly found high above in the clouds and are seldom seen on land. They're not aggressive, but they attack intruders who trespass into their territory. Kittenpillars are cats with bodies like caterpillars. They are tame and mild but not good at fighting. Well, they can perform a bit of nature magic, but it cannot do much harm to their enemies. They are peace and nature lovers. A kittenpillar can spend a millennium dwelling in the woods all by itself. Finally, dogfishes are dogs with scaly fish bodies. They're able to breathe underwater but can live on land as well. Like the dogs in the mortal world, they, too, have four legs. Aggressive animals they are, second to bearnixes."

"Kittenpillars are my favorite," said Eileen softly. "I love nature, too. I can communicate with flora and fauna. It was a gift I was born with."

"Did it make you feel different from others?" Ms. Jackson asked, gazing expectantly at her.

Eileen nodded.

The road split into two, and Ms. Jackson took the right fork. Another four statues of the magical creatures, one of each, were erected by the road. The bearnix was spouting fire from its wide mouth. The unibird was examining its wings while the kittenpillar was holding a half-chewed leaf in its paws. The dogfish, on the other hand, was scratching at the back of its head.

"Ms. Jackson, *who* are you?" Alexandria asked as politely as she could manage. "Why did the king and queen send you? How long have you lived in the Otherworld?"

"I'm a member of the Court of the High Advisors. This is my tenth year. We, the advisors and courtiers of the king and queen, are known as the Elders. There are about two hundred of us, but the actual number can fluctuate at any time. Some of us are assigned to go on missions, but we also have new recruits every season. We all have our own positions. There are fifty Elite Elders, including Zack and I." She pointed to a shiny silver badge on her chest, which had the words *Elite Elder* engraved on it.

"Hang on...." said Alexandria. "I heard a familiar name. Zack...that's Mr. Valentino, isn't it? You're not the only Elder who's disguised as a mortal teacher, right?"

"I'm not. In fact, there are about five in our school. The Representative Elder herself is also one."

"Interesting...." I was silently hoping that our annoying language arts teacher, Helen Edmunds, was not one of them.

"What do you Elders do?" asked Clarissa. She scanned Ms. Jackson from head to toe, "You don't just party all day and check your reflection in the mirror every once in a while, right?"

"Of course not. Do I look like a socialite to you?"

Acknowledging the fact that she had touched a nerve, Clarissa muttered a quick apology.

"Maybe it's because of the way we dress." Ms. Jackson smoothed the ruffles on her gown and continued. "But in fact, we hardly ever get to enjoy life. We don't spend every day frolicking in the courtyard, checking our wardrobes, or enjoying grand feasts in the ballroom. We don't have time to enjoy all these privileges. We've got battle plans to discuss, and as an Elite Elder, I have more than twenty meetings a week to attend. We also have training sessions every day—archery, swordplay, dressage, and skills on wand magic. Being an Elder is not as easy and fun as it seems."

"All right," said Clarissa. "So there are fifty Elite Elders. Do you guys have a leader?"

"The Representative Elder. She has served the king and queen for fifteen years. She's forty, the oldest and wisest among us, and we've always had a lot of respect for her. However, a dreadful accident took place a few months ago, in which she was involved. It greatly damaged her reputation. We've always fielded questions about that misadventure." Ms. Jackson gave a sigh at that mention.

It was Eileen who ruptured the silence following Ms. Jackson's words. "You've got an interesting dress code, haven't you? I like the color you're wearing."

"Indeed. The depth of the color depends on our position. Lilac gowns or tuxedos for regular Elders, lavender for Elite Elders, and a rich, deep shade of violet for the Representative Elder. Maybe you'll get to see her today."

A buzz of excitement issued from the others. I looked up, and an immense white palace loomed into sight. Towers, turrets, and spires with golden embellishments stood around the palace like soldiers.

"How are we supposed to get across the moat?" Alexandria was the first to notice the reeking moat that segregated the bricked path from the palace. Clarissa and Eileen were still gaping at the gilded towers.

Ms. Jackson snapped her fingers. A part of the wall fell forward instantly, creating a drawbridge. Amazed, we crossed it, and into the courtyard, we went.

Four arches were carved on the four walls, one leading to the drawbridge while the other three to dark passages. It seemed like it had been a beautiful courtyard before; however, it was now dull and untidy. An almost dried up pond could be seen at the far end of the courtyard. In the middle of the pond perched a small octagon gazebo blackened with grime and clotted with lichen; sparkling cobwebs stretched between the eight columns. The white wooden bridge that led to the gazebo was soiled and caked with dirt. Withered vines of wisteria and bare branches lay haphazardly on the canopy. The glossy marble statues of the four creatures were either headless or wingless. The colorful flowers had wilted, leaving a few dried leaves and petals. A three-tier fountain that bore intricate carvings was located in the middle of the courtyard. The water was shallow and had yellowed, fallen brown leaves and dead bugs gathered at the bottom of the fountain.

Eileen gazed, depressed, at the courtyard. I knew she loved nature very much and was heartbroken to see everything looking so lifeless and dreary. Suddenly, she let out an excited squeal. I looked in her direction and saw a creature lumbering towards her.

"Oh! A real live kittenpillar!"

The endearing creature had a furry mint-green body and a white head with whiskers. Triangular ears poked out from either side of its head.

"Ella," Ms. Jackson greeted her. The kittenpillar meowed. "I suppose she would like you to pet her, Eileen. Keep in mind that you shouldn't call her Wee Ella, or she'll use your face as a scratching pad to sharpen her claws."

Gingerly, Eileen edged towards the kittenpillar named Ella and reached out a hand to stroke her. The kittenpillar meowed contently.

"Wow," murmured Eileen.

A few minutes later, Ms. Jackson spoke. "Follow me, please. We're running out of time. King Patrick's not exactly the best definition of the word 'patience.'"

"Sorry, Ella," said Eileen. "I have to go now."

"Meow." Ella purred and nuzzled her affectionately.

"I'll pay you a visit later, I promise. Bye."

The kittenpillar licked Eileen, purred again, and wriggled away, heading for a wilted yellow rose bush. Everyone's eyes followed her as she left.

Ms. Jackson led us through the arch on the left side of the courtyard, and we delved into a winding passage. It was lit with blazing purple torches hanging on the walls, giving off an ancient, mysterious feeling. I took a closer look at them and saw that the flames were in different shades of purple—lilac, lavender, and violet.

"Are those real torches?" asked Alexandria. "I've never seen purple fire before." She touched the flames gently and smiled.

I uttered a little scream. "How did you—?"

"I was born immune to fire. Sometimes, the flames can even heal my bruises and cuts."

The fact that Alexandria was immune to fire did not surprise me that much after being transported to a different world by a fountain and learning about the exotic fauna of the Otherworld. After witnessing so much proof of magic today, I was beginning to doubt if anything was actually impossible.

We turned left. Then right. Then up a steep spiral staircase with carved banisters that went up for seven stories. After an exhaustive effort, we reached the seventh floor, panting and sweating.

A bright hallway with marble pillars, gold-trimmed walls, and a carpeted floor stretched in front of us, leading to a pair of double doors with antique brass handles. It looked a lot less mysterious than the passages downstairs. Tall, gilded candelabras with lit candles stood on either side of the hallway, painting everything in golden hues. Ice sculptures of bearnixes, unibirds, kittenpillars, and dogfishes lined the right side, while fire sculptures of the four creatures were displayed on the left.

Two guards, a real live bearnix and a dogfish, were standing in front of the gigantic doors. The dogfish was standing on its two hind legs on its fish body. He bowed at the sight of Ms. Jackson, and the bearnix raised a vermillion wing in a salute.

"Wow," breathed Alexandria.

"They all have their own ways of greeting the Elders," said Lilith. "Dogfishes and kittenpillars bow, and bearnixes and unibirds salute."

"Lady Lilith," said the dogfish. "Who are your companions?"

"They can speak English?" I whispered to Eileen.

"They're probably trained to speak English because they guard the palace," she guessed. "That would make it easier for the Elders to communicate with them."

"Young ladies who aren't yet aware of their true identities," Ms. Jackson explained briskly. "His Majesty summoned them. Now, may I enter?"

"What do you think the whole 'secret identity' business is all about?" Alexandria muttered to Clarissa.

Eileen exchanged a look of wonder with me. It suddenly occurred to me that the curiosity of an unknown world had thawed the invisible barrier between us.

"Well, my lady, surely your four companions aren't going into the Throne Room dressed like *that*?" the dogfish replied, smirking at us.

I looked down at my clothes and immediately regretted not wearing something else than my see-through blouse and tattered jeans.

"Noir," the bearnix frowned at the dogfish. "Don't say things like that."

"I know, Bessie, but His Majesty and Her Majesty and all the Elders have their dress code, and—"

"I don't care," said Ms. Jackson, her voice rising. "Let us in right now! His Majesty might turn me into a dogfish, or who knows what if I'm late! Now, are you going to let me in or not?"

"As you wish, my lady," said the bearnix nervously, nudging her colleague in the fish body.

The enormous doors opened, revealing a massive room with a resplendent interior. Milky white marble reigned the Throne Room, from the ceiling to the walls to the floor, like a giant pearly cave. A fancy chandelier the size of a car hung from the vaulted ceiling. The king and queen were seated on the two thrones parked in the back. About two-hundred Elders, all clad in lilac and lavender, were sitting on smaller thrones of equal proportion on both sides of the room; a few vacant seats were visible among them. The Elders whispered to each other, glancing curiously at us.

A stately woman with wavy black hair stood on the end of the carpeted aisle, facing the thrones and giving a report. Unlike the others, she wore a velvet ball gown in a deep shade of violet with a lacy high collar and long, tight sleeves that puffed at her shoulders and flared at her wrists. A voluminous skirt fanned out from her upper waist, finishing in a chapel-length train that trailed behind her. The hem was interspersed with tiny amethysts.

"Is she the princess?" Eileen asked quietly, unable to take her eyes off the woman.

"Definitely not," said Clarissa. "Look at her outfit. Remember what Ms. Jackson said about their dress code? She must be the Representative Elder."

"She seems quite attractive," Eileen said.

"What?" I chimed in. "She's forty and…." Clarissa fought hard to keep a straight face.

"Whatever," Eileen gushed. "I love what she's wearing. It's so elegant."

"Am I the only one who thinks she looks like an oversized purple pumpkin?" I quipped. Clarissa burst into a fit of silent giggles.

Eileen glared at me. "Listen up. Do me a favor and shut your mouth!"

"You're just saying that because her voice sounds like Helen Edmunds's, who gave you a hundred on your last language arts test!" I retorted.

Ms. Jackson turned away from us, but I could have sworn I saw the slightest hint of a smile on her face.

The king and queen did not seem to take notice or perhaps chose to ignore our arrival. The king wore a golden crown inlaid with amethysts and was attired in a bejeweled robe of golden brocade and purple velvet. An ornate scepter lay on the armrest of his throne. The queen looked like a mortal housewife, nothing special or magical. Her curly red hair was tied in a loose side ponytail, and an amiable smile played on her lips. Yet her pearl necklace, her crown of diamonds and crystals, and her frock, a luxurious purple gown with golden beaded appliqués and tiny jewels, signified her nobility.

"Thank you, Helen," she said, beaming at the Representative Elder, who curtsied. "You may leave."

The four of us exchanged looks of shock. *Helen? Not Helen Edmunds?*

The Representative Elder turned to face us. She was indeed my least favorite teacher, annoying Helen Edmunds. I cursed under my breath, and fortunately, she took no notice of my swearing.

"Elders, Elders! Settle down, please." A hush fell upon the room. "We have some visitors to welcome." The king pointed his golden scepter at us.

"Greetings, Your Majesties," said Ms. Jackson. "I hope we're not late." She curtsied, and we did the same rather clumsily.

"Perfect timing," said the king. "Very well done, Lilith. I personally requested to see these four young ladies."

The Elders' gazes were fixed upon us, some curious, some perplexed, some excited. Some cupped their hands around their mouths and gossiped with their neighbors.

"Take your places before the king and queen, now," said Ms. Jackson in an undertone, giving us each a little nudge.

Eileen, the shyest among us, pushed Clarissa to the front. We followed her and made our way down the aisle as the queen studied us, her expression unfathomable.

The king, on the other hand, had his gaze focused on Alexandria the whole time. It was not until we had approached the thrones that he spoke.

"Alexandria Matilda Richardson, my daughter. Finally, we meet."

Chapter Four

THE ROYAL FAMILY
(ALEXANDRIA)

I gazed blankly at the king, my mind whirring ten thousand miles an hour.

Me? The king's daughter? Princess of the Otherworld? No, they are bluffing. They have to be.

"Excuse me, Your Majesty. I...I'm an orphan living with a foster family. My parents abandoned me when they were alive, then...both died from leukemia, three years later."

There was a buzz of whispering from around the room.

"Perhaps she isn't the one, Your Majesty," one of the Elders, a brown-haired woman in heavy makeup, said.

The king chose to ignore her. "As unbelievable as it seems, my child, we, the queen and I, are your true parents. We gave birth to you and sent you to an orphanage when you were two months old."

My mouth opened and closed like a goldfish's. A wide variety of answers flashed across my mind simultaneously. I could have sneered and disregarded his words, greeted him like a father, or laughed it off as if it were a colossal joke.

But I was thunderstruck. Too stunned to speak. I gaped at the glamorous king and queen, whose expressions were solemn.

"No, no," I heard myself mumble. My gaze dropped to my feet. "There must be some sort of misunderstanding."

"You don't believe us, do you?" the queen said, her voice brittle.

I looked up, expecting them to laugh at my foolishness for taking this joke seriously. But I was wrong. For a split second, it seemed as if the two rulers were terrified that their only daughter would not accept the fact that they were her true parents.

If the queen wasn't telling a falsehood...if my parents had actually been safe and sound all these years instead of lying indifferently in a tomb...if, after years of wondering and dreaming, I finally got to meet my biological parents in person.... For a fraction of a moment, I felt overwhelmed by torrents of disbelief, mingled with relief and ecstasy. However, those emotions were subtle compared to the intense confusion. Millions of questions floated to the surface of my mind like bubbles in the ocean, but I didn't know which one to begin with. Instead, I shook my head to clear my thoughts.

"All right, then," I said slowly. "But this doesn't explain why I got sent to an orphanage in the mortal world and grew up there instead of the Otherworld."

"Daughter," said the queen, "we owe you an apology for that. For not being able to grow up with us, unaware of your true identity, and considered as a troubled student. But we sent you to the mortal world for your own good."

Did my ears deceive me? I felt as if the queen, my mother, had just injected poison into my blood, which was circulating around my body and making me sick.

"For *my* own good?" I demanded. "Your Majesty, you'll have to clarify that." I wondered how she would respond to my confrontation. Would she wave her scepter and wipe me out right on the spot? After all, I had no idea whether she was a villain or not.

"You, as the princess of the Otherworld, would be a tremendous threat to the infamous Underworld. The Underworld is another magical world, yet unlike the Otherworld, it is full of dark magic. It's ruled by the Siblings, two tyrants by the names of Alta and Alto."

I blinked, trying to absorb her words. Then, something completely irrelevant clicked into place.

"I knew it. I knew everything. I've dreamed about the Otherworld before, and the four creatures, too," I thought without realizing I was saying all this aloud.

"This attests to the fact that you are the princess of the Otherworld."

"Your dreams were no coincidences. You have magical blood running in your veins."

"Your blood, you mean," I said, a wave of disgust washing upon me. "You just told me that I, as your daughter, am a big threat to the Underworld. In other words, I wasn't meant to be born. If so, why have you ordered Ms. Jackson to bring me here? To kill the daughter you never claimed? And why are Clarissa, Eileen, and Daphne involved? What have you been plotting?" I felt as if I were swimming in a pool of deepening exasperation and confusion.

Some Elders tutted disapprovingly and glowered at me.

"We want you to fight the evil Underworld for us," answered the king.

Waves of anger flooded upon me, and for a moment, I didn't care anymore. "Oh, sorry about my poor memory, I forgot all about the world of evil," I snapped. "So, let me get this straight: fourteen years after disposing of your only daughter, you're going to use her to fight some villains." Sparks of fire danced wildly on my fingertips as I felt my temper rising.

A buzz of disbelief rumbled among the Elders, which quickly mounted into murmurs of disapproval.

Go on, call me an awful person for raising this terrible accusation. My life's already ruined. I don't care anymore, I thought, my hands balled into fists. My nails cut into my palms, sending throbs of pain down my arm. However, it was nothing compared to the stabbing pain in my chest.

"You have to fight the rulers of the Underworld for us," the king went on, this time firmly yet coldly.

I raised my eyebrows in skepticism. "What if I say no?" It was all I could do to restrain my anger.

"You have to, whether you like it or not because you're our daughter."

I sighed and decided to approach them in a more composed manner rather than yelling like a barbarian. "But...must I fight them? Must the Otherworld antagonize the Underworld? I'm a peace lover." Many Elders sneered at this statement. "And I know for a fact that you don't have to use violence to bring peace back. We could reason with them, we could convince them — "

"They are not the type for reasoning with or convincing," said the king matter-of-factly, as if explaining a simple math concept to a kid. "They'd murder you the first chance they had. Plus, as the princess of the Otherworld, you are destined to be a warrior. It's your job to get rid of the Siblings. Sometimes you have to fight for the ones you love, for what you believe in."

The more serene the king acted, the more it agitated me. *Destined? My job? For the ones I love?* This was getting more and more absurd. My parents, for fourteen years, had never bothered to visit or care for me. Now, they handed out a perfunctory apology and asked me to get rid of some foul world of magic for their sake? And told me to love them? After everything they had done to me for the past fourteen years?

"I can't," I answered through gritted teeth.

A collective gasp echoed among the Elders. Clarissa, Eileen, and Daphne looked at me, mingled fear and sympathy written on their faces.

"Say that again," said the king softly, cold fury audible in his voice.

"I can't," I repeated, my temper reaching boiling point. "And I won't!"

Before I knew it, I lashed out at them, the anger, the anguish, and every drop of hurt and hatred pouring from me like a flood unleashed by a reservoir. "Have you ever thought of all those years I managed to survive in the orphanage? Fourteen years I've been kept in the dark! Have you two checked on me at least once to see how I was doing? Have you any idea how beastly the kids in the orphanage were? No! I was terrified for all these years, and I bet anything that the two of you were having a good laugh over my misery all along. Enjoying life in this palace, having these Elders do your bidding. And now you somehow want me to defend your pretty little realm because you're afraid the Underworld will take over. Have you an inkling of how terrible it was to be abused and bullied?" I smirked, "Oh, of course not. I forgot the two of you must have grown up as pampered aristocrats, born with silver spoons in your mouths. You'd totally deserve it if the Otherworld got overtaken by the Underworld. What's more, you have no right to call them evil. What you did to me was evil personified. For fourteen years, you didn't care or show any support for your daughter, who had been thrown into a horrible orphanage for some puny reason! Does this make you feel like you're any better than Alta? Or Alto? Why did you even have me in the first place? I want the truth! I demand to know why I was discarded as a baby and sent to an orphanage!"

Shocked silence. It had become so quiet that I could hear my own heartbeat.

I surveyed the spectacular room with utmost guilt and savage pleasure bubbling in me. The Elders gaped at me. Floored. Flabbergasted. At a loss for words. Some eyed me with resentment, some wrung their hands in anxiety or bit their lips, but most stared incredulously at me, pitiful, astounded, yet at the same time fascinated by my defiance. I cast a quick glance at Ms. Jackson, whose eyes welled with tears. She had her gaze fixed on the ruffles of her gown.

Clarissa, Eileen, and Daphne mirrored each other's expressions of utter disbelief and awe. Paying no attention to them, I glared into my parents' eyes.

The king's face turned blotchy red; the queen devoted her attention to her lace gloves instead of making eye contact with me.

I thought I had gone too far, and I braced myself for death.

"Alexandria…." It was the Representative Elder, Helen Edmunds, who broke the silence. "Do not judge your parents so harshly. They've been through difficulties that you could never imagine." Her voice was soft yet firm.

"That will do, Helen," said the king sternly. Then, in a gentler voice, he addressed me. "Alexandria, you have every right to yell at us. We offer our sincerest apology."

This was so ridiculous I almost laughed instead. An apology? Was an apology going to set things right? Could an apology dispel all the trauma I'd been through?

The king went on. "We have made a mistake, and I'm not going to cover it up."

"A mistake?" I repeated. After releasing the accumulated anger in me, I found myself face-to-face with sorrow. Here were my parents, apologizing for giving birth to me, in front of my friends and all of their advisors.

"My daughter…." This time, it was the queen who spoke. "I understand how hurt and angry you must be. However, you must know that a story has two sides. Please give me a chance to clarify all the misunderstandings. Let me tell you my story."

Taking my silence as a yes, she continued. "Several decades ago, when only one magical world existed, there was a perfectly ordinary family known as the Williams." She inhaled deeply, then exhaled as if praying for the courage to go on. "The couple had three children—two girls, Alta and Alti, and a boy, Alto. The three young ones had a very strong bond with one another. They were each other's shadows. Everything had been dandy and harmonious for the family, but all changed when the youngest child, Alti Williams, turned twenty-three. Alti had always wanted to go to the mortal world and apply to the best university in an advanced country. She had a thirst for knowledge and wanted to learn more about the remarkable world mortals had created. Things such as electricity, the Internet, and air-conditioning had piqued her curiosity and enchanted her deeply for a long time.

"Her parents encouraged Alti to pursue her dream, yet Alta and Alto were anything but supportive of her decision. This led to a severe quarrel between the three of them. Alta and Alto were furious at their sister, under the impression that she was abandoning them. Alti, on the other hand, criticized her siblings for being narrow-minded and conservative. Alti won the argument, having no idea she would face devastating loss and regret her choice in the future. After two years, she returned from the mortal world, only to find that her parents had passed away in her absence, and her siblings had changed — the departure of their sister and the death of their parents had caused them to lose belief in everything but gaining wealth and power. They developed an infatuation for dark magic and became more and more addicted and obsessed with it, discovering and learning more sinister brands of magic every day. Alta and Alto eventually became so hungry for power that they decided to take over the entire magical world, which involved planning regicide to dethrone the king and queen. Then, they themselves were going to take over the throne, rule the magical world, and make it a realm of evil. Eternal glory, that was what they were after. Alti did not know about this, for her siblings had estranged themselves from her since her return. However, she did start to acknowledge the fact that Alta and Alto were no longer and never would be the same as before.

"One day, Alti couldn't stand it anymore. She ran away from home, eloped with her lover, and married him. To force herself into forgetting her siblings, Alti changed her name to Marianne, taking her beloved mother's name. Meanwhile, Alta and Alto had successfully assassinated the rulers of the magical world. In less than a year, it became theirs, and they dubbed it the Underworld. Alta and Alto went even further. They were now not only blinded by power and wealth but had also become bloodthirsty devils who slaughtered anyone who dared to defy them. Guiltless inhabitants were imprisoned, tortured, or killed only because they spoke ill of their rulers in public. The Siblings' reign of terror showered the streets and towns of the Underworld with innocent blood. The civilians had no choice but to obey their tyranny, or they'd end up losing their lives.

"Marianne and her husband Patrick decided to take action. With their powerful magic, they created another world — the Otherworld, a realm of felicity and peace. Many terrified

Underworldians were eager to leave the Underworld and join the Otherworld, yet most were brainwashed or coerced to pledge eternal allegiance to their rulers. When Alta and Alto learned about the Otherworld, they were enraged and decided to murder their sister and her husband. The Siblings launched an assault on the Otherworld, expecting an easy victory. But much to their surprise, the Otherworldians rose valiantly to the occasion and fought back with remarkable strength and skill. That made Alta and Alto decide to retreat their forces and return to their realm of darkness. However, the Siblings secretly vowed to either get rid of the Otherworld or rule it. Their ultimate goal was to unite both magical worlds and make it a totalitarian kingdom of utmost evil.

"Unfortunately, Patrick and Marianne, who were ignorant of the Siblings' ambition, thought the coast was clear and settled down in the Otherworld with their citizens. Some of their worshippers moved into the palace with them and served as Elders, while the others built their own village, ready to live happily ever after with their families. Then, one day, Patrick and Marianne had a baby girl. This baby, the princess of the Otherworld, was rumored to be an exceptionally powerful Otherworldian. Word reached the Underworld, and the vengeful rulers cooked up another plan, a plan to wreak their hatred towards their sister—they would take the princess's life. Patrick and Marianne had no choice but to send their daughter to an orphanage in the mortal world, a place where no Underworldian would dare enter. The Internet and television could spread news worldwide, and it would be a matter of time before the bloodthirsty rulers got arrested for attempting to break into an orphanage."

That was a redundant sob story, but it answered none of my questions. "So, what does this story have to do with me?"

"You, Alexandria, are the princess of the Otherworld."

The truth hit me hard, striking me like a bolt of lightning. *I was the princess, the baby the Siblings wanted to kill.* A sudden wave of shame and guilt assailed me—I had misunderstood my parents. They had no choice and had done everything for the best, protecting the Otherworld as well as my life. They did send me to the mortal world for the greater good.

"This is a lot to take in, I believe," the queen went on in a soothing voice, "but take a quick look at the Elders."

I did and met the gazes of Ms. Edmunds, Mr. Valentino, Ms. Jackson, and several other teachers I'd seen in morning assemblies but had never talked to.

"I believe you recognize a few familiar faces — your caring teachers at school. You think you encountered them by chance, don't you? You think they taught at your school by coincidence? No. We were behind it, me and Patrick. We stationed those Elders at your school to keep an eye on you. We cared for you as much as any ordinary parent, or perhaps even more. But Alexandria, you were right. You have every right to hate us for not being able to grow up in the Otherworld, where you truly belong. We thought everything would be fine with you. Also, we've had numerous battles with the Underworld over the past few years. We didn't... we were too focused on preserving the Otherworld."

I looked down at the purple plush carpet, not daring to meet their eyes. I wished I could unsay the ignorant words of accusation that had escaped my lips.

Silence loomed upon us for a while until Clarissa broke it. "Your Majesty? Then...why have you sought us?" She indicated Eileen, Daphne, and herself. "Why are *we* here?"

The king sighed. "Another redundant tale, I'm afraid. A precious artifact — the Gem of Hope — was stolen from the Otherworld yesterday. The Gem of Hope is an enchanted gem that is able to protect the Otherworld from dark magic. However, once it's gone, all the Otherworldians will fall into a coma, and our realm will fade away to nothing in less than a week. The gem, if in an Underworldian's hands, will be destroyed soon, along with the hope and peace left in our world."

"So it's gone?" asked Clarissa, her eyebrows locked. "Stolen by an Underworldian?"

"Whoever stole the gem smashed a vial of Forgetfulness Nectar at the guards, which made them unable to recall anything about the thief. A vile, pathetic attempt to mask the thief's identity.

This verifies our theory that an Underworldian is behind it."

"But why aren't the Elders asleep?"

"They live in the palace, the two hundred of them, and they are protected by each other's magic. It would be extra difficult to enchant a place with so many powerful Otherworldians gathered together."

"So the cloudy weather and the eerie village all make sense," Daphne muttered to herself.

"Indeed," the king nodded.

"You called for us because you want us to find the Gem of Hope," I said, the hidden agenda dawning on me.

"Precisely."

"Does that have anything to do with the reason we were transported here by a fountain?"

"I charmed the fountain in your school and made it a portal. The aquazombies were there on my orders to drag you into the fountain and bring you here."

"But why us, though?" said Clarissa. "We're ordinary teenagers."

"Why not send the Elders into the Underworld?" suggested Daphne.

"We did that last time, and it was disastrous," replied the queen, looking ill at ease.

A murmur erupted throughout the Elders.

"My young guests, you may seem ordinary, but in fact, you each have a second identity. Several centuries ago on Earth, the first four humans with magical blood and elemental powers, our ancestors, were born. Because their innate powers made them different from mortals, they were regarded as evil witches and wizards. As a result, they created a world of magic with the help of each other's elemental powers for their families and humans who, like them, had magical blood. Among the four Creators, Ember was the goddess of fire, Zeru the god of the sky, Fern the goddess of nature, and Walters the god of water. The gods and goddesses also created bearnixes, unibirds, kittenpillars, and dogfishes — spirits of fire, sky, nature, and water. Although the four Creators were extremely powerful, that did not stop them from aging and passing away, like regular mortals. One day, when they were all elderly people, they sought the ancient seer, Delphia, who had the ability to foresee the future. That night, the four Creators, who never bore children, each chose an heiress from the future to inherit his or her elemental magic."

"Are you saying that we—me, Clarissa, Eileen, and Daphne—were the chosen ones?" I said slowly.

"Precisely. Do you need proof? Tell me, then. What made you feel different from others? What can you do that they can't?"

"I'm prone to deep, intense emotions, and I set things on fire whenever a powerful wave of anger hits me," I admitted, recalling everything extraordinary that had happened to me before. "And I'm immune to fire. It…it heals me."

"The more emotional heirs or heiresses are, the more intense their elemental powers get," remarked the queen. "Alexandria, you are not only our daughter but also the heiress of Ember, the goddess of fire. What about you, Clarissa?"

"I'm an expert on skydiving, but that's not very special, is it?" she said quietly.

"At such a young age? That's what makes you unique. You are the heiress of Zeru, the god of the sky. Eileen?"

"I…I have an inexplicable connection with nature," whispered Eileen, her voice trembling with fear or excitement. I wasn't sure which. "I've been able to communicate with flora and fauna since I had a memory. And…and I know the scientific names of all the animals and plants by heart."

The king nodded. "Fern's heiress. Finally, Daphne?"

Daphne's gaze dropped to her feet. "I've told nobody about this before, but…well, when I was three, my parents…well, they died in a shipwreck on a family trip. I was with them. We were on a cruise, and an unexpected storm hit us. I was the sole survivor among the thousands of passengers aboard." Her voice shook a little. "They—the rescue workers found me floating on the sea, crying for food. It was a miracle I managed to survive."

I looked at Daphne in astonishment, unable to believe she had harbored such a harrowing secret for so many years. At that thought, my hatred for her receded into pity.

"You, Daphne, are the heiress of Walters, the god of water. All four of you have proved yourselves as the heiresses of the four Creators in your own ways. After centuries of conjecturing, the four heiresses have been confirmed."

Many Elders whispered and pointed fingers at us. Some frowned, some gaped in shock, some shot admiring looks at us. I felt uncomfortable, like a helpless animal trapped in a display case.

"But...but how can it be?" said Eileen. "My parents have no magical blood. How could I possibly be a...an heiress of a... goddess?"

"Three of the Creators—Zeru, Fern, and Walters—chose mortals as their heiresses. Now, since—"

"This isn't true...it can't be." Daphne shook her head in disbelief.

"Daphne, you've never gotten along with Alexandria, have you? Fire and water are innate enemies, and your enmity with the heiress of Ember is able to prove this."

Daphne shot me a half-frightened, half-exasperated look and scooted as far away from me as possible.

"As the heiresses of the Creators, you have elemental powers that no Otherworldian or Underworldian can rival. Therefore, we want to send you on a mission to retrieve our stolen gem from the Underworld."

"You're sending us into the world of evil, weaponless and defenseless?" I said incredulously. It sounded so absurd I almost burst out laughing.

"You'll be armed well, and you've got more than each other," replied the king. "Two Elders will accompany you on your mission."

"Patrick, are you sure?" Queen Marianne whispered in his ear, looking apprehensive. "Are we really going to do this? They... they're only fourteen! There will be only six of them! And they don't know the first thing about battling! This mission sounds like, and probably is a suicide mission!"

"We've talked this over, Marianne. Do you want the gem

restored or not?"

"I...oh, of course, but—"

"All right, then," the king said with a touch of finality. "Heiresses, are you all willing to participate in this mission?"

"Sounds like a fun challenge," said a grinning Clarissa, who did not seem to find any of this overwhelming or astonishing at all.

"Daphne?"

"Yeah, I'll...I'll do...my best to try...and help—"

"I'm taking that as a yes then. Eileen?"

"I'm...." She eyed Clarissa, whose look of encouragement goaded her into accepting. "Perhaps. Yes, I guess."

"Very well," said the queen. "Eileen, there's nothing to fear."

Yeah, nothing to fear, I thought sarcastically, *entering a world ruled by two devils who are completely rotten to the core.*

"You must learn to step out of your comfort zone and discover your true self," the queen went on, gazing intently at Eileen.

"What...what are you talking about, Your Majesty?" said poor Eileen, looking flustered.

"Your heart is masked by your parents' high hopes and ways of pleasing them. You have to discover the real you, the true Eileen Spencer, who is hidden underneath the endless expectations of others. Perhaps you'll be able to, after this mission."

"I'll try, Your Majesty."

"Good girl. Alexandria, are you willing to do us a—?"

"Fine, I'm going. But this is because I hate Alta and Alto and what they did to the innocent Underworldians. This is not a favor for you two." Suddenly, a horrifying fact flashed across my mind—Alta and Alto were my aunt and uncle. I felt my stomach churning, unable to digest the fact that my relatives were ruthless, cold-blooded mass murderers. What's more, I was deprived of a healthy childhood because of them. I loathed the Siblings with all my heart, and I wanted their lives as much as they wanted mine.

"Heiresses, I can't thank you enough. The gem meant everything to the Otherworld, and we'll do our very best to ensure your safety. Now, for the Elders. Any volunteers?"

I turned around to see their reactions. Almost all of them shrunk back into their seats, each trying to seem less obvious than the other.

"Your Majesty, as an acquaintance of the four participants, I believe it is my duty to take part in this mission and protect them," said our English teacher, Mr. Valentino.

King Patrick nodded thoughtfully. "Interesting, very interesting. Yes, you may join them, Zack."

The other Elders started buzzing in protest.

"Your Majesty, you haven't forgotten about the accident last time, have you?" the woman with brown hair who had spoken earlier said in a whining voice, frowning reproachfully at Mr. Valentino.

"You're really going to trust Zachary Valentino to…to…," an Elder sitting beside the brown-haired woman added, giving him a funny look.

"That's enough, Jenkins and Benson," snapped Queen Marianne. "How about the two of you join the search?"

"No, Your Majesty, we didn't mean…," replied Jenkins hastily, exchanging a fearful glance with Benson.

"Do me a favor and be silent, then," barked the queen.

"Your Majesty," Ms. Edmunds began in a quiet yet firm voice. "I feel the need to accompany —"

Half of the Elders sniggered and shot skeptical looks at her. However, King Patrick and Queen Marianne took no notice of their reactions.

"Helen, are you sure?" said King Patrick. "I must impress upon you the importance of this mission, as it entails the safety of the four heiresses, including our only daughter. There will be no room for mistakes."

Ms. Edmunds nodded.

"Oh, are you sure, Helen Edmunds?" said Jenkins, smirking. "This is Alexandria Richardson, the princess of the Otherworld we're talking about, not just some pathetic apprentice of yours. What if she ends up the same as Evonne Fitzgerald? Would you like to deal with the consequences, in that case? Would you want this poor, innocent child to suffer from your incompetence?" She looked at King Patrick and Queen Marianne and spoke in a sanctimonious manner. "Your Majesty, the last time—"

"I'm perfectly aware of what happened, thank you very much," said the queen coolly. "Helen, here's a chance to prove yourself. You will be the leader of this mission, and keep this in mind: there is absolutely no room for failure. Helen, Zack, the two of you are now dismissed. Go and get dressed for your mission. Patrick and I are going to take our young guests to the weapon chamber, and the two of you will meet us there."

"Then we'll take our leave," Mr. Valentino and Ms. Edmunds said in unison. He bowed, and she curtsied before exiting the room.

King Patrick and Queen Marianne got to their feet. "Come, heiresses, follow us."

Dazed, still unable to perceive everything, the four of us followed the king and queen out of the Throne Room, then through another heavy, carved door on the right side of the hallway.

We found ourselves in a small, circular room with walls that stretched all the way up to the skies, giving us a weird feeling of being trapped in a tower. The candelabra beside the door provided the only light. Swords, spears, shields, and all sorts of weapons were dangling from the soaring walls. Four colorful velvet pouches sat on a wooden shelf across from us.

King Patrick surveyed the room. "Here, the weapon chamber—"

"I'm telling you, Alexandria isn't...!" a voice shouted from the Throne Room.

I poked my head out of the door.

King Patrick ignored the voice and carried on with his introduction of the history of the weapon chamber. "So, we hoard the most refined weapons in—"

"Your Majesty, may I go to the restroom?" I lied, desperate to find out what the Elders were saying behind me.

"Sure. Ask Noir the dogfish or Bessie the bearnix, the two guards outside the Throne Room, to escort you to the nearest restroom."

I tiptoed into the huge hallway. Noir and Bessie were standing guard outside the Throne Room. I walked up to them.

"Princess—"

"Please move aside, I want to—"

"Eavesdrop?" Noir frowned at me.

"Yes. You got a problem with that? I'm the princess, technically your mistress."

"No, no, Your Highness," said Bessie quickly, dragging her colleague out of the way.

I pressed my ear on the enormous double doors.

"Jenkins, you haven't even gotten to know her yet," said Ms. Jackson's voice. "Why are you jumping to conclusions so soon?"

"Don't be foolish. The child disgusts me. For goodness's sake, she's not even good-looking! Having such a hideous princess in the Otherworld! Oh, I might die of shame."

I peeked through the tiny crack between the doors and saw many Elders bobbing their heads up and down in agreement.

Ms. Jackson snorted. "How shallow are you? It's no wonder you've got no beauty beneath that pretty little face of yours."

"Stop deceiving yourself," said Jenkins, smirking. "Haven't you seen her repulsive attitude, the way she talked back to His and Her Majesties?"

"The child can be excused," another Elder joined the conversation. "Anyone would be furious to learn they've been kept in the dark for fourteen years."

Jenkins yawned. "Kept in the dark, eh? You know perfectly well that the king and queen kept her in the dark in order to protect her. Anyway, back to my main point—a princess should never be rude or aggressive. We all know what princesses are supposed to be like, right? Dainty, demure, yet delicate, which is why they all need princes to protect them. Alexandria Richardson possesses none of these traits. She's not even pretty, so I wouldn't be surprised if she never finds a spouse. Dear, dear, I'm starting to worry about the future of the Otherworld."

"I'd watch my mouth if I were you, Kerry Jenkins," a man in a lavender tuxedo warned her."

Jenkins, regardless of his words, went on. "I think Alexandria should spend more time on her appearance and her wardrobe instead of going on that ridiculous mission. Anyone agree?"

Ms. Jackson looked so furious I half-expected to see smoke wafting out from her ears. "How can you say that? Alexandria's going on that mission to save our lives! You've gone too far. As an Elite Elder, I have the authority to banish you from this—"

"Nah, sis, you got it wrong. It's the Representative Elder who has that power. Speaking of dear old Edmunds, I'm amazed at how shameless she is. She nearly got Evonne Fitzgerald killed—"

"She's already had her killed," Benson, the Elder on Jenkins's left, said spitefully. "Look at poor Evonne, now lying in the infirmary. It's all Edmunds's fault."

"Galen Benson, you have no right to talk about Evonne. You only want a reason to hate Helen because you're jealous of her. Plus, His Majesty—"

"Is always taking our useless Representative's side and speaking up for her when she's in trouble," finished Jenkins.

"Shut up, or I'll report you to the king and queen," said a young Elder.

"Oh, Robert, no need to be so harsh on me," Jenkins said in a sickly-sweet voice. "We were best friends, don't you remember?"

"I'm glad to hear you using the past tense because that was before I recognized your true colors. I don't want anything to do with you now. You're an awful, shady, ghastly—"

"Just save your insults, Robbie."

"Don't call me Robbie!" Robert cringed at his nickname.

Jenkins yawned again. "Whatever. Oh, where was I? Yeah, back to Edmunds the failure."

"That's out of order!" yelled Ms. Jackson. She stood up and whipped out a stick that glowed fiercely lavender, which I assumed was her wand. Purple sparks danced menacingly on the tip.

"Well, we mustn't get all pessimistic," Benson piped up. "Who knows? Perhaps it might be a good thing that Edmunds has gone on this mission. It'd be great if she had Zachary Valentino or one of the heiresses killed. His and Her Majesties will be bound to banish her. Or better, let's assume that dear Edmunds herself ends up dead. That'd be perfect!"

Several Elders dissolved into peals of laughter.

"SHUT UP!" hollered Ms. Jackson. "HOW DARE YOU INCITE THE OTHERS! YOU DON'T DESERVE TO BE SITTING HERE!"

The other Elders watched this epic debate unfold with rapt attention. Their gazes switched from Ms. Jackson to Jenkins and Benson, as if enjoying an exciting game of tennis.

"Wait and see, Jackson. Let's see if the losers will make it back alive."

"It'll do us no good if they don't," said Robert, his expression solemn. "The Otherworld will fade away sooner or later if they don't find the gem."

"Oh, Robbie, I'm afraid you misunderstood me," replied Jenkins sweetly, her voice like poisoned honey. "Fingers crossed that only a few of them will come back alive with the gem. Let's cross our fingers for a second time that Edmunds *won't* be one of them. Last but not least, we should cross our fingers for a third time that I'll step into her position as the Representative Elder." Then, she and her worshippers exchanged wide, devilish grins.

There was another torrent of screams and shouts, but I cared no more. I felt my insides flaming with anger as I had realized two things. One, I was hated and discriminated against only because I did not match the traditional impression of a princess. Two, I had to return to the Otherworld, safe and sound, to prove both Jenkins and Benson wrong. Despite the overflowing anger in me, I wondered what had gone wrong on the previous mission and why everyone detested Ms. Edmunds so much. I decided to eavesdrop for a little longer when —

"Alexandria!" someone shouted from behind. "What are you doing there?"

I cursed under my breath and saw Clarissa. "No…nothing. Aren't you supposed to be in the weapon chamber? Why are you here?"

"King Patrick's handing out scepters!" she squealed. "Look at what I've got! A unibird's horn!"

"What? You ripped a horn from —"

"No, it's an heirloom! The exact same scepter the god Zeru had!"

The two of us returned to the weapon chamber. Eileen was examining her scepter — a ten-inch stick made of vines and leaves. She gave it a swish, and a stream of tiny green leaves and pink flowers emitted from the tip and rose up into the air. Daphne, on the other hand, had inherited from Walters a trident made entirely of ice. She scrutinized the delicately carved snowflakes on the hilt and ran her fingers over them.

"Alexandria, come here," said King Patrick. He flicked his scepter, and an orange stick zoomed out of nowhere, now hovering in the air.

I jumped about a foot in surprise. "What's that?"

"It's a scepter made of lava. Here, hold it."

The scepter glowed warmly as my fingers enclosed around it.

"Give it a wave!" whispered Clarissa, dancing on her tiptoes.

I did, and large fireballs erupted from my scepter.

"Watch that!" yelled Daphne, extinguishing them with her trident.

Clarissa clapped her hands. "Cool! This is amazing!"

King Patrick let out a chuckle. "Seems like you've all gotten familiarized with your scepters." He turned to Clarissa. "But it'd be safer if you had this." He gave her a sword with a glowing blade.

"Advanced technology in the Otherworld? Wicked!" Clarissa waved it happily in the air. Sparks of lightning flew everywhere, zapping in all directions.

Eileen screamed. "Stop that! What if you hurt one of us by accident?"

"Alexandria, yours." Queen Marianne handed me a spear. "Be careful with it."

"How will I know how to use this? I've never handled a weapon before."

"Oh, you *will* know," said Queen Marianne, a twinkle in her eyes. "You all will, naturally. It's in your blood."

"What about me?" demanded Daphne. "Am I getting a new weapon?"

"That trident of yours can function as a weapon as well as a scepter, so you won't need one. As for Eileen—"

"I'll stick with my scepter, thanks," squeaked Eileen. "I'm...not good at weapons."

"All right, then. All set, everyone?"

The door flew open, and in came Mr. Valentino and Ms. Edmunds, who had her long hair held back with a purple barrette. Both were garbed in jeans and mortal clothes. It was the first time I had seen them dressed as mortals since I entered the Otherworld.

"Great timing," Queen Marianne smiled at them. "You got your belongings? Wands? Weapons?"

The two of them nodded grimly.

"Now, Helen," said King Patrick, "lead the others down to the fountain, where you'll begin your mission. I wish you all the best."

I could tell he was nervous, but he was good at suppressing his emotions.

"Young heroes, I have something to give each of you," Queen Marianne said. She took the four velvet pouches on the wooden shelf and handed each of us one.

"Wow, a gift? Thanks, I'm going to open mine right—"

"No, Clarissa," said Queen Marianne. "These are magical

pouches. I've placed a charm in each of them, and you're supposed to open them during the mission when you face your darkest hour. Use it only when times are desperate when nobody nor anything can save you. Also, every pouch can only be used once throughout the whole mission, so choose your time wisely. Now, you'd better get going. Helen, Zack, may luck be with you." Queen Marianne shook Mr. Valentino's hand and enfolded Ms. Edmunds in an embrace. "Farewell, heiresses."

Eileen, Daphne, and I nodded rather stiffly since nobody except Clarissa was able to digest everything that had happened in the last hour.

"Let's get going, then." Ms. Edmunds and Mr. Valentino led us out of the weapon chamber.

I looked at Queen Marianne, my lips parting.

"Alexandria, you have something to say?" she asked.

A pause.

"Goodbye, Your Majesties. I...I won't disappoint you." Then, terrified to see my parents' reactions, I turned on my heels and raced to the others—

"Alexandria, wait!" King Patrick called. "I...I see something."

"You saw something?" I knit my eyebrows. "Um, Your Majesty?" I added hastily, trying not to sound offensive.

King Patrick looked embarrassed. "Perhaps I never mentioned this to you before, but the ancient seer, Delphia, also had an heir. This is a secret between you, me, and Marianne."

"And...you're the heir?" I guessed. His words threw me for a loop.

"Yes and no. Delphia was a member of the Richardson family, and the ability to foresee the future passed on from one generation to the next. When your mother and I were fighting for the Otherworld, Alta struck me with a horrible jinx, damaging my seeing ability. I've never been able to tell complete prophecies since then. However, I sometimes see or sense illusions from the future, and I just saw something. About you."

His words sent a chill down my spine. "What exactly do

you see, Your Majesty?"

King Patrick closed his eyes. "You'll...wait, the image is clouded by mist, but I can make out...yes. Listen, you'll...you'll end where...you started. And...you'll find happiness one day while facing a mirror."

"Huh?" I stared blankly at his apologetic expression.

"I'm sorry, Alexandria," he said. "Sometimes, my visions get a bit...twisted. And...well, you've also inherited my damaged seeing ability. I'm so sorry, dear. If only I could explain it." King Patrick gave me a meaningful look, as if wanting to say more, but then thought better of it.

"Alexandria, come on!" shouted Clarissa.

I waved goodbye to the king and queen and hurried towards the staircase. Halfway along the hallway, I looked back to get one last glimpse of my parents. King Patrick nodded sheepishly at me, and Queen Marianne rippled her fingers in a shy wave. I wanted to apologize for my impertinence, but the words got stuck in my throat. Instead, I forced a smile at them and left the seventh floor to join my companions.

"Took you long enough," muttered Daphne as we followed the two Elders down the endless flights of stairs. "Scared, little princess?"

"Not as much as you are," I retaliated with a glare.

Soon, we reached the lifeless courtyard. Eileen's eyes darted from tree to tree, from bush to bush, probably looking for Ella. However, the kittenpillar was nowhere to be seen.

"How are we going to get to the Underworld?" asked Clarissa, bouncing up and down. She was obviously not taking notice of the Elders' dark expressions. "Perhaps we could fly on unibirds? Or...hitchhike?"

Ms. Edmunds silenced her with a stern look. "I don't like that giddy attitude of yours, Clarissa Dawson. We're not going on a picnic. This is a mission. You never know what will happen next in the Underworld. We either succeed or face something worse than banishment." She turned to Mr. Valentino. "Everything packed? We might be staying in the Underworld for more than one night."

"What?" The four of us exchanged looks of consternation.

"Nobody mentioned camping outdoors!" Daphne whined. "I'm not staying out for more than—"

"There's no turning back now, I'm afraid," said Mr. Valentino. "Heiresses, please get into the fountain. The only way to journey to another world is to take an aquaportal, a water portal. There's a fountain two miles away from the palace that leads to the mortal world, but we can only get to the Underworld via this one."

"What?" I groaned. "Not again! We almost got killed by the two aqua—"

"You heard Zack," said Ms. Edmunds fiercely. "Go."

We obeyed, and the two Elders followed suit.

"I'll do a countdown," announced Ms. Edmunds. "When I finish, raise your scepters and shout our destination aloud—the Underworld. We're taking off in three...two...one!"

"The Underworld!"

I squeezed my eyes shut as I felt myself flying through cool darkness.

Chapter Five

THE UNDERWORLD
(ZACK)

Splash!

Alexandria inhaled a gulp of water and coughed as the six of us climbed out of the fountain. She tapped her scepter on her palm, and a neat ball of fire burst from the tip. The flames hissed as the fireball blazed vigorously. As the heiress of Ember, she not only was immune to fire but could also summon it when in need. One by one, she dried everyone's clothes with the fireball.

The sun grinned at us from above as I tried to recover my spatial awareness. This time, the portal had brought us to a savanna. It was a bizarre sight, a fountain perched in the middle of a vast, grassy savanna. The water rippled gently, gleaming under the sunlight. Tall tufts of grass grew here and there in the distance, their thin, yellowish-green blades protruding from the meandering meadows all around us. In the distance stood a lonely tree with leaves greener than emeralds. Sure enough, the weather here was much better than the Otherworld.

It's because of the gem they've got, I thought, feeling slightly disturbed by everything in the Underworld.

Helen's words rang in my ears: *You never know what will happen next in the Underworld*. At that thought, I cast a glance at her, and she caught my eye. We exchanged a knowing look at that moment.

The fountain was not stationed here the last time I came with her. Helen had told me the first time I set foot into the Underworld that it was a world of utmost evil and could actually read people's minds. The Underworld was a terrain-shifter—it was able to shift its topography in order to confuse travelers. Unlike the regular fountain portal that connected the Otherworld to the mortal world, the entrances and exits to the Underworld changed every time. The aquaportals would never take us to the same part of the Underworld twice. I was fine with the ever-changing entrances, but the ever-changing exits were another matter. Anything with water, from a big river to a small creek to an ancient fountain, could be the aquaportal back to the Otherworld. According to my past experiences, we had to try almost every river, fountain, or stream in the hope of striking it lucky and guessing the right one. Although we made it back to the Otherworld on our fifth guess the previous time we were here, that didn't stop the mission from being a total disaster.

Six months ago, Helen, Lilith, a young Elder named Evonne, and I came to the Underworld on a mission. It was so horrendous I would give anything to have that experience erased from my memory. Even though I was terrified, Evonne, who was still an Elder-in-training, would have been more traumatized if she could recall it.

We were trapped in a humongous labyrinth of granite pillars and separated by two identical passages, grouping me and Lilith together and Helen and Evonne in the other. Just when I thought Lilith and I would still be able to escape, a shroud of mist formed and separated the two of us, which meant I was on my own. The passages twisted and turned, toying with my mind. While fighting my way out, I came across terrifying monsters I had never dealt with before. There were formidable dragons that killed enemies by embedding their talons in the victim's throat and enormous twenty-legged spiders with gleaming green eyes and wicked smiles etched upon their faces. I had only two choices then: one, to fight them, or two, to let them finish me off. It was the first time I had to face these terrifying creatures all by myself, and I was scared to death. I could still recall the disgusting taste of my sweat mingled with blood and tears.

Luckily, after killing a giant poisonous scorpion, I found Lilith right behind it. It turns out that Lilith and I had both swung our swords at the same time without knowing and confused the creature. Then, I stabbed my blade into its unprotected belly and saved the two of us. After meeting up with Lilith, my worries dissolved. With the help of each other, we fought and slayed many monsters along the way and eventually stumbled across Helen, who was in the middle of a duel with a bearnix. The sudden advent of Lilith and I distracted it, and that gave Helen enough time to confuse it with mist. Then, the three of us got away just in time. However, we still couldn't find Evonne, and we were worried sick since she was the youngest and least experienced among us.

After a few twists and turns, we finally found her lying unconscious in one of the false passages. The terrifying image of Evonne sprawled in a puddle of blood, her dark blonde hair mingled with green liquid that resembled poison, her face chalk-white, and her forehead coated with blood was permanently engraved in my memory. The sight of Evonne's mangled body almost drove the three of us insane. I had never seen Helen's face that pale or Lilith's eyes that wide with fear. As for me, I cried like a startled baby. I had never seen anyone looking so dead in my thirty-five years of life.

Evonne barely made it back alive. The three of us took turns carrying her as we hurried to the adjacent fountains and rivers, trying to find the portal back to the Otherworld. After four failed attempts, we finally succeeded. Evonne was seriously injured, and no incantation nor potion could heal her. King Patrick and Queen Marianne did everything to save her, but her situation was touch-and-go. After two weeks, Evonne finally managed to regain consciousness, but unfortunately, she had lost her memory. We tried everything to help her recall her past, but our efforts were to no avail. Her memory was wiped blank. She remembered nothing, not even her childhood nor parentage.

The whole episode took a heavy toll on Helen, and she was never the same again. She began to retreat into herself, focusing more and more on her duties rather than socializing with the Elders. I didn't blame her since the misadventure not only damaged her reputation but also was the reason the Elders practically imploded. Almost half of the Elders lost faith in their Representative and kept their distance from her. Some, though neutral, refused to have anything to do with her. It was obvious that they were jealous of her because she had been the Representative Elder for fifteen years. Helen, like her name, was like the moon shining brightly amidst the innumerable stars, dimming them with her radiant beams. Of course, the stars that were outshone — the jealous Elders — were eager to have a reason to start vilifying Helen in public since she'd failed on a mission.

A hearing was held because of this. King Patrick, Queen Marianne, and all the Elders were there, interrogating the witnesses of the disastrous mission. After Helen had explained and clarified everything, we voted on whether her Representative title should be withdrawn. In the end, her position was preserved, yet barely. This voting result dissatisfied many Elders. They did horrible things to Helen, spread rumors about her, and justified their evil deeds by claiming they were defending Evonne. A young Elder, Jill, poisoned the unibirds in the royal stables and pushed the blame on Helen, but her plan backfired when Helen herself brewed a healing potion and saved the unibirds. After the king and queen investigated further, they discovered the truth, and as a result, Jill was banished from the palace. Another Elder, Vincent, told a downright lie to the king and queen and claimed that Helen was planning regicide on them because she wanted to take over the throne. However, this was such a farfetched story that the king demanded that the guards lock him in the dungeons for a month.

Fortunately, not all of the Elders were against Helen. Lilith and I promised her that we would both support her until the end, no matter what.

Helen refused to mention or recall anything that had to do with Evonne's accident. To her, that harrowing event was an emotional trigger that led to an endless pit of depression and sorrow. I understood how she felt, so I never blamed her for fielding it, as I had also suffered from that incident. Nightmares about that misadventure haunted me. A zombie with bloodshot eyes, a skeleton with rattling bones, and a dogfish whose mouth reeked of blood accompanied the image of a nearly dead Evonne. I knew that Helen must have taken the situation worse since she was the leader of that mission. Every time I passed her in the hallways, her gaze was melancholic. The cheerful Helen I once knew was gone. Lilith and I told her countless times that Evonne's accident was not her fault, but she never forgave herself.

I was certain that Helen would rather have a swim in the moat than return to the Underworld, so I was shocked when she volunteered to participate in this mission. Perhaps it was because she wanted to be the hero, or maybe she wanted to prove herself to King Patrick and Queen Marianne. Either way, it was unarguably brave of her to face this cursed world again after that traumatizing event.

***

Anyway, while I was lost in my thoughts, Helen cleared her throat.

"Battle plans," she said curtly.

"What would you suggest, Ms. Edmunds?" asked Alexandria.

"How many times have I told you to just call me Helen?"

"No need to be so cranky with me," casually answered Alexandria. "By the way, this is the first time you've told me so." Then, after catching a glimpse of Helen's stony expression, she added meekly, "Oh, um...sorry — Helen."

"So what in the world are we supposed to do?" said Daphne. "Finding a tiny gemstone in the Underworld is like searching for a needle in a haystack."

"Our ultimate goal is to get to the palace, where I assume it's being hidden," said Helen, her gaze sweeping across the five of us as if to see who dared to challenge her.

"You mean the Gem of—" began Clarissa, but I clapped my hand to her mouth before she could finish.

"Don't say it out loud!" scolded Helen. Then, her voice dropped to a whisper. "The Underworld is a terrain-shifter. The terrains here shift around randomly to confuse us, so we'll get to see a myriad of landscapes today. However, I know for a fact that the palace is the hub of the Underworld. In other words, the terrains revolve around it, like planets orbiting the sun in the solar system. But if we go—"

"Did you just mention that this world can read our thoughts?" Eileen cut in, looking anxious.

"Something like that. It toys with our minds."

"Has anyone…died or gotten seriously hurt here before? On your past missions?"

"Many people are sent into the Underworld, but few ever come back alive," I said perfunctorily, casting a quick glance at Helen, who gave me a look of gratitude. This was a touchy subject for her, and I knew she wouldn't want to go through the details again.

"So—" said Daphne.

"So one day you see a peninsula here, but the next day, it becomes a glacier, and you find yourself in a tundra. The day after the next, this glacier turns into a fjord, and the next after the next, you wonder, where did that hummock come from? Then, the hummock changes into a savanna. Well, it goes on and on like that, and you get confused."

Alexandria and Eileen both frowned as though having trouble comprehending my words.

Clarissa blinked. "What was that bunch of scientific mumbo-jumbo? Can you speak English?"

"Of course!" I said, grinning. "I'm your English teacher—you haven't forgotten about that, have you?"

The puzzled expressions on Alexandria, Clarissa, and Eileen's faces wore out, and they cracked up. Daphne looked sourly at them.

Helen's lips thinned. "Excuse me, but I'm the leader of—"

but the rest of her sentence was cut off by a deafening —

"ROAR!"

The creature that had appeared out of nowhere had the vertical slit pupils of a cat and the caramel-colored fur of a lion. It narrowed its red eyes and bared its yellow teeth at us.

"Which way should we go?" yelled Alexandria.

"There!" I pointed in a random direction. "Come with me!"

Without another word, we bolted across the savanna, the beast on our heels. Helen turned and fired three arrows at a time, a few hitting the lion-cat. It staggered but then advanced on her to get revenge. Luckily, Alexandria hurled a fireball at the monster and distracted it.

The lion-cat was injured yet undefeated. It let out another roar and sprinted after us.

Things were not going well in front. As the topography ahead changed, we found ourselves facing a suspension bridge with ropes hanging on either side. Below it was a fifty-foot valley and a creek with craggy boulders in it. White waves swished and leapt over the rocks furiously as if racing through an obstacle course.

"We have to cross this thing, quick!" Helen, who was far behind, hollered at us. "Zack, go last! Make sure the four of them get to the other side!"

Alexandria was the first to pluck up the courage and go. She took a deep breath and set off. But halfway across the bridge, the plank beneath her feet cracked. She let out a yelp and seized the ropes, leaving her legs dangling in mid-air. For a few moments, she remained suspended in the air as if calculating her next move. Then, warily, she let go of the left rope and held on to the right with both hands.

"Cling on tight and swing yourself forward until you reach the other side!" I called out to her.

"I'm not doing it!"

"Now's not the time to argue back!" Helen, who had caught up with us, yelled. "Eileen, go! And hold on tight to the ropes!"

Eileen managed to get through the first five planks, but when she was about to set foot on the sixth, it cracked.

"What should I do?" wailed Eileen.

"The left rope! Move along it with your hands!"

Eileen obeyed. She proceeded along with great caution by swinging herself forward, gripping the rope with one hand, and letting go of the other as she inched her way towards her destination. Left, right, left, right.... We watched her edge closer and closer to the other side, and she finally succeeded while Alexandria was still struggling on how not to fall.

"Now, Clarissa—"

Crack! To my horror, the entire bridge collapsed as if smashed by an invisible force. Our only hope of getting to the other side was to swing on the ropes.

"Don't worry, I know what to do," said Clarissa. Before I could stop her, she gripped loosely on the left rope and slid to the other side as if playing on a zipline and landed gracefully.

Then it was Daphne's turn. With trembling fingers, she clenched her fists around the rope and began moving forward. She reminded me of a fragile leaf swaying in the wind; her whole body shook, and her blue ponytail quivered in little wavelets. I held my breath, praying that she would make it to the other end. However, halfway through the bridge, her hand slipped, and she lost her grip.

I clapped a hand to my mouth, and Helen gasped, clutching her heart, but Alexandria seized Daphne's wrist just in time.

"Let go of me!" Daphne's hysterical screams split the air.

"I won't," said Alexandria. She had somehow managed to cling on tight with one hand and hold on to Daphne with the other.

My mouth dropped open. *The heiress of Ember saving the heiress of Walters?*

"Why don't you just let me die? I hate you, and I don't want to owe you one! Let go of me!" Daphne made an attempt to break free, but Alexandria had an iron grip.

Two unibirds were quarreling in the clouds and had

stopped to look at them. I would have wiped them out if I hadn't been so surprised by what I had just witnessed. Helen, looking fascinated, also had her gaze fixed upon the two heiresses.

"No," said Alexandria firmly, hoisting Daphne up.

Daphne's fingers closed around the left rope once again. She stared at Alexandria. "Why are you doing this?" I heard her ask, her tone more incredulous than spiteful.

Alexandria didn't answer her. She gripped the rope with her right hand, let go of her left, and swung herself forward. Then, she looked over her shoulder and shot Daphne a grim look. "As much as I used to dislike you, we're both Otherworldians, like it or not. We are on the same boat, and I won't let it sink."

With a few more swings, Alexandria landed on the other side.

Daphne, who reached her destination moments later, looked at her sheepishly. "You...you didn't have to do that."

"I know I didn't," replied Alexandria, shrugging. Blushing a little, she devoted her attention to combing her tangled red hair instead.

"Thanks," a grudging Daphne said to the mossy ground.

"You know what? You owe me big time."

Daphne smiled. "You know what?"

Alexandria raised her eyebrows.

"Perhaps I really do."

Helen and I arrived after a few seconds, both sweating and panting.

"Now what?" I asked her. She opened her mouth to speak, but—

"Hello," came a boy's voice. Nine handsome boys emerged from behind a flower bush. They had charming eyes, perfect noses, and soft, moistened lips. Most of them were wearing light makeup and were so attractive the heiresses' eyes were glued on them, with Alexandria being the only exception. That was what I liked most about her. She wasn't vain, nor did she judge people based on their appearance.

Helen narrowed her eyes at the boys. "I would appreciate it if you mind your own business and get out of our way."

The boys chose to ignore her. Instead, they beamed at Eileen. "What a beauty!"

"I've never seen one like her in years!"

"What's your name?" one of the boys laid a hand on Eileen's shoulder. "I'm Frank."

"What do you think you're doing?" Alexandria stepped in between the boy and Eileen.

"None of your business, carrot-head," another boy said to her. The others sniggered.

"You always want to be the center of attention, don't you?" Eileen rounded on Alexandria, her tone uncharacteristically vicious. "Now's my moment, and don't you dare take my spotlight!"

"Calm down, beauty. Boy, your little girlfriend is jealous, isn't she?"

Alexandria caught my eye and tried to warn me that something was wrong.

I tightened my grip on the hilt of my sword while I saw Helen getting out her bow. Clarissa, Eileen, and Daphne were still gazing into the dark, mesmerizing eyes of the boys as if they had fallen under a spell.

Fallen under a spell.

I suddenly recalled what Helen had indicated during our penultimate Elders' meeting—her newest discovery. She had found out that devils and devilines, male and female devils that roamed the Underworld, could change their appearances to fool their enemies.

Then, it hit me—these boys were monsters in disguise. I glanced at Helen, who apparently was thinking the same.

"Fight," I mouthed to her.

"Now's not the time," she said in an undertone. "We'll attack on my command later."

"How about giving me a kiss?" said the boy named Frank, gazing profoundly into Eileen's eyes.

"Don't, they're trying to trick you," I whispered to her, but she was deaf to my words.

Frank and Eileen edged closer to each other. Closer and closer they got, and—

"Attack!"

Helen, Alexandria, and I were the only ones prepared. Clarissa and Daphne, still rooted to the ground, remained motionless, their eyes staring out of focus.

Helen fired an arrow at the monsters and injured one of them; it pierced a boy's leg, and he fell to the ground, moaning and groaning. Alexandria pelted another with huge fireballs. I brought my sword to the neck of a boy and slashed at him.

The others gasped.

Frank stopped making kissy faces at Eileen. "Well, it's all over." His voice was sharp, metallic, and somewhat bloodthirsty. "Show them our true colors!"

With a leap and a twirl, the boys' handsome faces melted off their skin.

Alexandria gasped in horror. "What the...?"

"Devils and devilines. Male and female devils. Experts at disguising themselves." I watched, thunderstruck, as the remaining monsters snarled at us. The devils and devilines had completely transformed; they now had wrinkly green skin and eyes without pupils. Large turquoise horns stuck out from their heads.

"Get them!" hissed ex-Frank.

"Don't just stand there, Zack, do something!" Helen was dueling one-on-two with the devilines. With a well-aimed blow, one of them collapsed.

I fired a streak of purple light at ex-Frank and got her long hair tangled up with her horns. She snarled and growled, but it was no use.

"Mrrrr!" I turned around and saw two devils coming in my direction. I brandished my sword and stabbed one of them in the stomach. Just as I was dueling the other—

"Grr!" Ex-Frank dashed towards me with her horns sticking out.

"Take that!" Alexandria dived in ex-Frank's way and hurled a fireball at her. She waved her hand, and a wall of fire formed behind the devil I had been dueling.

I seized my opportunity and gave him a kick in the kneecaps, and he lost his balance and hit the firewall, his hair burning and his body melting. However, I could still hear ex-Frank growling. She obviously wasn't deceived or killed by the firewall.

Helen aimed an arrow at ex-Frank's heart, but for a fraction of a moment, I saw a look of hesitation in her eyes. She lowered her bow, her fingers quivering.

"Helen!" I shouted. "We've got to kill them!"

"Couldn't we just hurt—?" she looked pleadingly at me.

"No, they've put the heiresses under a spell, and the only way to break it is to kill them!"

Alexandria conjured another fireball and chucked it at ex-Frank, causing her hair to catch fire. Ex-Frank screamed, tugging at her burning hair, and that gave Helen enough time to shoot her. Bullseye! The arrow pierced her neck. Ex-Frank slumped to the ground, writhing in agony and eventually ceasing her struggle.

"Well done," I breathed.

"At least I didn't have to activate the hurler," said Helen.

"What's that?" asked Alexandria.

Helen's hand plunged into the pocket of her jeans, and she produced a ball of iridescent light that changed color with each glance. "This is the hurler, the most powerful and deadly weapon in the Otherworld."

"You should've had it activated. I really thought we were dying over there!"

"You haven't seen a worse situation," I replied. "The second time I came here with Helen and another Elder named Arthur, there was this huge swamp that had all of us immobilized. But luckily, Arthur saved—"

"You've killed him!" a voice screamed. "How could you!"

"Not another deviline?" I whispered, glancing at Helen.

"Another…?" Alexandria tightened her grip on her scepter.

"HE WAS MY TRUE LOVE, HOW DARE YOU?!" the

speaker fired a spiky black rose at Helen.

I turned, just in time to see—

"EILEEN SPENCER! HAVE YOU GONE MAD?" Alexandria, who had witnessed everything, shouted in dismay. She waved her hand to create another firewall, intercepting Eileen's spiky rose.

Did my eyes deceive me? No, not Eileen. I knew her. She would never do—

"Ugh...," came a groan from below.

I looked down and saw ex-Frank's eyes snap shut.

Eileen blinked twice as if rousing from a trance. Clarissa and Daphne exchanged blank looks.

"What...what have I done?" Eileen ran over to us, looking appalled. "I...I'm sorry, Helen! I really am! I...oh, I swear I didn't mean to, I didn't know! I wasn't myself!"

Sparks of fire danced furiously on Alexandria's fingertips. "What if you actually killed one of us?" she bellowed at Eileen, who lowered her head.

All of a sudden, everything dawned on me. Helen caught my eye, and I had a feeling she understood everything, too.

"Eileen, can you recall what happened?" Helen asked, looking concerned.

"I remember...a boy called Frank or something. He was nice...and so romantic. He...he said he loved me. The rest....I... well...."

Clarissa dashed over to us. "What in the world happened?"

"Was there...a battle?" Daphne looked at the bloody corpses of the devils and devilines.

"I…sort of fell into a trance, and there's been a big blank in my memory for the past twenty minutes and...." Eileen's voice faltered. "Oh, I didn't mean to! I just couldn't...."

"It's all right," said Helen, her voice hollow.

"Helen?" I asked. "Is it...what I'm thinking?"

"Yes," she replied, slowly at first, then faster and faster. "Here's my interpretation of what just happened. The devils and devilines disguised themselves as handsome boys to fool us, then used their own brand of magic to...to enchant Eileen, then manipulate her mind and use her against us. Their brand of magic allows others to see an illusion—somebody or something that attracts the seer. For instance, a person who believes in romance will see the devils and devilines as ideal spouses; a person who longs desperately for wealth will see them as bags of gold. They also put Clarissa and Daphne into trances, wiping their memories blank before planning to finish them off."

Once again, Helen impressed me deeply with her wisdom and incredible logic.

"But you, Zack, and Alexandria weren't affected," Daphne pointed out.

"What did you expect?" said Clarissa. "The Elders are far more powerful and experienced than we are."

"But what about Alexandria?" Eileen asked, eying her with wonder.

Helen sighed. Her weary eyes seemed a hundred years old as if she had beheld too much of the ugliness and suffering of the world. The hardships, the difficulties, and the horrible memories of her past seemed to revisit her mind. "I...I don't know about that."

"It might be more difficult to enchant a princess of the Otherworld since her blood is purer than any of yours," I suggested.

"That might be it," decided Helen.

Clarissa gasped. "Hey...look at that...." She pointed to a winding cobblestone path that was forming all by itself.

A pause. Everyone gazed at it as though hypnotized.

"So, what are we waiting for?" said Helen finally. She made her way along the path, motioning for us to follow.

My pulse thudded in my ears, and my heart slammed against my chest as we trailed behind her. An ominous feeling licked my insides.

This, usually, was a bad omen. The writing was on the wall.

Chapter Six

ERIC
(ALEXANDRIA)

We proceeded along the cobblestone path and ran into four bearnixes and kittenpillars that had been lurking behind shrubs and trees, but the two Elders got rid of them in a blink of an eye. Daphne caught sight of two unibirds hiding behind a cloud and gestured at Helen to shoot them.

"Helen, please!" Eileen, the animal lover, begged. "They haven't done anything to us!"

"It'll be too late if they have," Daphne chimed in. "We must finish them off, or it'll be the other way around."

"No! They didn't attack us!"

"They will, sooner or later," Zack piped up.

Helen silenced all of them with a harsh look. Meanwhile, the two unibirds had flown away.

"Look at what you've done!" Daphne snapped at Eileen.

I was about to step in when the cobblestone path ahead split into three forks right before my eyes. "Can somebody tell us what to do next?" I asked, trying to end their pointless argument and have them concentrate on our mission instead.

Everyone shot intuitive looks at Helen, who glanced helplessly at Zack.

"Well, I trust your judgement, Helen," he said with a chuckle.

"Oh, great. Let me think...."

At that moment, I noticed a bedraggled teenager standing by the left fork. The boy looked about fifteen and seemed exceptionally tall for his age. He had pimples on his forehead and cheeks, making him look like a regular adolescent boy instead of a handsome monster, like the ones we had just encountered. His suspenders and white shirt were dirty, and his boots were smeared with mud. His untidy red hair was like a bird's nest.

I made my way towards him. "Sir?"

"Who are you?" said the boy with a scowl. "What do you want? And why are you here?"

"I'm Alexandria, and I come from the Otherworld."

The boy's eyes narrowed with skepticism.

"I'm here on a mission—to find the Gem of Hope."

The boy let out a sneer. "I don't believe you. King Patrick and Queen Marianne know better than to send a little girl into a world of evil. They—"

"Are my parents."

His disdainful expression instantly faded, replaced by a rather curious look. "Interesting...so you're the princess of the Otherworld?"

"I am."

"I'm sorry," he said, looking flustered. "I didn't mean to—"

"Quite all right. Just tell us which path leads to the palace of the Underworld. We're trying to get there."

"Take the left fork."

"Thanks," I replied, ready to rejoin my companions. I turned, only to find them coming in my direction. "The left fork, guys. We can just go on and—"

Eileen drew nearer to the boy and took a sharp intake of breath. "Oh, Zack! Look at his blue eyes and straight nose! He looks just like you! Almost like a doppelgänger!"

For a moment, I saw a look of mild astonishment on

Zack's face, but it soon wore out. I studied the boy and realized that Eileen was indeed right. I suddenly knew why the boy had caught my attention in the first place—he resembled Zack in miniature. Except for his red hair, thick eyebrows, and pimples, he looked almost the same as Zack.

"What's your name?" I said, my curiosity getting the best of me.

"Eric Williams. I'm fifteen." His gaze drifted to Clarissa, Eileen, Daphne, and the two Elders. "And who are your... friends?"

"Helen and Zack are both Elders. Clarissa, Eileen, Daphne and I are heiresses of the four Creators. Like I said before, we're all from the Otherworld."

Helen groaned; Clarissa gave me a violent nudge; Daphne rolled her eyes and muttered, "Hopeless."

"Oh," said Eric.

A bleeding gash on his arm caught my eye, and a ripple of sympathy touched my heart. It triggered my awful memories of the orphanage. "How did you get that?"

Eric hung his head. "I don't want to talk about it, but you seem like a nice listener."

"Really? Go on, then, if you don't mind."

"My mother, my only living family, hates me. I mean nothing to her. I'm nobody. She always said I reminded her of my father a lot, and she wreaks her hatred towards him by hurting me." He rolled up his sleeves, revealing more cuts. Some had formed scabs, while fresh blood was still oozing from the others.

Pity for Eric welled up within me. "That's horrible!"

"You're the only one who's ever said that. I just ran away from home yesterday. I flew on a unibird and probably would have made it further if someone hadn't shot it and landed me here."

"What? You...you ran away? But where are you heading for?"

"In fact, I was hoping I'd make it to the Otherworld. I don't belong here in the Underworld. Nobody needs me."

"But what about your mother? Why did she keep you then

if she hates you so much?"

"I've been asking myself that question for my whole life. I guess it's because she wanted to make me miserable. My mother doesn't care whether I live or die. She treats me as if I'm unworthy of her affection. I don't call my family a family, nor my home a home. I'm a misfit in the Underworld."

Something in Eric's tone and expression convinced me he wasn't lying. "I'm sorry to hear that. I know what it's like, after spending the first ten years of my life in a dreadful orphanage. The older kids played games that involved me getting hurt. I was fostered by a couple four years ago, but they never loved or cared for me. I'm just like you, and I understand how you feel — nobody to trust." After a moment of hesitation, I added, "But... you can trust me."

"You? Why?" Eric shot me an incredulous look.

"Because," I lowered my voice to make it audible only to him, "we are the same. Unappreciated. Unloved. Unwanted."

Eric nodded wistfully, then started talking again, this time faster than before. "My mother believes in the evil and worships King Alto and Queen Alta, regardless of their immoral leadership. They think the meaning of life is to have control over everything and make people yield to them. They hate the Otherworld and despise King Patrick and Queen Marianne for being peace-lovers. It's King Alto and Queen Alta's ambition to rule the Otherworld one day and turn it into a realm of utmost evil, which is to say, the second Underworld."

"What about you? You don't want them to, do you?"

Eric shook his head. "Of course not. They're being ridiculous. The Otherworld is a place I'd love to be a part of. It's a world of peace and hope, completely different from the Underworld." His lips parted as though wanting to ask a question but then decided against it.

"What's wrong?" I said gently.

"You said you're from the Otherworld. Are you really?"

I nodded.

"Take me there, please."

My jaw dropped open. "You're not serious, are you?"

"Please. I need somewhere to escape to, something to believe in, proof that there is some light left in this terrible world." Eric's gaze was pleading, his eyes shone with fierce desire, and his voice was filled with unmistakable longing.

"But what will your mother say?" Daphne chimed in.

"She doesn't care about me, and vice versa."

"What? You're her son!"

"Yes, physically. But mentally, no."

Daphne stared at him, shock written on her face.

"You may think of me as an ungrateful whiner, but in fact, you have no right to judge me because you have never gone through what I have. My mother has made my life a living hell."

Daphne took a step back at his fierce turn of attitude. Clarissa and Eileen exchanged dark looks.

I looked expectantly at Zack, who bit his lip, and Helen, whose eyebrows were knitted.

"Eric," said Zack after what seemed like a long time, "You may join the Otherworld. But since you are an Underworldian, you must first pledge an oath to Helen, the Representative of all Elders."

Helen's scowl had become more pronounced than before.

"If you are ready, repeat the words of the oath with her," said Zack. "But, as a reminder, I must tell you that this oath contains an exceptionally strong brand of magic, and such a powerful oath cannot be broken. If you break it, it will take your life. Consider well, my boy."

"I'll never break the oath!" Eric's eyes glittered with hope, and his voice quivered with excitement. "May I start pledging allegiance right now? I've waited for fifteen years, and it's been my dream since I was a child. Please allow me to prove myself to you. Help me out of here. *Please.*"

Daphne glanced at Clarissa. "I wouldn't admit a boy who wouldn't trust his own mother," she muttered, running her fingers through her hair.

"Eric, I'll ask you one last time before you pledge the oath. Have you made your final decision?"

"Yes. Lord Zack, I've made up my mind to join you."

"Wait a second," Helen interrupted. "Eric Williams, I'm going to have a word with Zack. In the meantime, consider carefully. This is a decision that will affect your whole life."

The two Elders then disappeared behind an enormous bush.

I went in their direction to eavesdrop while Clarissa, Eileen, and Daphne debated about the matter.

"You may have shown compassion to the boy, but this is ridiculous! Outrageous! Absolutely unacceptable!" Helen's face flushed red with anger. "The boy is from the Underworld, and everyone and everything in the Underworld is evil. How could you even *trust* him? Have you stopped to consider the ramifications of such a promise?"

"I sense no animosity from Eric," began Zack, his tone placid. "He has been through a lot. Eric Williams is not beyond redemption, don't you see? We might be preserving an innocent soul if we reach out to help him. We have an invaluable opportunity to change his fate and show him that not everything in the world is evil. Eric hasn't been influenced by his mother, and he needs *something* to believe in. Anyway, the oath is enchanted. If he chooses to betray us, he will die. I see no reason to prevent him from joining us."

I thought such an impeccable speech would be enough to convince Helen, but as usual, I was wrong.

"This is way too dangerous, and I will not permit it," she sniffed with dignity. "You disappoint me, Zachary Valentino. To be frank, I had higher expectations for you. I thought you knew better than to act on impulse. Surely I taught you better than that."

I knew deep down in my heart that Helen was right, but at this point, I couldn't help feeling a surge of resentment towards her. I could relate to everything Eric had said about being mistreated. He was like a reflection of my past self, and Zack was right. Eric needed something to believe in.

"With all due respect, Helen Edmunds, I must say that

you are way too sensible sometimes."

"Is that an insult? No Elder has ever dared to challenge my authority, let alone a former apprentice of mine."

I held my breath, sensing that a quarrel was about to break out among the two Elders.

"I most certainly did not challenge your authority," Zack started off cautiously.

"Then what do you mean?" Helen crossed her arms in front of her chest. I wouldn't have been surprised to see smoke billowing from her ears and nostrils.

"Helen, I never meant to insult you. But just put yourself in Eric's position. How would you feel if you were him, nobody to trust or love?" Seeing that Helen did not reply, he went on, gently yet firmly. "I am in favor of letting Eric join the Otherworld. He is a brave young man who hasn't been tainted by darkness. He abides by his own morals, and he defied his mother instead of being brainwashed and turning into a monster like her. Helen, I'm certain you'll understand this because you're so intelligent: some people turn on society and become evil because society turned on them first, smothering their hope by rejecting and disappointing them again and again. Surely you wouldn't want Eric to become the next Alta or Alto, would you? I'm sure your answer will be no because I *know* you. You have a kind heart and a fine mind. I will intervene no more and leave the final decision to you because I trust you as much as King Patrick and Queen Marianne do. You will make the right decision."

I felt a wave of respect for Zack. His interpersonal intelligence had to be the best among all of the Elders. Nobody could have delivered a better speech than what I had just heard.

"Zack," Helen began slowly, her anger unraveling. "You do know that...this is like taking a gamble, don't you? If we win, we gain a powerful new member. If we lose...." She grimaced and shook her head. "I wouldn't want to imagine the consequences. We might lose not only our positions but also our lives."

"I know. But I have faith in your judgement."

The two of them were silent for a solid minute, both lost in their own thoughts.

Helen inhaled deeply, then exhaled. "Yes, then. I'm going to make an exception for Eric. And Zack... I should never have called you a disappointment." She let out a sigh. "People who have grown older like me tend to ignore the advice younger ones provide."

"No worries," replied Zack, trying to suppress the wide grin on his face.

"Will Eric be coming along with us, then? Journey with us to retrieve the Gem of Hope, a treasure stolen by people from *his* world?" Helen tried to restrain the tiny hint of sarcasm in her voice.

"That's the only way," answered Zack, heaving a sigh of satisfaction. "We can't send him back to the Otherworld on his own, can we?"

The two Elders emerged from behind the bush. Eric, who had been pacing and staring at the ground, looked up at them.

I blinked, assuming the conversation would have lasted longer than that.

Helen looked grimmer than usual, but at least she did not look furious enough to feed anyone to an angry bearnix. "Eric," she said solemnly. "Your time has come. This choice of yours can change your future, your fate, your everything. Choose wisely."

"I choose to join the Otherworld."

Helen got out her wand, which, unlike Lilith's, was plum-purple and bore elaborate carvings. Eric, without another word, followed suit. Then, they crossed wands.

"Your full name?"

"Eric Ethan Williams."

"Repeat the oath with me. 'I, Eric Ethan Williams, solemnly swear to pledge my allegiance to the Otherworld. I shall try my very best to create peace, get along with my fellow Otherworldians, and respect the Elders. I refuse to join or have anything to do with dark magic, and I shall remain faithful to King Patrick and Queen Marianne for an eternity.' Then, your name and today's date."

Eric repeated the oath without hesitation. Streaks of purple and turquoise lights radiated from the two wands as he uttered the final word.

"Purple for the Otherworld, turquoise for the Underworld, right?" I muttered.

"Yes," said Zack half-heartedly. His gaze was focused on the two glowing wands.

"I, Helen Wisteria Edmunds, as the Representative Elder of the Court of the High Advisors, accept Eric Ethan Williams as a new member of the Otherworld. Do you, Eric Ethan Williams, accept your new identity as an Otherworldian?"

Nobody spoke or made the slightest movement. As though we had entered a sacred shrine, everyone remained still and silent.

"I do."

Purple sparks emitted from the crossed wands, which exploded into innumerable tiny stars. They swirled around Eric and erupted into celestial starbursts, beaming rays of silver light and enveloping him in a pearly glow.

Helen drew back her wand. "Finished. You are an Otherworldian now."

"Lady Helen, Lord Zack, I can't thank the two of you enough," said Eric, bowing. "You made my dream come true. I am forever indebted to you for your kindness, and from now on, I shall serve both of you well."

"Addressing me directly by name will do, young man. I wouldn't have compromised if Zack had not insisted. Do not make me regret giving in. Prove yourself worthy."

"Shall we keep moving on, then?" I suggested. "Eric, as I said earlier, we're on a mission to find the Gem of Hope, a precious artifact stolen from the Otherworld."

Eric nodded. "I see. I'll help you in every way I can."

We moved along the cobblestone path, and I walked over to Zack. "Hey, thanks for letting Eric come with us."

"He has a pure heart and an undefiled soul. Like I said to Helen, I sensed no animosity from him."

"I felt the same. Thanks a million."

Meanwhile, Helen spotted a kittenpillar attempting to

ambush us from behind a tree. With a well-aimed arrow that penetrated the kittenpillar's tail, it let out a yowl and stumbled out of view.

Eric glanced at her and gave me a slight nudge. "Is that Helen as pompous as she seems? I don't like her. She thinks she's superior to all of us, doesn't she?"

I gave him a hard look. "No, she doesn't. Eric Williams, you keep this in mind: just because you are now an Otherworldian does not mean you can insult my friends in front of me. Keep your complaints about them all to yourself, or I'll make you regret it." Sparks of fire shot from my fingers as I felt my temper rising.

Eric took a step back. "Sorry."

"It's all right." Suddenly, a wave of tenderness flooded upon me. Being mistreated, Eric probably had no friends and didn't know it was wrong to speak ill of others. "You know, Eric, we can be friends if you want."

"Really?" A smile crossed his face.

I nodded.

"Nobody has ever wanted to be friends with me."

"Hey, I told you that you could trust me, remember? So, friends?"

"Yes then, with great honor." He bowed.

"Well, I prefer saluting," I joked.

Eric looked flustered and went red in the face. "Excuse me. Didn't know that a princess like you could be so tomboyish." He laughed in spite of himself.

"Just joking, Eric," I said, liking him more every moment. He didn't act like a tragic hero, dwelling in his misery all day long. On the contrary, he was a rather cheerful person.

"Stop goofing around!" said Daphne. "We've got something else to worry about."

I looked up, and right she was. Coming from the opposite direction was an army of about twenty bearnixes, kittenpillars, and dogfishes. They took their places and remained static as if waiting for a command to begin their attack.

"Your attention, everyone!" said Helen. "We've got a battle

to fight. Alexandria, Clarissa, Zack, and I will be on the attacking team, and Daphne, Eileen, and Eric on the defense team."

"What? How?" said Daphne frantically. "What's defense? What does a defense member have to do? Somebody help!"

"Will you calm down?" scolded Eileen. "You're not the only one who's nervous! Helen, what now?"

Helen looked at her, flabbergasted as if she had never seen anyone as foolish. "Set traps everywhere with thorn bushes and poison ivy!" she almost yelled at Eileen. "You also have to pay attention to the battlefield. Help anyone on our side."

"Got it," Eileen breathed, clapping her hand to a screaming Daphne's mouth.

"Alexandria, attack the dogfishes, throw fireballs, and perform any spell —"

"But I don't know any!" I protested.

"Just do everything to stop —"

The army of creatures advanced on us.

"Take your places right now!" shouted Helen. "Don't act irrationally. Think before you strike!"

I threw a fireball at the nearest dogfish, who dodged it with great ease. It retaliated by flinging a spiky ball of ice at me.

Zack leapt out of nowhere and slammed his shield at the icy ball. It bounced off his shield, smacking the dogfish right on the nose. It shrieked and howled in pain.

"Uh, thanks," I said.

"Don't mention it."

"Where did you get that shield?"

"I had it with me all along. We Elders keep our weapons shrunken and hidden in our pockets for safekeeping and enlarge them with our wands whenever we need them."

I spotted a bearnix trying to ambush him from behind, and at that precise moment, an arrow whizzed towards us. Zack deflected the arrow with his wand, causing it to strike a nearby kittenpillar, who meowed in agony.

The bearnix that had tried to kill us roared, and fire spouted from its wide mouth. My vision was clouded with flames, a giant, sizzling blur of vermillion and orange and yellow. From the corner of my eye, I saw the bearnix getting out a knife and aiming it at Zack.

"NO!" I brandished my scepter, ready to attack—

All of a sudden, the waves of fire vanished. The knife dropped to the ground and clattered as it hit a stone, and the bearnix keeled over. In its place stood Daphne, looking slightly embarrassed. I nodded to show my gratitude, then devoted my attention to the battlefield.

The enemies were down to less than ten, thanks to Eileen's traps. A dim-witted bearnix burned down the poison ivy in an attempt to free its trapped companions, but its plan backfired. Instead, it caused the leaves to burn and ooze with smoke. The poison of the ivy spread and killed the other prisoners in less than a minute.

"Hey!" Eric roared at the monsters.

Three bearnixes came rushing towards him. With a flick of his wand, he sent a colossal ball of turquoise fire zooming at them. The three bearnixes collapsed into a heap, black liquid oozing from their eyes and ears.

I watched, stunned by Eric's powers. "What was that?"

"Dark magic. Underworldian magic."

"But aren't you now an Otherworldian?"

"Yes, but technically, I'm an Underworldian who switched his allegiance. I will have Underworldian magic as long as my mother's blood runs in my veins. Since I have switched my loyalty to the Otherworld, my magic is now fatal to Underworldians. This is because I have betrayed my world, especially my mother."

"Your mother? But—"

"There! Behind you!"

I turned and saw an army of dogfishes charging towards me. I tossed fireballs at them, but they converted them into icicles and chucked them back at me.

"Over here! Help!"

Helen noticed me and sent a sea of arrows sailing towards the dogfishes, who scampered away frantically. I raced to the others to see if anyone needed assistance. Eileen was dueling a bearnix one-on-one with her scepter. Clarissa and Daphne slammed another to the ground as it let out a roar, fire spouting from its mouth and singeing the ends of Daphne's blue ponytail. Two dogfishes and a kittenpillar lunged at Zack, but I thrust my spear at the monsters and saved him in the nick of time. One of Eric's turquoise fireballs struck the kittenpillar, and it slumped to the ground.

Meanwhile, Helen got out the hurler. It gleamed red, yellow, green, and blue at the same time. The remaining enemies looked horrified. They knelt down clumsily at the sight of the spherical weapon. The dogfishes whimpered and whined as though trying to communicate with us.

"Helen, they're talking to you," said Daphne. Seeing the looks of perplexity on our faces, she explained, "I know what the dogfishes are saying."

"But why can't I understand them?" said Eileen. "I'm the heiress of Fern, so I should—"

"Yes and no," explained Zack. "As Fern's heiress, you are able to talk with all the animals in the mortal world. However, you can only communicate with magical creatures who share the same brand of elemental magic as you. In your case, it's kittenpillars. Bearnixes for Alexandria, unibirds for Clarissa, and dogfishes for Daphne."

"But what about Noir and Bessie, the guards in the palace?"

"They're different. They speak English all the time, so—"

"Right," Daphne cut him off and turned to Helen. "The dogfishes just said, 'My lady, I beg your pardon, we didn't mean to offend you.'"

Helen's eyes narrowed. "Why should I believe you?"

Daphne, with a lot of barking and growling, translated Helen's words into the dogfishes' language.

The dogfishes responded by woofing this time.

"They said, 'We're sorry, my lady. Please have mercy,'" said Daphne.

The dogfishes looked pitiful as they shivered and shed tears.

Just when I thought Helen was going to strike, she lowered

the ball. "Fine, then. Don't ever come near us again, or I won't spare your lives next time. Now go before I change my mind."

Daphne repeated her words in the dogfishes' language. The dogfishes bowed their heads and scuttled away from us.

Zack stared at Helen as if she had taken leave of her senses. "You let them off the hook?"

"Yes," said Helen vaguely, her lips pursed. It occurred to me that she was wondering if she had made the best decision.

"Why didn't you finish them off?" asked Zack. "You would have scored at least fifty points and gotten a bonus of about...." He calculated with his fingers.

"What are you talking about?" I said.

"Our monthly bonus depends on how many Underworldian creatures we kill that month," explained Zack, shifting his weight from one foot to the other in uneasiness.

Helen frowned. "I never liked that bonus-counting program. It was supposed to encourage us to fight for justice by slaying monsters, but many times, I wonder if killing off all those monsters actually makes me one instead. How can someone destroy a monster without becoming one? I try to hurt and weaken the enemies instead of killing them during battles, but sometimes...."

"I agree with you," said Zack. "The whole thing's ridiculous. After all, not every Underworldian is evil."

"That's true," said Helen with a sigh.

"Hang on, you didn't think that way before meeting Eric," replied Daphne.

"No, I realized that *after* getting to know him." Helen turned towards Eric. "I owe you an apology for making negative assumptions about you before. Since you have proven yourself to me, Eric, I sincerely welcome you as a new member of the Otherworld. I'm proud to have you as a part of our team."

Eric bowed deeply at these words.

To my surprise, Helen shook Eric's hand as her solemn expression broke into a warm smile.

Chapter Seven

MY ELEMENTAL POWERS
(CLARISSA)

As we walked on, Eric and I got into a conversation. To my great delight, the two of us got along surprisingly well. We chatted about the flora and fauna in the Underworld and Otherworld, and I was enchanted by the biodiversity in both magical worlds. Trying to get Eileen to listen to her favorite topic, I gestured at her a few times. However, Eileen kept shaking her head, though she stole a few curious glances at Eric. I guessed she was too shy to join our conversation.

The weather today was lovely. Immaculate white clouds gazed down at us as they sailed across the azure sea hovering above us. The trees that lined our path were draped with vivid green blankets of leaves. Filtered through the green canopy above, dapples of sunlight played hide and seek on the ground. The lush green fields around us were sprinkled with red wildflowers, filling the air with a sweet floral aroma.

We passed a white rose bush on the left side of the winding path. I spotted a black butterfly on one of the flowers. It fluttered away when I neared and reached out a hand to stroke it.

Eric heaved a sigh.

"What's wrong?" I asked.

"I knew a beautiful lady who was punished by the Siblings and turned into a black butterfly. Bella, that was her name."

"Why was she punished? And why didn't her family protect her?"

"The Siblings had already taken care of that. They murdered Bella's parents before dealing with her."

"That's terrible. What did Bella do to deserve this?"

"She fell in love with a young man. As they were both believers of kindness, they planned to elope together and flee to the Otherworld, but were unsuccessful."

"Why? What went wrong?"

"The young man was Alta's son, the prince of the Underworld. Unlike his mother, he hated everything in the Underworld, from the lack of freedom to the brainwashed citizens who were all in favor of their tyrants. However, the night he planned to elope with his lover, Alta, who somehow got wind of the news, turned her son's lover into a butterfly forever. As for her son, he had no choice but to stay with his mother."

"So Alta loved her son—" I said, starting to see the whole point.

"No, she didn't!" Eric snapped, a savage look in his eyes. His features were contorted with rage.

Taken aback at his reaction, I took a step backward. "Um...I'm sorry?"

Eric's angry expression immediately wore out. He rubbed his eyes. "Oh no, Clarissa, don't apologize. I shouldn't have yelled at you. It's just that...I lost my father because of Alta, and I cannot imagine how that...." He paused, grasping for a word horrible enough to describe Alta. "That beast would love anyone." Eric took a deep breath before going on. "Alta is rotten to the core, and so is her wicked brother. They slaughtered countless Underworldians and creatures only because they stood up to their immoral leadership. I don't and will never believe they know the meaning of love."

I nodded, then suddenly recalled something he'd mentioned earlier. "Hold on, Eric—so Alta had given birth to a boy before, right? Did she have a husband or—?"

"It was her boyfriend, a man who had loved her *before* she turned evil. The man broke up with her after seeing her true colors."

"What happened to him later?"

"He was murdered by Alta herself," whispered Eric, grimacing.

My heart skipped a beat. "Wait a second—she got rid of her boyfriend because he broke up with her and turned Bella into a butterfly?"

"Not precisely. Well, to be accurate, her boyfriend allegedly disappeared. Rumor has it that he sailed away in a ship, far, far away, beyond the threshold of the Underworld. Yet others claim to have seen Alta kill him. Many people believe the latter, including me, since the Siblings have always been known for mass murdering."

"What are you two talking about?" Alexandria called out to us cheerfully.

"Oh, um...nothing, nothing in the world," Eric replied, looking a little uneasy.

"Not flirting with each other, are you?" said Alexandria, shooting us a sassy look.

I laughed. "Don't be ridiculous. That's impossible!"

Eric, on the other hand, didn't seem that amused. He kept on walking with his eyes staring out into space as though in deep meditation.

The cobblestone path was now winding and curving like mad, but we eventually had to stop. A giant yellow canary approximately two stories tall was blocking the road. It laughed at the sight of us.

"Looky looky what we've got here—an ugly hag, an old man, a traitor boy, and four little girlies! Ha! You think you can beat me? Never!"

The bird's shrill voice sounded exactly like a human's. A shudder ran through my body.

"Of course we can beat you," said Daphne, brandishing her trident. "You're just a silly old bird, aren't you?"

Zack glanced at her and put his index finger over his lips. He mouthed the words, "We'll figure out a way to leave, don't make it mad."

"A silly old bird? For goodness's sake! I'm the Chirpy Bird! Nobody gets away from me!"

Helen groaned as quietly as possible. I saw her exchange dark looks with Zack and mouth "Not again" to him. It occurred to me that this was not the first time they'd dealt with the bird. The signs Helen and Zack had displayed triggered my curiosity. I wondered what had happened the last time they went on a mission.

"You'd better brace yourselves for death," bellowed the bird. "Or maybe if you all bow to me, I might let you go, unharmed. I'm feeling rather merciful today."

Eric's hands were balled into fists. "We'll go down fighting instead!"

The bird laughed shrilly again and mimicked Eric's voice. "You think you stand a chance against me? What a fool! I'd love to see you die fighting! Ha!"

Alexandria stepped forward.

"Don't," the two Elders said together. I grabbed Alexandria's arm, but she broke loose.

"Leave him alone and get lost," she said to the bird through gritted teeth.

"Defending Mr. Traitor, eh?" the bird let out another laugh. "Hmm, how touching."

Alexandria jump-kicked off the ground and brought her spear to the bird's neck. However, the blade bounced off as harmlessly as a rubber ball when it hit the bird.

The Chirpy Bird let out a scream of mirth. "HA! I'm invincible! No weapons can hurt me!"

It was a grotesque sight. Drool oozed from the corners of its beak as it guffawed.

I glanced at Alexandria, who was now deep in discussion with Eric. A few moments later, Alexandria nodded. Eric then walked up to Helen and muttered something in her ear. The two of them exchanged a few urgent whispers, and Helen told him, "Be quick."

"What?" I mouthed to Eric, giving the bird a quick glance.

He came up to me. "Do you know that you can draw clouds from the sky? Just point your scepter at a random cloud up there. Then, concentrate on getting it down. Trust me, it'll work."

I looked at him as if he was demented. "Don't be silly. We have to get out of here as soon as possible!"

"You're the heiress of Zeru, aren't you? That gives you the ability to steer and ride the clouds, just like him. So listen to me carefully. One, draw a cloud from the sky and get on. Two, levitate it, then glide across the air and above the bird. Three, send a few raindrops to warn us, and we'll back away. Finally, use your scepter again. Concentrate really, really hard, focus on your elemental powers, and zap the bird with lightning."

"I'm not flying solo! I need a—"

"Well, like it or not, you've got to do it. It's the only way to get us out of here."

"But the Chirpy Bird's immune to magic!"

"To weapons, more like. The bird just said no *weapon* could hurt it. You have the power to summon rain and lightning. You can do this."

"But I can't charm the cloud, not here."

Eric pointed at the white rose bush we'd just passed. "Hide there. We will buy you time and distract the Chirpy Bird. Go! We have no time to waste!"

Reluctantly, I headed towards the bush as I heard Alexandria taunting the bird.

"You've got a rather stupid name, haven't you? Who in their right mind would call themselves 'Chirpy Bird'?"

The Chirpy Bird made a snatch for Alexandria with its human-like fingers, but she was too quick for it.

I crouched behind the bush, got out my scepter, and pointed it at the sky. *Please,* I prayed to Zeru, *please help us. We are in grave danger.* I squeezed my eyes shut and visualized myself flying on a cloud.

A weird sensation washed over me. I opened my eyes and

blinked, only to find myself surrounded by wet, warm clouds.

Eric had said I could actually *steer* a cloud. He was serious, wasn't he? With my heart pounding eagerly, I clambered onto the nearest cloud, and as I did, it solidified immediately. I gripped my scepter with my trembling fingers.

"Levitate," I whispered, my voice shaking in feverish anticipation. I blinked, surprised that a valid command came to my mind so naturally as if an intuition.

The cloud jerked upward and rose up into the sky, slowly at first, but got faster and faster and —

"Stop!" I shouted. The cloud jolted to a halt. Gingerly I laid my scepter on the cloud, which was now hovering in midair. It was wonderful up here. Clouds here, clouds there, some layered, some streaked, some plump, some slender, some solid like clumps of cotton, some gauzy like strands of gossamer. Every cloud was unique in its own way, dotting the vast, pure blueness above me. It was not until a minute later that I finally tore my gaze away from the mesmerizing sky and took a look at the scenery beneath me.

"Oh, wow…" I whooped with joy as I saw the vistas of green fields and hills unfurling below me, blurring into an endless mosaic of blended hues of green. Excitement and elation flooded upon me as I gazed greedily at the landscapes in miniature, as though I could never get enough of it. Words failed to describe how perfectly ecstatic I was, sitting high up in the clouds as the chilly wind caressed my cheek, sibilant whispers echoing in my ears. I waved my arms, ready to surf the skies like an enthusiastic explorer —

Then, without warning, throbbing pain coursed through my arm. An arrow had pierced it. I cursed and looked up to see if the assailant was nearby. Sure enough, a unibird with a pink mane was glaring at me. I suddenly recalled what Ms. Jackson had said about unibirds: *They're not aggressive, but they attack intruders who trespass into their territory.*

"Who do you think you are, intruding upon my land?"

"Sorry," I said, raising my hands in surrender. The last

thing I wanted to do was to offend these terrifying monsters from the world of evil. "I'm...from the Otherworld, and I'm here on a mission—" But this, apparently, was the wrong thing to say.

"I'm an Underworldian, and I will only *destroy* people who aren't!"

With an angry squawk, the unibird steered her cloud at me.

I accelerated my own cloud to gain distance and drew my scepter. "Harm," another command came out of my mouth intuitively.

Golden sparks emitted from my scepter and zapped at the unibird. She shrieked and lost her balance, falling off her cloud.

I had no time to see whether she had escaped or wanted revenge since a fight was already raging between my companions and the bird. To make matters worse, it looked like we were about to lose, which meant I had no time to delay.

"Hey," I told my cloud. "Zoom up above the battle that's raging over there."

The cloud seemed to know exactly what I had in mind, and I found myself hovering above the Chirpy Bird in less than five seconds.

"Rain!" I commanded. A few raindrops fell from my cloud.

"What the—?" shrieked the bird.

I took a deep breath and raised my scepter. "Lightning."

A trickle of yellow sparks shot down at the bird, but it wasn't enough to do any harm, nor did the bird feel it. To my utter dismay, it lunged at Daphne and grabbed her trident.

I lowered my cloud to keep a closer eye on the bird. "Rain harder!"

The rain was practically pouring. I tightened my grip on my scepter and concentrated with all my might.

"Lightning!" I shouted.

A wave of sparks zoomed at my adversary, but it still wasn't enough to overpower it. I noticed that the bird was swiping away the sparks of lightning with Daphne's trident. At that thought, torrents of anger took over me, and like Queen Marianne had said, the more emotional we heiresses were, the more intense our powers got. My scepter was vibrating so furiously I had to make an enormous effort to hold on while at the same time struggling to keep my balance on the cloud. I gripped my scepter as though my life depended on it. Finally, an exceptionally violent spark struck the bird in the eye. It staggered, then slammed to the ground, unconscious. The Chirpy Bird fell with such force that it must have caused an earthquake.

"Stop," I told my scepter. The lightning stopped abruptly. My cloud descended to the ground, and I dismounted. "Levitate!" I commanded once again, pointing my scepter at the cloud. It ascended up into the bright blue sky.

"Nice timing, pal," muttered Daphne, who shot me a very dirty look. She went up to the bird and retrieved her trident. Her lip was bleeding and cut. "That stupid bird pecked me, and I put up a fistfight with it," she explained, dabbing at a cut on her lip with her bloody finger.

"You mean it kissed you, pecking you right on your lip," joked Alexandria.

"Oh, shut up." Daphne's face reddened.

I looked at the others, who were no better off than Daphne. Eric, who had obviously led everyone into battle, looked the worst. There were gashes and cuts all over his face.

"Where in the world have you been?" thundered Helen. "We would've died if it weren't for Eric!"

A glint of pride shone in Eric's eyes when his name was mentioned.

"I'm sorry I didn't arrive in time," I said. "There was a unibird in the clouds, and she introduced my arm to an arrow." I pointed at the gash on my arm.

"Never mind," said Helen, pursing her lips. "Let's go. We've got better things to do than dawdle around."

As we set off on the path once again, I noticed that Eric's enthusiasm had mounted after the fight, perhaps because of his new-gained confidence. He joked and laughed and showed off the facts he knew about Chirpy Birds, a species of giant flesh-eating birds that roamed the Underworld.

"Know what the funniest part is?" he said. "They can't fly! Chirpy Birds can't fly! Isn't it a disgrace to be called a *bird* and not know how to fly?"

Everyone lapsed into peals of laughter, and even Helen cracked a smile.

"That's ridiculous!" exclaimed Daphne.

"Crazy, huh?" said Alexandria, suppressing a giggle.

"But why would they need to if they can run faster than flying?" came a shrill voice from behind.

Eric gasped.

The next second, we found the Chirpy Bird towering over us, a look of triumph gleaming in its eyes. "HA! Nobody escapes me!"

The seven of us took off sprinting along the path, with Daphne and Eric taking the lead, Eileen, Zack and I on their heels, and Alexandria and Helen behind. The bird, roaring and snarling, was following us closely. It made a few snatches for Helen, the slowest among us, but Alexandria tossed fireballs at it as a distraction. The fireballs did save Helen, but the bird somehow dodged every one of them. I tried in vain to draw clouds from the sky, for I was unable to concentrate.

The landscape around us began to change. Before I knew it, we were in a copse. The cobblestone path was still visible, and I could see it weaving its way through the trees ahead. A tang of fresh dirt teased my nose, and twigs, dried leaves, and all sorts of foliage cracked and snapped under our feet, brown and crisp.

The Chirpy Bird guffawed. I looked over my shoulder, and a chill went down my spine. Its outstretched claws were only two feet away from Helen.

"Eileen!" I screamed. "Do something now!"

Eileen turned, made a slashing movement in the air with her scepter, and cut down a pine tree, tripping the bird and buying us time.

When I was about to stop and catch my breath—

"Oh no!" I heard a yell of frustration coming from Eric.

"What's wrong?" shouted Eileen.

"We're in big trouble!"

"Well, you don't say!" I roared, barely managing to catch up with him.

"He's not talking about the Chirpy Bird," said Daphne, her voice strained. "We've got a major problem ahead."

Alexandria and Helen arrived five seconds later. They, too, looked tired and puzzled.

"How do we cross this?" Eric bellowed, pointing straight ahead.

I walked up to where his finger was pointed. "Oh my...."

The road had terminated by itself. In front of us—no, right beneath us—was a huge waterfall that looked at least thirty feet deep. The current in the stream below was exceptionally swift, and that did not look good against our dangerous circumstances. We would either have to jump and risk drowning or wait for the bird to finish us up.

"We must jump," decided Helen. "There's water below to shield the impact. Then, we'll have to ford across—"

"What?" Alexandria cried in dismay.

"I'm going first," Helen pressed on, ignoring the continuous protests that came from Alexandria. "If anything happens to me, go back into the little forest and take refuge behind the trees or whatever."

"But what if—" started Zack.

"I'll send you a sign when I'm down there. Zack, could you go last? Make sure everybody follows if I survive the—"

"I'm not jumping into the waterfall!" shouted Alexandria.

"It's the only way to get us out!" insisted Helen.

"But—" Alexandria argued.

"HA!" A roar came from behind. "Nasty little scoundrels, trying to get rid of me by a pathetic tree?"

"Just do it!" yelled Helen. "We've got no alternative, now that the bird's caught up with us! Jump as far as you can, and don't hit your head on the rocks. On my count, three...two...one! Go!"

Both Helen and Daphne dived into the stream below the waterfall. Eileen and Eric exchanged a quick glance, and both followed suit.

Alexandria, Zack, and I were the only three left. "Now what?" I asked.

Before either of them could answer, the Chirpy Bird loomed into sight. I gulped.

"I'm not going underwater!" wailed Alexandria.

"Neither am I!" I protested. Plunging into the stream like that was way too dangerous, and I wasn't going to take any chances.

"Do you trust me?" asked Zack.

"Yes!"

"Then—go!"

Zack pushed both Alexandria and me into the waterfall. It was like flying—flying face-first into the swift current. Not as bad as I imagined. I landed with a deafening splash and was followed by Alexandria.

"I...I CAN'T SWIM!" screamed Alexandria.

"Oops, looks like I should've given it a second thought," came Zack's voice.

"Here I come!" The Chirpy Bird made a snatch for Zack, who barely got away. With a leap, he descended into the waters gracefully.

Swimming was no big deal for Daphne since she was the heiress of Walters. I wasn't especially good at swimming, but at least I didn't drown. As I paddled towards the riverbank, I could hear the waterfall's continuous thundering and feel the tiny droplets of water raining over my head.

Alexandria kicked in the water, flailing her arms and coughing. "SOMEBODY HELP!" she screamed at the top of her lungs, inhaling a few gulps of water. Finally, under the assistance of Daphne, she reached the shore after the rest of us did. Alexandria's face flushed red as she murmured a quick thank you to Daphne.

"Enough exploring," muttered Helen. I couldn't help associating her with a shaggy dog when she ran her fingers down her wavy hair and shook it. "I'm so done with everything today. Come on, let's find a place to camp out for the night."

I never imagined that I would side with Helen, but right now, I couldn't agree more with her plan. I, too, had enough of the cunning Underworld. It was toying with our minds and fighting skills in every possible way.

"You got the tent, Zack?" Helen asked.

"Right here." Zack withdrew from his pocket a small pouch and pulled out a purple handkerchief. Then, he tapped his wand on it twice. The little handkerchief swelled, growing larger and larger until it was big enough for me to realize it was actually a shrunken tent. Then, the two Elders busied themselves with the rest of our camping gear.

I was about to ask Alexandria if she was all right when—

"Squawk!"

A loud squawk startled me. I turned and saw a unibird with a purple mane. Its eyes were swollen and red-rimmed.

"Lady Clarissa, please help me! My wife is hurt! She's bleeding like mad, and she's on the verge of death!"

I looked down at my scepter, then at the unibird. "But I'm not sure if I can save her. I've never tried.... I don't know if my elemental magic can—"

"You're Zeru's heiress, and you have the power to heal unibirds. Please, she's dying! I don't know how much time she's got before it's too late.... At least come with me and take a look at her, I beg you!"

"Lead the way, then," were the words that came from my mouth. "Listen, I got to—"

The others looked questioningly at me, and it dawned on me that they couldn't understand the language of unibirds. Quickly and clearly, I translated its words into English.

"What?" said Daphne, crossing her arms. "This is nuts."

I glanced at Helen for permission. There was a strange and rather soulful look in her eyes. For a split second, I thought I even saw tears sparkling. She took a moment to collect herself, then said softly, "Just go, Clarissa."

Surprisingly enough, Zack took a different point of view. "Hold on for a moment. What if he's trying to trick you? He might do you in as soon as you're out of our sight. I won't risk losing one of us, not like the last time Evonne—" Zack stopped in mid-sentence immediately and cast a scared look at Helen, who wore a pained expression at that mention.

It occurred to me that he had touched a nerve by mentioning this seemingly sensitive subject, and maybe it was better to abstain from it. Eric put on a puzzled expression, and Eileen and Daphne, who both registered Helen's odd reaction, exchanged looks of curiosity.

"What if we found Evonne and saved her just in time?" Helen said to Zack, her tone almost beseeching. "And what if that unibird is dying out there, like Evonne last time, and Clarissa could have saved her if we'd let her?"

"Who's Evonne?" Alexandria, who was a lot less tactful, chimed in. "Is it the Evonne we know? Ms. Fitzgerald?"

"I—no, nothing." Looking flustered, Zack's face reddened as he carefully averted both Alexandria and Helen's gazes.

"But you can't go alone, Clarissa," Eileen insisted, breaking the awkward silence. "Zack's right. We can't afford to lose anyone. You never know what might happen."

I turned to the Elders. "Please."

"All right then," Zack gave in. "But I insist on going with you."

A fountain of gratitude welled up in me. "Thanks."

"Come quick!" the unibird cried as he flew into a nearby forest.

Zack and I hurried towards his direction, and soon he came to a stop. On a mass of twigs and leaves lay a female unibird with her long legs crossed, and to my horror, it was the exact same one I had injured while steering the cloud.

The unibird looked fragile of health, and blood was oozing out from a deep gash. I recognized the wound as being where I had zapped it. A wave of guilt washed upon me. I felt ashamed of myself, hurting a unibird just because she was in the wrong place at the wrong time. In fact, the unibird seemed hardly alive. Her breathing was shallow, the golden glow in her horn was fading, her mane was dirty and jagged, and her wings were bent at a strange angle.

"Save her, I beg you," the male unibird implored.

"I'm...I'm not sure if I can help," I answered. "I've never tried healing before."

"You can do it. As the heiress of Zeru, you must be powerful. Please. At least try."

I placed a hand over the wound, which was still bleeding copiously, and took out my scepter. "Heal," I commanded. Nothing happened. Summoning all my willpower, I concentrated again and gave it a second try. No luck. I cursed in frustration. Never had my scepter failed me — what had I done wrong?

But still, there was another way. I reached into my pocket and got out the golden pouch. It beamed and shone as if grinning at me.

Use it only when times are desperate when nobody nor anything can save you. Also, every pouch can only be used once throughout the whole mission, so choose your time wisely. The queen's words rang in my ears. I could only use it once, but was saving the unibird worth it?

I glanced at Zack, hoping for advice. "It's your decision, Clarissa. I won't interfere."

Hesitating, I unfastened the golden ribbon and dumped whatever was inside onto the unibird's wound. Golden liquid dribbled onto the deep gash.

I waited for a few seconds, gazing expectantly at the unibird, but nothing magical happened. *Perhaps the unibird is going to die after all.*

But no.

At that moment, the unibird's wound began to heal, bit by bit. The blood vanished, and the gash sealed. Gold color filled her beautiful horn once again, and her mane turned back into a beautiful, vivid shade of pink. She opened her eyes and blinked.

"Oh, Mary!" The male unibird galloped over to his wife and nuzzled her, tears of joy glistening in his eyes. "How are you feeling?"

"Much better." The female unibird's gaze drifted to

the golden pouch in my hands, then to my face. I held my breath, worried that the unibird would acknowledge me as the perpetrator and get her revenge. I was ready to make a run for it.

"Thank you," she neighed. "You saved my life."

"Well, it was the least I could do," I said, shrugging. "I didn't mean to...you know."

The unibird shook her head. "I know you didn't. Now I come to think of it, you were just protecting yourself when you attacked me."

I blinked twice, unable to believe she'd let me off the hook that easily.

"Lady Clarissa." The male unibird raised a wing in salute. "I can't thank you enough."

"You're welcome," I beamed at them. "Excuse me, but the others are waiting for me. I have to leave."

Both unibirds nuzzled me with affection, and as Zack and I departed, they both called out to us. "We'll return your kindness in the future!"

A grin crossed my face. It felt lovely to see the unibird couple reunited and looking so content.

We headed back to our camp and saw the purple tent being set up. Alexandria was lighting the fire. Helen and Daphne were nowhere to be seen. Eileen and Eric were glowering at each other as though they'd been quarreling.

"Why don't you just go and fetch a few twigs?" Eileen snapped at him. "Are you that lazy?"

"I'm not your dogfish!" retorted Eric. "Why don't you snap your fingers, conjure a little tree, then burn it down?"

"I create nature, not destroy it. Is it all Underworldians, or is it only you who treats nature without respect?"

Eric opened his mouth to argue, but Helen, who emerged from behind the tent, gave the two of them a stern look. "Enough."

To my surprise, Eric shut his mouth obediently. Eileen, with a snort.

"I just got the sleeping bags ready," said Helen, wiping the beads of perspiration from her forehead with her handkerchief. "Zack, why don't you, Alexandria, and Eileen go foraging for edible mushrooms and berries? I have some porridge here, and let's see if we have enough ingredients to make dinner."

Helen handed Alexandria a large basket and brushed her hair away from her eyes. She noticed me and stopped in her tracks, her lips parting as if wanting to speak. I nodded at her, indicating that everything was fine. Helen returned my nod and went back to her business.

Daphne emerged from behind a shrub, and I straightened the tent with her. The golden pouch slipped out of my pocket, and I stooped to pick it up. I thought of the two unibirds and smiled.

"What are you smiling about, Clarissa?" Eric, who came over to us, asked.

"Oh, no, no, nothing in the world," I laughed. "Seems like we'll be having a delicious dinner."

Eric made a funny face, and Daphne and I burst into laughter.

"You're really cute sometimes, you know that?" Daphne said to Eric, who blushed and busied himself with polishing his wand, a metallic ten-inch stick in a bright shade of turquoise.

"It's nice of you to say so. Eileen hates me, by the way."

"Don't mind her," I replied consolingly. "She'll cool down soon. By the way, where's my sword?"

"Over there," said Daphne, placing a purple flag on the top of the tent. "Helen just took it."

I raised my eyebrows, displeased that Helen had taken it without my consent. As I picked up my sword, I noticed a small piece of paper attached to it. Two words in Helen's handwriting were on the note.

Kindness personified.

I had never liked Helen much before, but at that moment, affection for her brimmed up within me. Beaming, I looked up and happened to catch her eye.

"Thanks," I said to Helen, a word that meant everything.

Chapter Eight

A NIGHT IN THE LAND OF EVIL
(ALEXANDRIA)

Eileen led the three of us to a secluded area of a dense forest. The chilly evening breeze hummed and teased at the rustling leaves. Tall trees shrouded by night loomed over us, casting ghostly shadows on the lichen-coated ground. Twilight reigned the sky, and the towering columns of trees around us darkened a shade every few minutes, giving off an eerie sense of foreboding.

"Please don't tell me our dinner is lying somewhere here," I said. "This place gives me the shivers."

"It'll be all right. Just wait and see," replied Eileen. "I'm certain I felt some nature aura here." She got out her scepter, looked around, and pointed it at the mossy ground. "Rise," she said in a whispery voice, lifting both of her arms.

I watched, amazed, as a sea of colorful mushrooms popped up from the ground and started growing in height and size. Overhead, clusters of red, orange, yellow, and green berries blossomed from the branches of the trees.

"Here," said Eileen with a smile. "All these mushrooms and berries at our disposal."

"I don't like this place. It's spooky." Colorful mushrooms,

for some reason, made me uncomfortable.

"We have to grit our teeth and do it." Zack took Eileen's side. "It's not like we have a choice."

Eileen plucked a blue mushroom with white dots from the ground. "This isn't poisonous, right?"

"Very clever, Eileen," said Zack.

"I thought colorful mushrooms were the poisonous ones," I suggested.

"It's the complete opposite in the Underworld," explained Zack. He picked a bright yellow mushroom and tossed it into the basket.

"So we'll be having colorful mushrooms-and-berries stew for dinner?"

"Something like that, yeah."

I crouched down and got to work. As much as I dreaded the thought of feasting on them, I had to admit that they were indeed beautiful. Some were glossy, others were luminous, and the rest bore exquisite patterns. The mushrooms in this forest were all unique in their own way, with different shapes and vibrant colors. Bold red, vivid green, ivory yellow, pale blue. Not to mention, none were identical.

"Hey." Zack scooted closer to me.

My eyes were still fixed on a glittering periwinkle mushroom. "Huh?"

"Why did you have your heart set on recruiting Eric?" said Zack, throwing a handful of purple, pink, and blue mushrooms into the big basket.

"You were the one who vouched for him," I said, slightly irritated at his pointless question. I plucked the periwinkle mushroom from the ground and threw it into the basket.

"I know, but what made you trust him in the first place?"

"Eric reminded me of my past—his life was like a reflection of mine. I could relate to everything he said about feeling like an outcast because I've been there."

Distracted by my words, Zack accidentally dropped a handful of green mushrooms.

Eileen frowned. "Don't drop our dinner, if you please."

Zack jabbed the dropped mushrooms twice with his wand, and they flew into the basket.

"You guys talking about Eric?" said Eileen.

I nodded.

She sighed. "Honestly, Alexandria, I just don't get why you trust Eric so much. He's an Underworldian."

"What difference does it make?" I stopped uprooting a yellow mushroom and looked at her sharply. "We are all human. We bleed when we are hurt. We cry when haunted by sorrow. We get angry when offended. We are equal, no matter Otherworldian, Underworldian, or just a regular mortal. There is no difference between Eric and me, except the worlds we used to belong in."

Eileen gazed at me, speechless. I thought she wasn't listening, so I stood up and checked the branches for edible berries. A golden strawberry caught my eye. I plucked it off and tossed it into the basket.

"That was very noble of you, Alexandria," said Eileen finally. "Defending Eric and everything."

"I'm just doing the right thing," I replied, shrugging. "Hey, you want to try this golden strawberry?"

Eileen frowned. "I'll pass."

"What about you, Zack?"

"Hmm, it looks nice." Zack sounded unsure, but I decided it wouldn't hurt to try. I took a bite of another golden strawberry dangling from the branches and gagged. It tasted like sour milk.

"Disgusting." I reached into the half-filled basket and threw the first golden strawberry away.

The next thirty minutes flew by as we chatted and played word games to ease our exhaustion. We collected berries and mushrooms until our basket was full, and fortunately, made it all the way back to our camp without running into any monsters.

Clarissa, Daphne, and Eric were sitting around the fire, gulping spoonfuls of porridge from small bowls. Their faces were tinted orange by the bright fire that burned in the middle of a pile of twigs. A big saucepan filled with porridge sat beside it.

"Ouwack?" mumbled Clarissa, her mouth full.

"Yeah, see what we've brought," said Eileen.

Helen came bustling over. "Well done." She got out some twigs and stuck a green mushroom on one, making a mushroom lollipop. Then she roasted it over the fire. We watched and followed suit.

"Mmm," said Eileen, "Not as bad as I imagined." She stuck a purple berry on her twig and leaned closer to the fire. "Wonder how a roasted berry would taste?"

"I wish we could have some meat," Eric whined. "Couldn't we go hunting?"

Eileen scowled at him. I knew she was a vegetarian and was against slaughtering animals. "Meat! Killing off innocent animals just because you want meat? Eric, have you got no feelings?"

"No need for that," said Helen. "We've got enough sustenance for two days. More porridge, Zack?"

"Sure," he replied. For some reason, Zack had managed to consume the whole bowl of porridge, which was something I would rather fight the Chirpy Bird again than do.

Clarissa caught my eye and stuck out her tongue. "You couldn't pay me to go for a second helping," she mouthed at me.

I nodded, thinking that the porridge didn't taste as well as I had expected.

"How did Zack even finish his first share?" whispered Eric.

"Search me," I replied, gagging as I forced another spoonful into my mouth. I had been starving after a long day of traveling, but the slimy, rubbery mushrooms pretty much ruined my appetite.

"You want something else to eat?" asked Clarissa.

"Well, it's not like we have a—"

She produced three packets of crackers from her pocket and handed me one. "Here you go."

"Thanks," I said, grateful to have something decent to eat.

"You want one, Eileen?" asked Clarissa.

"No thanks, I'm already full." Eileen enjoyed the roasted berries so much that she had gobbled up two-thirds of the berries we had picked.

The others seemed rather satisfied with our dinner. Daphne sighed contentedly. Zack slurped the last remnants of his share and smacked his lips.

"We're going to bed now, right?" said Eric.

"Of course not," Helen set her bowl on the ground, walked over to the tent, and came back with a scroll. "Now's the perfect time to practice and study battle plans! I have everything mapped out. Zack, take Alexandria and—"

Daphne yawned. "Relax, Helen. Let us sleep."

Helen glared at her and opened her mouth to argue but was stopped by Zack.

"It's been a long day for them," he reminded her gently. "Don't forget, it's their first time in the Underworld."

"Fine, then. Have some rest, everyone. But don't let me hear a peep from you."

"Wait a second—what about night watches?" said Daphne. "We're not going to camp out in the middle of nowhere and invite the monsters to dinner, are we?"

Clarissa smirked at that thought. Eileen frowned at her, and mouthed "That's not funny."

"Darn, I almost forgot. I will take the first shift. Here's the order: me, Clarissa, Eric, Zack, and Daphne. Alexandria and Eileen will be responsible for our breakfast tomorrow. The last one who was on duty will wake the next one up. Am I making myself clear?"

Eileen raised her hand. "What will we have for tomorrow's breakfast?"

"Our dinner's leftovers will do," answered Helen.

"And when can we have our baths?" added Daphne.

"We'll have them tomorrow morning at the stream, the one beneath the waterfall. Any more questions? No? All right, bedtime."

The rest of us crawled into the tent, one by one.

"So *this* is a tent?" said Eric. "Interesting—I've never seen one before. Oh, there's even a little window on the ceiling, and we can see the starry sky through it. This is so cool!" He beamed at Zack.

"Stop toadying the Elders, will you?" Eileen snapped at him. I could tell she was still mad about the stick incident.

"I'm not toadying them! Why do you hate me so much? Does that stupid little quarrel even matter now?"

"I don't—"

"Will you two give it a rest?" said Daphne.

Eileen raised her eyebrows. "Since when have you switched sides?"

"That's enough," demanded Helen, poking her head into the tent. "I don't want to hear a peep from you."

"But—" started Eileen.

"I said that's enough!"

Everyone crawled into their sleeping bags. I rolled onto my right side, and my eyes snapped shut almost instantly.

How I wished I didn't have that nightmare. In my dream, the Chirpy Bird was back. It hurled insults and snarled at us. The lion-cat and ex-Frank were standing by its side, smirking and making rude hand gestures.

All of a sudden, ex-Frank growled, "Attack!" and the monsters advanced on us. I watched in horror as the lion-cat pounced on Daphne and clawed at her throat. The Chirpy Bird struck Clarissa unconscious with its shield. Zack lunged at the bird with his sword, but the bird overpowered him and knocked him out as well.

The Chirpy Bird made its next move, this time targeting Helen. I dived between them, but ex-Frank shoved me out of the way and slammed me to the ground. The Chirpy Bird seized Helen and opened its beak, ready to eat her alive, but a roar of thunder startled the bird, and it dropped her. Helen landed with a loud thump. There she lay, motionless, with her eyes closed. Blood was trickling from her forehead. I heard Eric yelling Helen's name in despair, and every shout sent bolts of pain coursing through my body. The Chirpy Bird gloated over its victory, guffawing as it sauntered over to her body.

Temper heated my blood. I sprinted towards the Chirpy Bird, determined to end its life once and for all. But as I raised my scepter to attack, I heard someone, or something, hissing behind me. I turned, coming face-to-face with Eileen. Her eyes turned yellow, and she started babbling nonsense, as though manipulated by an evil spirit. Without a second thought, I ran, and Eileen, roaring gibberish, charged after me.

Just then, a creepy, rattling voice spoke. "They're back...."

"What's that?" yelled Eric. The two of us looked around frantically, but the speaker was invisible.

Thunder bellowed in the distance, and lightning streaked across the sky. Then, maniacal laughter filled our ears, masking the rumble of the thunder.

"I could not stop you from taking the Gem of Hope, but I can end your life," another disembodied voice said.

Before I knew it, an axe flew at me. I tried to move, but my feet were rooted to the ground. Eric bolted towards me, and I watched in horror as the axe pierced into his body instead. Terrified, I forced myself to look into his eyes. It shocked me to see how badly he'd been injured.

"Why did you do that?"

"I had...no choice," he mumbled.

The ground rifted, and the next second, I felt myself falling through a bottomless pit as if being transported to another world....

I jerked awake. My body was clammy with cold sweat. Torrents of relief flooded me as I realized it was nothing but a dream. I glanced up at the window and saw the tiny silver stars winking at me. It was still dark outside. I was trembling from head to toe because of that nightmare, but Clarissa and Eileen were snoring peacefully beside me.

I sat up and decided to find someone to talk to. I looked out and saw smoke billowing from the blazing campfire. Eric, who was sitting in front of it, had done a good job keeping the fire alive.

I tiptoed out to join him. "Hey."

"Alexandria?"

"Of course," I yawned and parked myself beside him. "Who else were you expecting besides me?"

Eric gave me a warm smile.

Uneasiness stirred in me, like a chilly gust of wind disturbing a sea of silent waters. My nightmare suddenly seemed twice as terrifying as I recalled that I possessed a damaged seeing ability. *What if my dream was a premonition? How much of it would come true in the future? Will someone...one of my companions...die today?*

"I thought you were asleep?"

"A nightmare woke me up," I said, sighing and rubbing my eyes. "How are you adjusting to being an apprentice of Helen and Zack's?"

Eric's eyes lit up with excitement. "Wicked! They're both geniuses! Do you get to do stuff like fighting monsters every day in the Otherworld?"

"Me? I grew up in an orphanage in the mortal world. I thought my parents were dead, but it turns out they were actually the king and queen of the Otherworld. I met them for the first time in my life yesterday. Don't you think it's ridiculous?"

"You said we were the same when you first talked to me. You were abused before, weren't you? Like me."

I nodded. "In the orphanage. The older kids were monstrous, and our caretaker always turned a deaf ear to our complaints."

"But at least your mother didn't torture you," said Eric vaguely.

"I'm so sorry, Eric." I tried to imagine his pain, speaking of his traumatizing past as though it had nothing to do with him. "Your awful mother, who is she?"

Eric closed his eyes. "A sadistic woman. My father left her when he discovered her true colors. I never got to know him."

"So...he's gone?"

Eric nodded bitterly. "Some say that my mother killed him."

"Wasn't she arrested?"

"The king and queen can do everything as they please. They can kill anybody they want."

"The king and queen? What does that have to do with your family?"

Eric heaved a sigh. "Well, you promise not to tell anybody? I trust you, Alexandria."

"Yeah."

"My mother is Alta Williams. The queen of the Underworld."

My mind went blank. *How is this possible? No, no. There must have been a mistake.* Eric was telling a falsehood. He had to be.

Strong gusts of wind roared in the distance. In the nearby forest, I saw two unibirds building a giant nest of branches and leaves. However, they seemed uninterested in us, so I decided not to attack them.

"Alexandria?"

"You're not serious, are you?" was all I could utter.

"I was too scared to come clean in the first place. You wouldn't have accepted me if I told you beforehand."

"Well, no, I—" I was speechless. Then, something in my mind clicked into place. "Does…. Does that make us…cousins?"

"I guess so," Eric answered shyly. Red blotches appeared on his face.

I was flabbergasted at that thought. Somehow, it made me uncomfortable to even think about it. Alta and Alto were the bloodthirsty rulers of the Underworld, and goodness knew how many innocent lives they'd taken. And what's more, Eric, like them, was my relative. A wave of anger washed upon me. I was furious at Alta, at Alto, at Eric, but mostly at myself, at the fact that I could not and did not have the power to change reality.

"Alexandria?" Eric's voice sounded so distant, so far away.

"Huh?" I wasn't paying attention, nor did I really care. I was starting to have second thoughts about taking Eric with us. Could there possibly be another Eric Williams, a treacherous, heartless version of him hidden behind the mask of the mild-tempered boy I knew? Dread crept into my stomach and twisted it. I could not bear to contemplate the existence of such a horrible possibility. How could I be related to the brutal Alta and her son? I felt certain that it was a matter of time before Eric switched his loyalty back to his mother, for she was more powerful and was blood-related to him.

Eric's conflicting emotions were reflected on every feature, and I could tell that he was extremely upset. However, I wasn't going to allow myself to pity him.

"I'm sorry." Eric's voice was almost a whisper. He looked on the brink of tears.

"You don't have to be." I cringed inwardly when I heard my voice.

"You didn't want anything to do with Alto and my mother, did you?"

"Listen, I...I...." I did not know what to feel. Guilt, mingled with anger, burned in me. I felt like a volcano about to explode.

Fortunately, I was saved the necessity of finishing my sentence by Zack, who emerged from the tent. "Eric, it's late. Go and get some sleep."

"Thanks," Eric nodded at him. "Good night, Alexandria," he said coldly and crawled into the tent without waiting for my reply. I registered the sharp change in his attitude, and I couldn't help resenting myself for being so harsh on him.

Zack took his place beside me. "Why aren't you asleep?"

"I had a nightmare."

"Sorry to hear that."

I didn't reply; instead, I devoted my attention to the sea of stars that hovered above us, shimmering like diamonds adorned on a black cloak. The wind howled, breaking the silence that drew upon us for several minutes.

"Blustery night, isn't it?"

I nodded absentmindedly. A voice in the back of my head kept nagging at me.

"You're so quiet. Didn't you always come to my classroom and chat with me after school? Where's my little chatterbox?"

I said nothing.

"What's wrong? You look worried. We can talk about it if that'll make you feel better."

"Well…." I sighed, debating with myself whether I should tell Zack the truth about Eric.

"I won't tell a living soul," said Zack gently. "You can trust me."

You can trust me. It pained me the way he said it. It made me think of Eric, of what I had said to him when I'd seen the scars on his arms. I promised him that he could trust me, but still, I hurt him when he revealed the truth about his parentage. I felt ashamed of myself; then felt angry that I felt ashamed.

But what if Eric hurt one of us? Clarissa, Eileen, Daphne, Helen or Zack? I couldn't keep Eric's secret. It would mean danger for the others, not knowing the true identity of our new member; it would be a form of betrayal, me and Eric against them.

Finally, I said, "Eric…he's Alta's son."

"Who told you that?"

"Eric himself. Minutes before his shift ended."

"You find it shocking?" Zack's voice sounded unusually serene.

I looked at him. "Don't you? He's the son of that witch, our biggest enemy! I'm worried he'll switch sides again, back to his mother. What if he betrays us? What if he's been scheming against us all along to gain our trust? I never should've insisted on having him join us. Helen was right from the start."

Zack laughed. "You needn't worry about that. Eric swore an oath, didn't he?"

I didn't know whether to be relieved that Zack wasn't upset or to be worried about his lack of vigilance. "But—"

"Alexandria, didn't you always believe in the kind? The good? Eric has been through a lot, yet he never gave in. He's chosen his side firmly and has demonstrated positive traits of every kind. He fought side by side with us today with extraordinary courage and loyalty. Is this, perhaps, not enough to prove his devotion?"

"I guess it is." Though still unconvinced, I decided to steer the topic away to avoid a quarrel. "By the way, Zack, you've been here before, right?"

"Yeah. I've been to the Underworld five times, not counting this time. The first few times went okay, but the last time...." His voice trailed off.

"What happened?"

"I don't want to mention it. It was a nightmare."

"What went wrong?"

My words had a dramatic effect on him. He took a deep breath and closed his eyes. Then, he opened them and gazed at the fire as if recalling the mission. The flames crackled and hissed like a snake.

"It was dreadful. There were four of us. Helen, Lilith, Evonne, and me."

"Whoa, wait. Helen? And Lilith and Evonne? Do you mean Ms. Jackson and Ms. Fitzgerald, our geography teacher and our former language arts teacher?"

"Yeah. One of us...."

I looked at him, curious. "Go on, please."

"I shouldn't have told you that," said Zack slowly, pursing his lips.

"You mentioned a few names," I plowed on, "Ms. Jackson, Helen—"

"What is it about me?" a voice came from behind us. It was Helen herself.

"Speak of the devil," I murmured.

"It's getting colder in the early mornings," Helen draped her violet shawl around Zack. "Here, that's a lot better."

"Aren't you supposed to be in bed?" asked Zack, looking anxious. But even so, he couldn't help blushing when Helen offered him her shawl.

"I'm an insomniac," she replied.

"Since you-know-what happened?" whispered Zack. Worry swept across his face like a shadow.

Helen gave him a significant look.

I somehow understood what was going on. "The last time you came to the Underworld. You dreamed about it, didn't you?"

"I...." Helen looked flustered. "How did you know about... that?"

"What exactly went wrong last time?"

"Alexandria." Zack shot me a look of warning.

I knew I had gone too far, for Zack had never talked to me in that way. I muttered a quick apology to Helen, assuming the case was closed.

However, to my amazement, she said, "Everything went wrong last time." Her voice was barely audible and full of regret.

I was so surprised by the sudden change in her attitude that I was at a loss for words.

Helen's eyes were glued to the fire as though she could find solace in the blazing flames. "If you really want to know...," she began in a hollow voice. "I'll tell you, then, if you're so curious."

"You mean the adventure with the four of you?" I said eagerly.

She nodded, brushing her hair away from her eyes.

"You're not telling her, are you?"

"Zack, I know what I'm doing," said Helen gently, yet with a touch of firmness.

Zack fell silent at her words.

"The Underworld is a world of utmost evil. Nobody would volunteer or be foolish enough to come unless it was a must. Six months ago, Queen Marianne made one last attempt to get Alta and Alto to change their minds. She sent four Elders into the Underworld."

I felt a wave of respect for my mother. Perhaps some would define her actions as folly, but she never stopped believing in her brother and sister. Her naïvety and her unrequited faith in her siblings was so moving that it made me sad to think about it.

Helen's voice, empty of emotion, trailed on. "At first, I tried to get the queen to stop fantasizing the truth. How could two mass murderers mend their ways just because of our persuasion? It was beyond preposterous. But of course, I was shouted down by the rest of the Elders."

Zack made a squeaky sound. "You were right, Helen. We should've kept our mouths shut. Evonne would've still been all right if we hadn't intervened." From the corner of my eye, I saw him wipe a tear from his cheek.

Helen wrapped an arm around him.

"And then...?" I asked quietly.

"We eventually went to the Underworld. Four Elders, like I mentioned—Zack, Lilith, Evonne, and I. Evonne, who was then my apprentice, was a fledgling Elder. The king and queen had only wanted Zack, Lilith, and I to go on the mission, but I insisted on having Evonne come along. For starters, I'd taken a strong liking to her, and she was like my sister. She'd been my apprentice for a year, and the two of us got along very well. Second, Evonne was not only brave but also talented at archery. She had a very nimble mind."

"She was the best strategist, only second to Helen," Zack chimed in.

I noticed that he was blinking back tears again. Something told me that Evonne either betrayed them or something horrible happened to her. I shifted in uneasiness at those thoughts, hoping that both of my assumptions were incorrect.

Helen went on with her story. "Evonne was an outstanding apprentice. Anyway, when we all got to the Underworld, we fought off a few monsters. The four of us worked seamlessly, and the fighting process went well—almost *too* well. However, when we thought we'd reached the palace, a maze of granite pillars appeared."

Zack shuddered and buried his head in his arms.

A chill went down my spine. "And?"

"The maze split the four of us into two passages. Zack and Lilith were grouped in one, Evonne and I in the other. Then, a thick shroud of mist formed, separating Evonne from me. That left me no choice but to proceed on my own. I ran into a kittenpillar with venomous fangs, and it followed me so closely that I barely escaped. When I finally did, a two-headed devil attacked me. I shot an arrow at one of his heads and hurried away, but he got me in the end. Evonne, who happened to pass by, attacked him and made him blind. The devil left me alone and went for her next. I ran after them, but all of a sudden, my vision blacked out. In fact, everything went dark. Moments later, a streak of turquoise light revealed three passages ahead. A disembodied voice whispered 'choose' to me. I heard a potion bubbling in the first one, a scream in the second, and a dogfish's groan in the third. Now that I come to think of it, I should've given it a second thought. But under the circumstances, I was so anxious and desperate to get everyone out that I acted irrationally. I hurried along the second passage, thinking it'd be one of the others." Helen's voice slowed down to a halt.

"And then?" I was able to visualize the whole adventure with the help of her description.

"The path led me to a female bearnix. She was the one who had screamed. The two of us dueled, and I probably would've collapsed if Lilith and Zack hadn't arrived in time. I confused the bearnix with mist and ran away with them. The three of us held hands, desperate not to let anything tear us apart. But there was still one problem. Our youngest member was missing. We called her name over and over again, and after a few twists and turns, we found her lying in one of the false passages." Helen made a brief stop.

Zack let out a sniffle.

I gulped. I did not want to push Helen to go on, nor was I sure if I wanted to hear the ending.

"She didn't die, but she was very close to death," Helen's voice dropped to a brisk whisper as if she wanted to get through the tragic climax as soon as possible. "Evonne was sprawled unconscious in a puddle of blood when we came across her. Lilith, Zack, and I, with her body, bolted out of the maze after a few wrong turns. When we finally got back to the Otherworld, Evonne was nearly dead."

I felt my stomach churning vigorously as trepidation throbbed in it.

"King Patrick and Queen Marianne tried everything to save her. She did, eventually, regain consciousness."

"Oh, that's great news!" I blurted out.

Zack silenced me with a harsh look.

Helen sighed. "I don't call what happened next good. Evonne met a fate worse than death—she lost her memory. She couldn't recall anything, not even her identity and parentage. Her memory was wiped blank."

I was too horrified to speak, nor did I know what to think. Poor Evonne. Her year of training had dissolved into nothing. I also felt dreadful for Helen, Zack, and Lilith.

"But what happened next?" These reckless words escaped from my lips before I could stop them.

"It was my fault that Evonne lost her memory, and everyone knew that. She never would've gotten hurt if I hadn't insisted on taking her along with us. After a hearing, the Elders had a vote on whether my position as the Representative Elder should be withdrawn. I wasn't allowed to vote and would've been deprived of my position if the king and queen hadn't voted for me. The initial result was eighty-one to eighty; eighty-one Elders wanted a new Representative Elder, while eighty didn't. Thirty-seven chose to abstain. However, the king and queen, who were dissatisfied with the result, joined the voting as well. They became the eighty-first and eighty-second to take my side. I was preserved, yet barely. Many Elders lost faith in me, but I never blamed them. They had every right to hate me. I disappointed everyone that time, and it was entirely my fault that Evonne almost...."

Helen wasn't blubbering. Her voice wasn't throbbing with emotion, nor did she seem to be wallowing in her misery, but there was a certain brittleness about her, implying her sorrow was beyond that. Revisiting the memory of a tragedy was not something one would desire, but she chose to, only because a heartless, ignorant fourteen-year-old wanted to hear a bedtime story. It was painful enough for one to harbor such dark secrets, but it must have been equally difficult for Zack to listen to the harrowing misadventure retold. However, a question that had me wondering was still left unanswered.

"Helen?"

She did not reply immediately. Instead, she combed her

long wavy hair with her fingers and stared fixedly at the flames. "What?"

"I'm not sure if you'd want to answer this, but why did you volunteer to come along on this mission after what happened last time?"

Helen's face was wrought with remorse. She turned her head away, and I thought I had offended her.

"Sorry, I didn't mean to—"

"No, please don't apologize." Helen rubbed her eyes, then spoke again. "I never forgave myself for Evonne's tragedy. King Patrick and Queen Marianne were understanding, but I could never dispel the guilt that plagued me."

"Hey, listen," Zack chimed in. "The rulers, Lilith, and I all agree that Evonne's misfortune had nothing to do with you. Nobody blames you."

Helen, though, took no notice of his words of comfort. She buried her face in her palms, where no one would see any sign of emotion on her features. When she spoke again, her voice was merely a whisper. "I blame myself. As the leader of that mission, I not only failed my duty but also spoiled Evonne's future. I volunteered to come again because I wanted to remedy my mistake. I know it's too late and—and Evonne's already lost her memory, but I...I had to make it up to the Otherworld." Helen's shoulder quivered slightly.

I was astonished to see her cry. It was not until then that I realized that Helen, despite her strict, stoic image as the Representative Elder, was a sentimental person deep down. She cared, even though she acted like she was way tougher than that.

"I've been trying to forget about Evonne's accident. I know it's terribly irresponsible of me to do so, but my past...it had no intention of letting me go. Every day, I wonder how much Evonne would have hated me if she could recall that tragedy. Countless variations of nightmares and flashbacks of that mission haunt me in my dreams. I hear Evonne screaming every time I fall asleep, and I can't help thinking what her version of events of that mission was. Who or what attacked Evonne and made her lose her memory? Was she mad at me for not protecting her when

I should've been with her? Was she scared? Whenever I woke up from one of those nightmares, I'd never be able to fall asleep again. Instead, I'd go down to the infirmary and sit by Evonne's side until the morning. I'd hold her hand and tell her how sorry I was. But no matter how many times I apologize to her, nothing will change. It's already too late. I destroyed her. Ruined her life. The irreversible damage—it's already been done."

There were tears in Helen's eyes, but she struggled to fight against them, the only thing left that she had control over. I wanted to comfort her, but I just couldn't find the right words nor the courage to speak up.

Zack put an arm around her. "Shh," he murmured as if coaxing a baby. "We've been making excellent progress so far, and we'll find the gem very soon. We're going to make it back to the Otherworld tomorrow."

"But what if—what if we don't? It was my fault the Otherworld lost a great Elder. Every night, I...I hear the wind whining and...and screaming like the female bearnix on our last mission, a reminder of the most crucial decision that I failed to make correctly. If I had given the three passages a...a second thought, I probably could've had a chance to save Evonne...." More tears welled up in Helen's eyes. She dabbed her handkerchief at them before they could flow down.

"The past is in the past," Zack reassured her, enfolding her in an embrace. "Everything will be fine this time."

"Helen, I'm sorry about that accident, but you can't be constrained by the past and paranoid about the future," I pointed out. "Regarding yourself as a tragic hero and dwelling in the past isn't going to do you much good in this case. Only you can free yourself from your past; only your change of attitude can brighten your future."

"Maybe," replied Helen, a weary look on her face.

We sat there in awkward silence, listening to the wind screaming dolefully in the distance like an abandoned infant's wailing.

"It's four o'clock now," said Zack, checking his watch.

"Let me finish my shift. You two should really get some sleep. I have a feeling today's going to be a long day."

Without a second thought, I crawled back into the tent, not realizing how exhausted I was until I fell asleep before my head hit the pillow.

Chapter Nine

TRAPPED
(ERIC)

"Eric Williams, how dare you betray your own mother!"

I was kneeling at the foot of Alta's throne. If looks could kill, I would have dropped dead right on the spot. Utmost hatred shot from Alta's eyes. She wore her long red hair in a loose side ponytail and was dressed in a turquoise gown, the one with tiny diamonds shaped like skeletons embroidered on the hem. Yet I knew too well that underneath that elegant façade was the heartless woman that had traumatized me for years. Alta's turquoise diadem, tucked firmly in place, was glowing, which wasn't a good sign.

"Betray?" It was probably reckless to do so, but I retorted. "I never betrayed you. I was never yours to betray."

"YOU'LL PAY FOR SUCH INSOLENCE!" Alta screamed, hurling her diadem at me.

The diadem exploded as it hit my arm, and I felt myself plummeting through blackness. A searing pain spread through my body. My injured arm was killing me; my lungs were on fire, and I couldn't breathe.

"Eric…Eric…Eric!" Somebody was beside me, pinching my arm.

"Mmm," I murmured.

"Wake up!" the voice shouted.

I opened my eyes and blinked twice.

There was no Alta, no throne, no exploding diadems. Only Daphne and my bruised arm. Daphne's blue hair was messy and tangled.

"Oh hey, it's you," I murmured. "Could you leave my poor arm alone?"

"I've been shouting your name for one solid minute, and you were still conked out."

"Okay, okay, I'm getting up. What's the time now? And where are the others?"

"It's eight in the morning. Alexandria and Eileen are making our breakfast. Clarissa's with them, and both Helen and Zack went for a bath. We've all got chores assigned. The two of us are supposed to get these sleeping bags, and the tent cleared and packed."

Yawning, I pulled myself out of my sleeping bag. "When can we have our baths?"

"As soon as the two Elders are back. In fact, the others and I have already taken our baths in the early morning, before everyone was up."

I crawled out of the tent and saw Alexandria and Clarissa debating heatedly about something. Eileen was pouring us bowls of porridge. Clarissa, who wore her hair in pigtails today, waved and said "Good morning" to me. Alexandria frowned and looked away immediately.

I understood her disgust at my mother, but it was definitely not my fault that I was Alta's son. Hatred for that madwoman bubbled in me, like water boiling in a pot.

"Eric!" shouted Daphne. "Stop horsing around and give me a hand!"

Reluctantly, I crouched down and started packing up the sleeping bags.

"I'm not lying to you! It's true, everything about Eric! We'd better talk about this somewhere else."

I poked my head out of the tent and saw Alexandria and

Clarissa arguing. From what I could make out, Alexandria had told her the truth about my parentage, and she obviously didn't believe her.

My heart sank at the thought of being an outcast again. Alexandria did not want anything to do with me, and soon, all of my cohorts would be following suit.

"Come, Clarissa," Alexandria whispered, beckoning for her to follow.

Clarissa looked hesitant, but Alexandria dragged her by the arm and led her behind a nearby tree.

I had to follow Alexandria in case she exaggerated the truth about me. Daphne had dismantled the tent and was trying in vain to shrink it with her trident. Eileen was stirring the saucepan and adding more mushrooms to the porridge. I seized my opportunity when they were distracted and tiptoed quickly towards the tree. I crouched down and pressed my ear to the trunk.

"This is a controversial matter!"

"You're not doing justice to Eric, and I don't even care who his mother is. I don't know why you're avoiding him, acting like he's contagious!"

"Clarissa, please be sensible. Alta is beyond wicked. Let's face it: she's a devil. How do you know Eric isn't a spy? Perhaps he was pretending to be innocent, so he could earn our trust and sneak into the Otherworld, where he can pry out the top secrets for his mother. Blood is thicker than water. Stop being ignorant and face reality."

"*You* are the one who's being ignorant. Don't you know it's wrong to judge people by their parents? You should never jump to conclusions about anyone before you get familiar with them."

"Like father, like son—haven't you heard of the saying?"

"Besides," said Clarissa, raising her volume, "don't forget that Alta abused him. I believe Eric will fight for us."

"Well...." Alexandria heaved a sigh of frustration. "Maybe we should give him an opportunity to prove himself, after all.

But I'd feel a lot more secure if Helen knew."

"Perhaps you can consult—"

"I will, thank you very much." Alexandria crossed her arms in front of her chest.

"You aren't fully convinced, are you?"

"No. Not at all, in fact. Eric could be dangerous if—"

"Will all of you stop goofing off?" snapped Daphne. "Eileen and I are the only ones who are actually working!"

I took refuge behind a small shrub in case Alexandria and Clarissa came close.

"Eric Williams, you come right here this instant!"

I gulped and rushed out of my hiding place.

"What were you doing?" asked Daphne. "And where were you?"

"Um...doing number one and two...well, behind the shrub over there," I lied, shifting my weight from one foot to the other.

"Humph," said Daphne. "You're the most irresponsible person in the world. Come and have breakfast." She handed me a bowl of porridge and colorful mushrooms.

I took a few spoonfuls of the sticky substance and grimaced. "Is this our dinner leftover from yesterday?"

"You got a problem with that?" demanded Eileen.

"Will you stop having a go at me?"

"What's going on here?" said a familiar voice behind me. It was Helen.

Before I could speak, Eileen squawked on me, "Daphne and I did all the work while he didn't even lift a finger!"

"What? That's—"

"Enough. Listen, stop arguing like a bunch of insufferable kids. I don't care how many reasons you give me, but we must work in peace. Honestly, can't you all just keep your complaints to yourself?"

Nobody moved a muscle while Helen spoke, not even Zack. Glowering at each other, the five of us nodded grudgingly.

"Very well, then. Now, stop wasting time and let's have breakfast. We must find you-know-what today, or else—"

"Helen, calm down. You have to show faith in them," Zack

whispered in her ear. "Settle down, everyone, and let's eat," he announced in a rather obvious attempt to sound cheerful.

We had a very silent and awkward breakfast. After ten minutes, I excused myself and went for a bath, for I couldn't stand Alexandria glaring daggers at me every five seconds. She cleared her throat and opened her mouth to speak the second my bottom left the ground.

As I headed towards the waterfall, my head drooped, and my shoulders sagged. I didn't know why, but I desperately wanted to please Alexandria. She was my cousin, as well as the first person to ever show kindness to me; however, she was steering clear of me just because my mother was the queen of the Underworld.

"I hate you, Alta," I muttered under my breath. "I hate you too, Alexandria."

But what good did hating do? Alexandria would never accept me as her cousin. It was unfair of her, but I could understand how much she loathed Alta and wanted to sever ties with her.

I let out a sigh as the waterfall came into view. It thundered down the cliff, spraying little drops of dew on my face. Like thousands of little mirrors leaping about, the stream gleamed under the morning sun. I wished the trip to the waterfall would have lasted longer than just that, long enough for me to analyze the situation and figure out my next step. While I was taking off my clothes, ready to take a dip in the water —

"Hello."

A voice scared the living daylights out of me, and I lost my balance. With a splash, I fell headfirst into the icy stream. Gasping and splattering water, I inhaled a lungful of fresh air. I paddled around, and the speaker came into view. It was a unibird with a purple mane, the exact one that had begged for Clarissa's assistance yesterday.

"Who are you?" I questioned.

"You have done well, son of Alta."

"What do you mean?" I said, this time more curious than annoyed. "Wait, you...you can speak English? I didn't know that."

"I can. I'm here to tell you to follow your beliefs, sonny. I see that your cousin is unhappy about your mother."

"Yeah. Wait, how did you know? You spied on me?"

"Sorry, but that's unimportant. Listen up, lad—you can't change the way others think, but you can choose your own ways of thinking, got it?"

"You're telling me to—"

"You care about your cousin, Alexandria, don't you? Well, it's not your fault that you're Alta's son."

"I know!" I said, my patience running low. "What's your point, anyway?"

"Eric, don't let people define who you are. Don't mind what Alexandria or the others say about you. Don't stop fighting for what you believe in. Don't let anyone or anything sway you if you're doing the right thing. Just keep being yourself and following your values. One day, everyone will accept you as you are."

"Oh. Um...thank you, sir. But...why are you telling me this? I mean, it's very uncommon to see Underworldians telling each other to believe in the good."

"It is unusual, but didn't *you* believe in the good yourself?"

He winked at me, and I couldn't help but give him a knowing smile in return. His words seemed to elevate the positivity flowing between us.

"Thanks a lot, but...well, how can you be sure that people will accept an outcast like me? How will they know I'm not faking it? I mean, no offense, but...you're not a seer. You can't predict what will happen in the future."

To my astonishment, the unibird smiled. "Young man, you're not wrong. I'm not a seer, nor can I foresee the future. But I give you my word. Just be yourself, and let your actions speak for themselves. Time will eventually prove everything. Now, I'd be more than happy to help you on your mission, but my flock's waiting for me. Good luck, sonny—you'll need it." The unibird galloped away and disappeared behind the trees.

I left the stream, dried myself with my clothes, and put

them back on. Then I strode back to our camp, feeling more positive and hopeful than before. I couldn't disappoint the unibird who believed in me. I had to show him I could do it, even though I would probably never see him again.

Soon, I reached our camp and dried myself by the fire.

"We're leaving in five minutes, everyone," announced Helen. "Listen to me while you collect your belongings: we will be journeying to the palace today. I don't know if we will eventually make it there, but that is no excuse for us to not do our best. We'll take a break after two hours of traveling and discuss battle plans. Then, we're going to rehearse for the final battle. We must be well-prepared, for I assume we will be fighting against the guards, or even worse, the Siblings themselves."

I noticed that Helen had left out my mother's name, and I felt a wave of appreciation for her. I did not need Alexandria's hatred to be triggered again.

"I don't know what monsters or challenging terrains we'll face today." Helen's voice quivered yet gradually got steadier. "But we've got to believe in each other, all right? Otherworldian or Underworldian, we are on the same level, like it or not. No one is better or worse, superior or inferior to one another." She glanced at Alexandria, who looked slightly abashed. "The monsters we meet today may outnumber us in people, but not in unity. We are stronger only when we're together." She took a deep breath. "Ready? Scepters and weapons prepared? Let's go, then."

"Okay, so—" started Zack.

"I see some familiar faces!" a shrill voice rang from far behind us.

Alexandria gasped. "The Chirpy Bird!"

"Follow me!" Zack sprinted in the direction opposite from the waterfall. "Clarissa, pull a cloud from the sky and leave, now!"

"No, I'm not leaving you," she insisted, catching up with us. "We're in this together, all seven of us. Either we survive together, or we die together!"

We gathered speed, running so fast the Chirpy Bird was far behind. Frustrated, the bird snarled and roared words of threat. I looked over my shoulder and saw the bird trip over its large clawed feet, cursing. The hilarious sight almost brought a smile to my lips, but this was no laughing matter — it was a situation of life-and-death. The bird got to its feet clumsily and made its way toward us, screaming nonsense on the top of its lungs.

"There's a desert ahead, everyone!" Eileen, the fastest among us, shouted.

"Can we take a detour to avoid it?" hollered Daphne. "I hate deserts!"

"We don't have anywhere else to go!" yelled Helen.

The sand dunes ahead got closer and closer, and before I knew it, I was in the desert. We huffed and puffed and panted, but —

"Keep running!" shouted Helen.

"No.... Let me...rest...," Daphne said, panting.

"Perhaps...we really...should...catch...our breath...." Clarissa, too, was gasping for air.

The Chirpy Bird reached the threshold of the desert and came to a stop. "Well, I wouldn't set foot in that desert if I were you," it said, grinning evilly. "Perhaps you should come out and be my breakfast instead."

"You wish!" I yelled, shaking my fists at the bird.

The Chirpy Bird laughed shrilly. "Well, then don't say I didn't warn you! You'll never make your way out of this desert. Mark my words!"

Then, the bird vanished right on the spot.

"What did it mean about not getting out of —?" began Alexandria.

"Don't worry about that," replied Helen. "We'll leave the way we entered. There, you see — "

Just then, as if the Underworld had understood her words, the oasis vanished. I looked around but saw nothing except for large waves of sand dunes staring at the cloudless sky above. They spread and stretched in all directions, a great, endless sea of yellow and brown.

"Great. We're trapped."

Everyone started talking at once.

"What if we can't find the way out?" said Alexandria.

"What if we can't even find water?" I said. "Daphne, can you conjure water or ice or — ?"

"I can't!" she wailed in frustration. She waved her trident, flicked it twice, and gave a few commands, but as if it had decided to turn deaf to her orders, nothing happened. "Oh, why is this darn thing not working?" she growled, hurling her trident at the sandy ground.

Helen muted everyone with a stern look, and silence drew upon us like a curtain. Only the apprehensive whispers from the two Elders were audible.

The air was thick and hazy with sand and heat. The sun flared at us from above, swallowing the entire desert with its blinding beams of light. Tiny beads of perspiration oozed from my skin, and I fanned myself. Alexandria and the others were exchanging hushed whispers.

Finally, after what seemed like a decade, Helen called for our attention. "All right, everyone. So, according to the emergency meeting I had with Zack — "

"There's only two of us. That doesn't count as a meet — " said Zack, but Helen raised her hand to silence him.

"So, as I was saying, we think we might be somewhere adjacent to the palace."

My mouth dropped open. Alexandria frowned in disagreement but otherwise showed no signs of contradiction. Clarissa and Eileen glanced at each other, skeptical.

"Remind me again, Zack, what does adjacent mean?" said Daphne, trying not to sound as sarcastic as she had intended to. "You mentioned it in your English class last week, didn't you? Does it mean very near or very far? The latter, right?"

"Adjacent means *close* to something," Zack replied enthusiastically. "Helen and I reckon we're adjacent, which means we're close to the palace of the Underworld!"

"And why is that?" Daphne plowed on, uttering one word

at a time. A funny expression was etched upon her face.

"Well, the palace might be sitting in the middle of the desert," said Zack. "So that fits the Chirpy Bird's words perfectly. It thinks we won't escape the desert because we'll find the palace and probably will get killed by the guards!"

"What?" I looked at Helen, expecting her to talk some sense into him. "The palace is right here in the desert? How is that — ?"

"We can't deny that there *is* a possibility," she said.

I exchanged looks of incredulity with the heiresses. "I really don't think — "

Strong gusts of wind assailed us, sending yellow dust and sand flying everywhere. The wind howled, tugging and clawing madly at my clothes. Large volumes of dust invaded my eyes. I choked and coughed as my throat burned in agony, powdered by the harsh, stinging floods of sand. Swirls and cyclones of dust scratched my limbs like a furious kittenpillar.

"It's getting into my eyes and ears!" I heard Daphne scream.

"It's a sandstorm, everyone, get down!" yelled Helen, crouching down and gesturing at us to follow. The wind clung to her long black hair as it flew wildly behind her.

I squeezed my eyes shut, burying my face in my palms as the sand raked my arms and legs —

Then, everything became still.

I opened my eyes. "Phew, now let's — "

"Behind you, run!" hollered Zack.

"What, the Chirpy Bird again?" said Alexandria, sniggering at her own joke.

"No, something ten times worse!" Zack grabbed Helen by the wrist and took off running.

I turned around, wondering what the Elders were fussing about. The sand behind me was ebbing, faster and faster as if the prelude of a horrendous tsunami.

"Eric, just go!" Eileen, thirty feet ahead, yelled at me.

I jogged over to her, wondering what exactly was wrong. The others had already disappeared. "Hey, what's — ?"

A massive shadow loomed over me. I looked up, only to see a thirty-foot sand-wave towering above me. It looked as if it would crash down and bury me alive at any moment. Petrified with fear, I froze in my tracks.

"It's a sand-tsunami!" shrieked Eileen. "What are you waiting for?"

Her words shook me awake. I darted towards her, my heart slamming against my chest. However, the huge wave of sand was right on my heels. Like a rolling snowball, it had gained not only height but also size.

"EILEEN, HELP!"

"It's all right, I've got you!" a voice from above called out to me. It was Clarissa! She had flown a cloud and risked her safety, only to ensure mine. "Eileen told me to come to check on you."

Eileen, who was also on the cloud, seized my hand and pulled me up.

"Accelerate!" Clarissa yelled at the cloud, waving her scepter wildly. The cloud zoomed across the desert, picking up speed.

The tiny figures of Alexandria, Daphne, Helen, and Zack dotted the vast desert below, all fleeing from the gigantic tide of sand. The wave gathered speed, now only a foot away from Helen.

"Want a ride?" yelled Clarissa.

Helen nodded, allowing the three of us to hoist her up. "Where are the others?" she said.

"There!" I spotted their tiny figures far ahead.

After a few seconds of climbing, pulling, and dragging, we were joined by Alexandria, Daphne, and Zack. Clarissa levitated our cloud, and we rose up into the sky. Silence loomed upon us for several minutes.

"That was a close call," I said, turning to Clarissa. "Thanks, we all owe you one."

"We would've been buried alive without you," admitted Alexandria.

Zack patted Clarissa on the back. "You're a genius."

"Perhaps we can go exploring and find the palace by cloud," suggested Clarissa. Wouldn't that be — ?"

But as if it had understood her words, the cloud beneath us evaporated right at that moment. The seven of us fell from the sky and landed on the soft sand. After a few seconds of groaning and moaning, complaints rent the air.

"Darn Underworld!" I cursed, rubbing my sore legs.

Alexandria stomped at the ground. "As if the sandstorm and tsunami haven't caused enough trouble!"

"It's no use complaining," said Helen, patting the dust and sand off her clothes. "Zack, emergency meeting right away."

The two Elders got into a discussion, and it took forever for them to finish.

"What should we do?" said Alexandria, wringing her hands. Clarissa stared blankly at the dull yellow dunes in the distance as though hypnotized.

The scorching rays of the sun beat down at the desert, drenching us in sweat. There was a throbbing behind my right eyebrow. I rubbed my temples to ease the pain.

"Where's Daphne?" Eileen noticed.

We looked around frantically, and Alexandria spotted her behind a dune.

"What are you doing over there?" I called out to her.

"I feel like throwing up." Daphne's face was turning clammy and purple. Before we knew it, she started vomiting. Then, her body went slack, and she slumped on the sandy ground.

My heart skipped a beat, and my knees turned to jelly at that sight.

"Daphne? Daphne, what's wrong?" I tried to help her up, only to find that her hand had become translucent.

"Helen! Zack!" Clarissa yelled for their attention. "Come quick!"

The two Elders hurried over to us and bent down to check on Daphne. Zack's face became chalky as he exchanged an uneasy glance with Helen.

"It must be the climate that's killing her," said Helen,

the remaining color draining from her face. "As the heiress of Walters, she's not supposed to linger in the desert for more than an hour. She'll fade away to nothing if we don't get out of here immediately."

"Are you kidding?" Zack almost yelled. "Then how did you forget about that in the first place?"

"Now's not the time to argue!" I chimed in. "We've got to leave this place immediately!"

"No way! She won't make it until then!"

The others exchanged frantic looks as if to see who could come up with a plan to save poor Daphne, whose legs were fading away.

"Alexandria, Eileen, you remember the little pouches Queen Marianne gave us?" said Clarissa suddenly.

They both nodded.

"They're supposed to help us in our darkest hour," replied Alexandria.

"Daphne's still got hers, right? She hasn't—"

"Yeah, but—"

"Then, QUICK!" Zack cut in.

Clarissa reached into Daphne's pocket. "Here!" she pulled out a cobalt pouch, untied the ribbon, then turned it upside down and dumped whatever was inside onto her palm. "How's a snow globe going to save her life?"

"Just smash it and pour the contents onto her body before it's too late!"

Clarissa obeyed, and all of us watched attentively, holding our breaths. Slowly, Daphne's limbs regained color and became opaque again, and her eyelids fluttered open.

"Oh, Daphne!" said Clarissa, almost throttling her with a hug. "We were worried sick! We thought we'd lost you forever!"

"So...what did I miss?"

"Not much," answered Helen, her inner anxiety reflected on her taut expression. "We have to get out of this desert, and I mean it this time. The climate here has proven to be fatal to Daphne, and we can't lose anyone." She bit her lip so hard it bled.

"We can't leave this cursed place on foot," I pointed out. "Not without Daphne collapsing for a second time. Plus, we can't be sure of how long the snow globe's magic will last."

"Cloud flying won't do," added Clarissa.

"So basically, we're trapped," Eileen said, shrugging.

"Don't worry," said Zack. "We'll figure out a way to leave, sooner or later."

"Don't worry. We'll figure out a way to leave, sooner or later." A hollow, metallic voice repeated his words.

It was an echo.

But echoes were not supposed to be in deserts.

"Shush, I heard something," I whispered. "I think it was an echo."

Eileen gave me a funny look. "Are you crazy? There are no echoes in deserts!"

"Are you crazy? There are no echoes in deserts!" A second voice repeated her words.

We looked at the two Elders, hoping for an answer.

"We're being followed," said Zack. "It must be a —"

"Perhaps we should stay low," Alexandria suggested. "That way, the monster or whoever's following us won't be able to see us clearly."

"No," said Helen. "Keep your weapons ready, but don't do anything. Not until I figure out what's going on."

"What?" asked Alexandria, her jaw dropping. "Do nothing? We just stand here and wait for the monsters to attack us?"

"Unless you can come up with a better plan!" snapped Daphne.

"Well, anything's better than just standing here and doing nothing!"

I walked away from them and stared at the sandy dunes ahead, trying to figure out where the disembodied speaker was. All was quiet, except for the howling wind that tore relentlessly at my clothes; all was still, except for the white clouds drifting leisurely in the sky; all was silent, almost too silent, like the serenity before a brutal storm.

A few moments passed in loud, roaring silence. Ahead of us, the blurry silhouettes of seven people came into view as they drew nearer. What I saw almost gave me a heart attack.

They were seven people that looked exactly the same as we — Alexandria, Clarissa, Eileen, Daphne, Helen, Zack, and me.

I turned around, but my real companions were still bickering. "STOP TALKING, ALL OF YOU!" I yelled, pointing at the clones. "WE'VE GOT ANOTHER PROBLEM!"

Helen and Zack looked up, mirroring each other's expressions of utmost terror. "RUN AGAIN! THE OPPOSITE DIRECTION!"

"Again?" Daphne moaned.

"Don't ask questions, just go!" hollered Zack, giving her a push.

The seven of us raced in the direction we had come from as fast as our legs could carry us. Clouds of yellow sand swirled in the air as our feet pounded against the mounds of dunes. The rapid footsteps behind us announced the proximity of our pursuers. They, too, were gathering speed to catch up with us.

"What are they? Monsters?" shouted Alexandria as she glanced over her shoulder.

"They're clones created by the Siblings!" yelled Helen. "They imitate our actions and repeat our words, and they've got powerful —"

"Why can't we just kill them off?"

"Of course we can't!" answered Zack. "They're clones, and they're made to confuse us! You might accidentally hurt one of the real us if you attack them! It's impossible for humans to discern between clones and real people!"

I looked behind and saw Helen lose her balance and trip. The monsters were only a short distance away from her. Without hesitation, I sprinted towards her and helped her up.

"Eric, you shouldn't have come," she groaned. "Perhaps I should sacrifice myself —"

"Don't even think about it. As a team, we're supposed to have each other's backs."

Supporting Helen by the arm, the two of us took off once again, only this time, the clones were ten feet away from us. With a pang of shock, I noticed that they were wearing the same clothes as we. The clones grinned maliciously and raised their weapons, aiming for us.

"Eric, leave!" said Helen. "Don't risk your life to save —"

"No!" I brandished my wand and unleashed a round of turquoise fireballs at our enemies.

"DON'T LISTEN TO HER!" another voice roared.

Alexandria and the others bolted towards me. The clones fired arrows and hurled spears at them, and one of the arrows whizzed past Eileen's ear.

"I told you to run, but you didn't listen!" bellowed Zack, slashing his sword at his clone. "Now we have no choice but to fight them!"

"ATTACK!" my clone commanded. "GET THEM KILLED!"

Panicking, I looked around for my real friends, but Zack's earlier warning had already dropped off the radar. The fourteen of us were battling and shouting incantations at one another. Both Zacks swung swords and hurled daggers at each other, attempting to end the other's life. Before I could figure out my next step, my clone pounced on me. I threw a turquoise fireball at him, but he converted it into a ball of sand with a lazy snap of his fingers.

It was complete chaos. Everyone was fighting with everything they had. Some fired charms, some shouted names, some hurled knives, and some were even wrestling and pummeling fists at each other. A blur of fireballs, lightning sparks, spiky roses, snowballs, and blades danced in the air.

I prayed silently that none of my real companions would get injured. From the corner of my eye, I saw one of the two Clarissas drawing a cloud from the sky and succeeding. To my horror, seven people dismounted from the cloud and joined our fight.

They were clones. Another seven clones.

"WATCH OUT, EVERYONE!" someone shouted, friend

or foe, I did not know.

Commotion reigned. The twenty-one of us—fourteen clones and seven real Otherworldians, were dueling, throwing punches, flinging swords, and stabbing spears at each other. Every single combatant was fighting to kill. Weapons of all sorts sailed through the air. To make matters worse, the new clones had guns, and they were opening fire at everyone they saw. It had become a riotous free-for-all.

"SQUAWK!"

I looked up and saw seven unibirds flapping their wings and galloping in the air.

"LADY CLARISSA!" a unibird with a purple mane squawked in English. "WHERE ARE YOU? WE'VE COME TO RESCUE YOU AND YOUR FRIENDS!"

"I'm here!" The three Clarissas waved wildly and jumped up and down, jostling for attention. The unibird flew over to one of them.

"NO, THEY'RE CLONES!" I screamed.

"ANIMALS CAN DISCERN BETWEEN CLONES AND HUMANS!" a unibird with a pink mane squawked, landing by my side. "COME, GET ON BEFORE THE CLONES DO!"

I scrambled onto her back and grasped her mane. The unibird kicked off the ground and flapped her wings. Then, she rose up into the air gracefully and galloped to gain height. "You got everyone?" she neighed at the other unibirds as they nodded. "Then let's leave the desert."

I rested my head on her long neck, watching the clouds come and go below my feet, all in different shades of white. I cast a glance at the others, who were bedraggled, fatigued, and still in a state of shock.

"You all right?" I whispered to Eileen, whose unibird was flying beside mine.

"Yeah, I guess." Her voice was shaky.

"Hey, it's okay to be scared," I reached out to hold her hand.

Eileen blushed a little and turned her head away from me.

"You...um...you still got your scepter?" I asked rather awkwardly.

Eileen nodded and gazed down at her unibird. "Sir, where exactly are you taking us?"

"Don't worry," neighed the unibird with the purple mane. "We're on your side. We'll take you to the nearest oasis, where I assure you will find water and a nice place to study battle plans."

"Thanks," I said. "No offense, but why are you helping us?"

"Lady Clarissa saved my wife yesterday," neighed the unibird. "We promised to help you in return, and we kept our word."

"What?" cried Clarissa. "It's really you?" A grin of surprise crossed her face.

"Of course," my unibird, who must have been his wife, replied. "Lady Clarissa, we meet again."

"Thank you so much," Clarissa reached out a hand and patted her gently on the head.

The unibird with the purple mane caught my eye, and the two of us exchanged a meaningful look.

Soon, we crossed the threshold of the desert and were now hovering above a clearing in the middle of a small forest. That was when an idea struck me. "Do you know where the palace of the Underworld is?"

"Sorry," replied my unibird, landing shakily. "Never been there before."

"Oh," I said, my heart sinking. "Then do you know if the Gem of Hope is hidden there?"

"Maybe. The palace is definitely the safest place to hide a precious artifact. However, it's almost impossible to break in—"

"It's all right," said Helen. "This is a perfect place for us to review our strategies and do a quick rehearsal battle. Thank you for everything."

The flock of unibirds neighed and nuzzled us.

"I'll see you someday, Lady Clarissa," the pink-maned unibird said. Clarissa caressed her fuzzy neck and planted a kiss on her forehead.

After bidding goodbyes, the unibirds turned, ready to depart.

"Wait!" Eileen's hand dived into the pocket of her jeans, and she produced a green velvet pouch. "This is a gift for all of you. Queen Marianne from the Otherworld gave us this, and we're supposed to use it in our darkest hour. It's a magical pouch, and it'll provide whatever you need when—"

"You are too kind! We wouldn't dream of having—"

"Just take it," insisted Eileen, looking pleadingly at them with her big green eyes. "We would never have made it out of the desert alive if you hadn't arrived in time. You came to our aid in our darkest hour, and you deserve something in return. Please, I want you to have it."

The unibirds raised their wings in salute, and Eileen took that as a yes. She tied the green pouch to her unibird's horn.

"Thank you," they neighed. "All the best on your mission!"

Then the unibirds took off, soaring higher and higher until they became tiny white specks and disappeared in the layered clouds.

Chapter Ten

ON THE HORIZON
(DAPHNE)

"Finally, it's noontime!" announced Zack cheerfully, glancing down at his watch. "Which means we've been in the Underworld for more than twenty-four hours. Well done, everyone!"

"I must say I'm very proud of you all for staying alive for more than one day," said Helen. "But don't get too relaxed. We haven't reached the toughest part yet—the battle with the palace guards, or worse, the Siblings themselves. Today, at twilight, we'll show them who the boss is." Her eyes glowed with fierce determination.

"And how are we going to prepare for that?" I asked. "We sit here, wait for some monster-passerby, and practice with it?" It sounded so ridiculous that everyone cracked up, with Helen being the only exception.

"No, of course not. Stop horsing around, and let's get to work."

"But we need enemies to practice with," said Eric.

"Yes, but not now. We're going to have a rehearsal battle after a tutorial of essential skills."

"A what?"

"A tutorial, Eric," explained Helen patiently. "First, we divide into two groups, attack and defense. Zack, lead the—"

"What's the difference between them?" asked Clarissa.

"The attack team is responsible for launching assaults during battles. On the other hand, the members of the defense team are in charge of protecting the others during a fight. They sometimes have to act as reinforcement, if necessary. Defense members will also learn about traps and how to set them up. Alexandria, Daphne, you're on the attack team, and Zack will be your mentor."

"Sweet," I muttered.

"Clarissa and Eileen, you'll be working with me. Eric, which is your strength, attack or defense?"

"Attack, I guess."

"Join Zack, then. Any questions?"

"How are you going to train us if you can't do any elemental magic?" I asked.

"We'll just teach you a few commands and strategies and give you a general idea."

"And when are we going to have lunch?" said Eric as his stomach growled.

"After the tutorial and the rehearsal battle, which is roughly two hours. Now, if you please, meet your mentors, and let the training begin."

Alexandria, Eric, and I walked up to Zack. "Everyone here? All right, so I'll be teaching all of you a few valid charms and basic skills, one by one. Alexandria, you're first. Daphne and Eric, you can practice dueling with each other while I teach Alexandria."

"Come on, Daphne," said Eric. "Perhaps I can teach you some stuff. You got any weapons besides that ice trident?"

I shook my head.

"Okay. When dueling, you must choose the fastest way to attack your opponent. For example, if you're dueling a bearnix, you can lure it to a lake and trick it into jumping into the water. I've already discussed this with Helen, and she agrees it's a useful strategy. Keep this in mind: fire and water are enemies. Bearnixes are spirits of fire, so they die immediately when making contact with water. You're the heiress of Walters, right? That makes it easier for you to deal with the bearnixes. Ice boulders and water will do the trick. If your opponent is a kittenpillar, jab it in the eye with your trident. Kittenpillars are the least aggressive among the four creatures, and you'll be able to get rid of them in ten seconds if you're skilled enough. Unibirds usually take refuge in the clouds while ambushing their enemies. They're trickier than the others. They usually attack people by shooting arrows, and they move with great velocity, so you have to aim well enough to attack them. Are you good at archery?"

"No. Ask Helen. She's the master."

"I will. Anyway, just throw ice cubes, ice boulders, or jagged icicles at the unibirds during a battle. Wiping them out will be hard, but you can at least injure or weaken them. As for dogfishes, you must watch out for their bites. They are more difficult to hurt or kill for you because both of you were either created or chosen by Walters and share the same brand of elemental magic. You'd better leave the dogfishes to Alexandria since she's the heiress of Ember. Just focus on the bearnixes and kittenpillars during the battle."

"But what if I have to duel one by myself?"

"Stab your trident at its fish body, the most vulnerable part."

"How do you know all this stuff? Did your mother teach you?"

Alexandria had told all of us the truth about Eric's parentage this morning, but I wasn't as worked up as she was.

"No. But I watched and learned whenever I had a chance to fight them."

"All right. Thanks."

"You remember the rehearsal battle Helen mentioned? You could work with Eileen and help her grow poisonous plants with your water magic. I suppose teaming up with Clarissa would also be a good option. The two of you could kill enemies by summoning lightning and water at the same time."

"Eric, you're next!" Zack called out to him.

I beamed at Eric to show my appreciation.

"You're welcome. I'm going to meet Zack, see you."

Feeling bored, I went over to Helen's team to check on the others.

"Daphne!" squealed Eileen as she saw me. "You'll never believe what Helen just taught me!"

"What, how to grow bushes with kittenpillar shaped flowers?" I quipped, snickering at my joke.

"No, it's THE SELF-RUNNING-FLESH-EATING-VENUS-FLYTRAP!"

"Okay, okay, please don't get so worked up," I said. "Eric just taught me a few strategies, and now, Zack's teaching Eric…," I glanced at them, "um…skills on swordplay. Maneuvering and striking, or at least something like that, I guess. Eric's pretty clever, and he suggested that we could team up you and me. I can help you grow poisonous plants with my magic. What else have you learned?"

"Oh, ever so much! The flesh-eating-flytrap, thorny rose bushes, an automatic twig-hurling tree, and…well, it'd take me an hour to go through all of them."

"Sounds interesting. I guess you'd really need my water magic to grow all that stuff."

Eileen nodded. She combed her long hair with her fingers and suddenly paused. "Hang on. You said that Eric…he tutored you? One-on-one?"

I nodded. "Yeah. Why are you asking?"

Eileen gave me a meaningful look, as if wanting to say more, but then thought better of it.

"What?"

But she was saved the necessity of answering by Zack, who called my name at that moment.

"See you later," I said.

Trying to be positive for my upcoming session, I told Zack, "I like you way better as an Elder than a regular teacher."

Zack smiled. "Well, thanks a lot, but let's carry on with the training first. What can you do?"

"I can conjure snowballs."

"What about slushballs, ice boulders and icicles? And cannons?"

I shook my head.

"To conjure one of those, simply picture one in your mind and concentrate wholeheartedly on it."

"That's it?"

"Right, the same way you conjure snowballs. It's a matter of willpower. You've got to have your mind wholly focused on it. Slushballs, unlike snowballs or ice boulders, are watery. You can drown bearnixes in massive ones. Ice boulders are good for reducing your adversary's stamina, as they are small and heavy, but personally, I think icicles are the best kind of ammunition. They're jagged and pointy and can penetrate objects easily. Try to avoid using snowballs in a fight—they're good for nothing except annoying your enemies."

"What about cannons?"

"Cannons are wonderful ammunition launchers, but you've got to make sure your ammunition doesn't run out in the middle of the battle. As for how to build one, get your trident ready and follow my steps. First, conjure two ice bricks. Make them as long as your leg and as wide as your shoulders."

I did.

"Then, carve them into reversed arches."

"What? I'm drawing a blank here."

"Dig a U-shaped channel in the middle of the surface, where you'll be putting your ammunition. Then, wave your trident and assemble the two bricks like this. I'm doing this one for you so you can see...." He traced his wand in the air and jabbed my bricks. "And then for the last part—conjure a muzzle and attach it to the end of the channel."

I shot him a puzzled look.

"Close your eyes and picture it in your mind. A hollowed cylinder block made of ice."

I had a hard time visualizing the object but eventually succeeded. An icy cylinder block of vapor whooshed from the tip of my trident and solidified, now hovering a few inches above my unfinished cannon.

"There you go." Zack plucked it from the air. "Now, attach this to the trench—the channel where the ammunition goes. Here," he pointed out. "Finally, tap your trident twice on the top and say 'automate.'"

"That's all?"

"Yes. Let's test your practical skills."

I followed every instruction with great caution, and in less than a minute, my cannon was finished.

"It looks great," said Zack. "Let's see if it can function properly."

I conjured an ice boulder and put it in the channel. Then, I adjusted the muzzle and automated the cannon. The boulder went soaring at the target, a lonely shrub perched nearby.

I beamed, looking at Zack. "Did you see that?"

"Well done, Daphne." He gave me a proud slap on the back. "You mastered this."

"Attention, everyone!" announced Helen. "Please end all tutorials immediately. Now's the big moment." She nodded at a grinning Zack. "We are going to have a rehearsal battle. Yes, a huge free-for-all."

Clarissa whistled, and Eileen glanced at me.

"You will have five minutes to discuss battle plans, and then, we fight. Zack and I versus the five of you."

"What?" I exchanged looks with my teammates.

"Your five minutes start...now!" Helen got out a notebook, and the two Elders began their discussion.

Eric looked at us. "So, perhaps we should divide into—"

"There's five of us and only two opponents," I pointed out. "We've already outnumbered them. Why bother preparing? We're definitely going to win."

"But they're Elders. They know better."

"There are more of us. Plus, we've got elemental powers and your Underworldian magic. The odds are against them."

Alexandria and Clarissa were already gibbering over

some piece of gossip instead of focusing on preparation.

"I'm tired from all that running and collapsing in the desert," I whined.

"Fine then," said Eric, yawning. "Let's all just kick back and take it easy for the next five minutes."

Eileen devoted her attention to a blue butterfly, watching it zigzag in the air. I wasn't particularly interested in butterflies, so I walked over to Alexandria and Clarissa, wondering what they were talking about.

"I was pretty surprised when she told me," Alexandria was saying. "I never knew she'd been through something like this."

Clarissa looked sad and shocked at the same time. "Now I finally understand why Helen's always acting so tough and rather haughty. I can't believe she's been holding on to this for the past few months. And it wasn't even her fault." She shook her head in disbelief. "You're right, Alexandria. We *have* to nail this mission. For Helen."

I was about to join them when Eric, who had noticed Eileen's obsession with the blue butterfly, skipped away in pursuit of it.

Eileen blushed furiously.

Grinning, I walked up to her. "Falling for Eric, aren't you?"

"He's sort of...cute, don't you think?"

"So you don't mind the fact about his mother?"

"Not really. He seems like a good...I mean....well, you know, a good friend. Gentle, caring—"

"And handsome?" I teased her.

Eileen averted my gaze as her face crimsoned.

"Hey, Eileen, look at this!" shouted Eric, running towards us. He had caught the butterfly by cupping his hands around it. The butterfly had smooth, fuzzy blue wings rimmed with turquoise. A swirling pattern of faint purple dots could be seen on its left wing.

Eileen scrutinized it. "It looks a lot like the Holly Blue, *Celastrina argiolus*, but unlike this one, the Holly Blue has black spots, ivory dots, and white-trimmed wings."

"Cool," said Eric. "Where can you find the Holly Blue, then?"

"They're mostly found in Eurasia and North America."

"Eurasia? North America?" repeated Eric, puzzled.

"They're parts of the mortal world," I explained.

"Interesting...so there *are* butterflies in the mortal world, too," Eric mused. "Perhaps you could teach me the scientific names of every animal in the mortal world. Oh, that is...if we...I mean, if I ever get a chance to visit the mortal world with you, Eileen."

Eileen nodded coyly. I winked at her, and she blushed again.

"You're not angry with me anymore, are you?" Eric looked anxiously at her.

Eileen developed a sudden interest in her feet. "Well, yes. Yes...uh, I mean...no, well...no, of course...."

Eric opened his mouth to reply, when—

"Time's up, everyone," said Helen. "For the rules, maiming and killing are absolutely banned. Both teams can request a truce anytime until two o'clock when we're going to have lunch. Now, the captains of both teams will have to shake hands." She stood out.

"Eric," said Eileen without hesitation, pushing him forward.

Helen and Eric shook hands, and the battle began.

We were no match for the Elders. Helen fired arrows everywhere to distract us. I barely managed to pull Clarissa out of harm's way as one of them whizzed past her arm. With all the dodging and ducking, it was impossible for our team to launch attacks. Alexandria and I hurled fireballs and slushballs at the Elders, but Zack deflected every one of them with his wand. He then came lunging at Eric, who drew his sword to fight. Unfortunately, one of my slushballs hit him smack on the face at that precise moment. Clarissa pointed her scepter at the sky, but before she could do anything, Alexandria's fireball ignited her pigtail. I extinguished it with a flick of my trident, but the next second, one of Eileen's thorny red roses hit me right on the nose. It was an utter disaster. The five of us were defeated by the two Elders in less than a minute.

"Truce time, please!" yelled Eric.

Our disgruntled teammates gathered around and started accusing each other.

"What were you doing?" Eric rounded on me. "You've dropped the ball!"

"It was your problem! Why didn't you dodge my slushball?"

"My problem? How am I supposed to dodge it when I'm dueling? And how am I supposed to duel properly when I've got a face full of slush?"

Clarissa and Eileen were also quarreling. "Why didn't you summon the cloud sooner? What were you thinking?"

"Are you blaming me? I haven't seen you do anything to help, except for hitting Daphne with that thorny rose!"

"Me? What about you? You were standing there and doing absolutely nothing!"

"We're not getting anywhere," Alexandria, the only one who had not joined the spar, pointed out.

"Fine!" snapped Eric. "I'm resigning. You go on and replace me as the captain, then, if you think you're so smart."

"Well, I suppose we could share the position," said Alexandria calmly.

Eric's anger faded away. "It's a deal. Or maybe you could be the captain, and I the vice-captain."

Alexandria smiled. "Fair enough, cousin. So now, we have two opponents. Let's divide into two teams. Eileen, Eric, and Daphne are team one, while Clarissa and I are team two. Team one will be dealing with Zack, while team two will tackle Helen."

"Nice planning," I said. "I'm glad I finally have an opportunity to take revenge on Zack for all the detentions he gave me."

"Hang on," interrupted Eric. "Only two of us in charge of Helen?"

"That's right. Eric, I put you in charge of Zack because of

your knowledge of sword fighting. Your job is to keep him busy and duel him. Try to lead him to the middle of the battlefield. Eileen, sneak behind Zack, exit the battlefield as soon as we begin, and design a few traps there. What's the most useful trap you've learned?"

"The self-running-flesh-eating-Venus-flytrap!"

"All right. But keep this in mind: don't get Zack swallowed or chewed up, all right? No maiming or killing, that's in the rules."

"Sure thing! I won't harm a hair on his head."

"I didn't mean...well, just promise me you won't get him maimed, okay?"

Eileen nodded.

Alexandria went on. "Daphne, help Eileen grow her flytrap with your magic. At the same time, chuck icicles at Zack when necessary to distract him. Of course, since Eric will be doing all the main work, you can also check on team two and deal with Helen. Anyway, look out for both teams. Send us signals if—"

"I can make an ice cannon that chucks ammunition at the target automatically," I suggested.

"Good," replied Alexandria. "I'm planning three major assaults. We'll launch the first two attacks, respectively, and the two teams will join forces on the third one. We're going to win this time." As Alexandria said this, her eyes gleamed with fierce determination that bore a striking resemblance to Helen's.

"It's good to see you guys actually discussing battle plans and working in peace, but it's been five minutes!" Helen herself yelled from the other side. "Are you done?"

"Not yet, ten more minutes!" answered Alexandria. Then she turned to us and pressed on with her plan. "The first assault will involve step A, which Eric will be in charge of. Eric, duel Zack and keep him busy. After one minute, execute step A: pretend you're tired or hurt, and sink to the ground. Then, Eileen and Daphne, execute step B immediately: begin your attack. Eileen, get your Venus flytrap done while Eric's busy. Daphne, run over to Zack and fight him with your trident after Eric surrenders.

You must get not only your cannon but also fifty icicles and ice boulders ready beforehand.

"As for you, Eric, quietly and quickly crawl away while Daphne's dueling. Exit the battlefield and join Eileen. The two of you will then execute step C: make your own ammunition — turquoise fireballs and spiky flowers, which will come in handy in the battle later. Make more than a hundred in two minutes, so don't waste time. After Daphne's ammunition runs out, put your own into the cannon. Daphne, pay attention to Eric, Eileen, and the cannon while you're dueling. Pretend to surrender as soon as Eileen and Eric are done. Then, leave the battlefield and let the cannon do the work. Now, for step D: Eileen, grow thorny rose bushes all over the battlefield and trap the Elders."

"But what about you and Clarissa?"

"I'll explain later."

"But how are we going to attack the Elders if we're separated from them?" I said.

"No more attacks for you guys. Mission accomplished. But don't just watch the rest of the battle from the sidelines. Pre-make some ammunition for our third assault."

"But what if Helen and Zack break out of —"

"They won't. Don't forget the self-running-flesh-eating-Venus-flytrap. It would totally come in handy at that moment, and we don't even have to lift a finger."

"Nice plan," I said. I couldn't help grinning as I visualized the Venus flytrap running in pursuit of the two Elders. "But what next?"

"That's when Clarissa and I come in and be the heroes."

"Wait a second," said Clarissa. "What will we be doing when they're fighting Zack?"

"We'll be having fun and taunting the two Elders high above in the clouds," replied Alexandria. "Now for our part, Clarissa. Draw a cloud from the sky when the battle begins, and we'll get on together. Helen might shoot arrows at us when we're flying up there, and I'm going to convert the arrows into fireballs and chuck them back at her. That's step E. Clarissa, we will launch major assault two as soon as Eileen's done with her thorny bushes. Next, step F: summon lightning to distract the Elders."

"Lightning? What if the Elders get killed?"

"I never told you to summon a *powerful* streak of lightning. You get what I'm saying?"

Clarissa paused and nodded.

"Then, lower the cloud and move us over to Daphne's cannon. Step G: I will conjure a firewall separating the Elders from the cannon. After that, we'll move it onto our cloud and return to the battlefield by flying. We all know what the two Elders are good at, don't we?"

"Archery for Helen, and Zack...swordplay."

"Right. They've got their advantages, and they're much more skilled compared to us, so we must plan our attacks creatively. They have experience, brains, and strategies, but we've got creativity, and that's more than enough for us. We can relax and let the cannon work its magic as soon as it's on our cloud. Assault number two accomplished.

"Now, last but definitely not least...assault number three — the five of us ally. After the ammunition in the cannon runs out, Clarissa and I will exit the battlefield by cloud, and we will pick you up. Then, all of us will launch our final assault in midair, this time without the cannon. Step H: unleash the remainder of our ammunition — the stuff you guys made while Clarissa and I were fighting Helen. Just pelt them with everything we've got. Then we can start cheering for our well-earned victory. Got it?"

"Wow," said Clarissa in awe.

Despite the fact that Alexandria and I were meant to be enemies, I had to admit that her plan was indeed flawless. I was actually starting to admire her after everything we'd gone through together.

"Your idea looks good on paper, but are you sure about its feasibility?" said Eric, frowning. "Everything seems a little too perfect."

"It'll work fine as long as you have faith in yourself. I know this isn't an easy task, but as a team, we will win. By the way, let's review everything from scratch. The battle begins, and—"

"I'll duel Zack and do a silent countdown from one minute before executing step A: pretend to give up and wait for Daphne to take my place," said Eric.

"Right. Eileen?"

"I'll exit the battlefield and get the flytrap done as soon as possible!" said Eileen, bouncing up and down with excitement.

"And I'll get the cannon and our ammunition ready for steps B and C when Eric's fighting Zack," I added. "After Eric collapses, I'll take his place in the duel and at the same time pay attention to my teammates."

"When Eric's back, we'll get turquoise fireballs and thorny flowers ready and stack them in the cannon after Daphne's icicles and boulders are gone," said Eileen. "Then—"

"I surrender, exit the battlefield, and leave Zack to deal with the cannon," I went on, picturing the battle in my mind.

"Then, it's my turn to make a contribution—the loveliest rose bush with the deadliest thorns!" Eileen chimed in.

"And Eileen, Daphne, and I will be out of the battlefield, preparing ammunition for the final assault," said Eric.

"Great," Alexandria smiled at us. "And what next, Clarissa?"

"I'll draw a cloud from the sky as soon as the battle begins, and we will get on together. You will execute step E: convert Helen's arrows into fireballs and chuck them back at her. Then, immediately after the first assault, I'm going to summon lightning to distract the Elders. You'll create a firewall, and then we'll get the cannon onto our cloud and let it do its work."

"And finally, for assault number three, you and Clarissa are going to pick me, Eric, and Eileen up, and we'll fight the Elders with everything we have," I ended.

Alexandria looked pleased. "Wonderful. Now, take your places! Of course, you'll have to play it by ear if something unexpected happens. Oh, and one last word, everyone: nothing is impossible, just do it!"

"Nice pep talk," I heard Eric whisper to Eileen. "At least it's way shorter than the one Helen gave this morning."

"Time to resume play?" Zack called out to us.

"Are we going to make it?" Eileen muttered to herself.

"Yes," said Eric. "We must think positively."

"We're ready. By the way, I'm the new captain," Alexandria flashed a confident smile at the two Elders. She and Helen shook hands, and the rest of us formed a queue behind her.

"Now, on my count," said Helen. "Three...two...one, begin!"

Eric and Zack started dueling, Eileen fled the battlefield as fast as her legs could carry her, and Clarissa pointed her scepter at the sky. Unfortunately, Helen fired an arrow right at her before she could do anything. I tossed an ice boulder at Helen, which she ducked narrowly. She then came in my direction to get revenge. A jet of purple light zoomed at me, and I leapt out of the way, narrowly avoiding it.

"Look what we've got here!" a voice sounded from above.

Helen looked up, only to see fireballs and lavabricks pouring from a cloud. I froze in my tracks, confused, as this was not a part of our plan. But then, it dawned on me that Alexandria was distracting Helen and buying me time to run away. I bolted for the exit and joined Eileen, who was charming and automating her flytrap.

"Daphne, I saw what you did over there. Nice work!" shouted Alexandria.

I smiled, then started working on my cannon. After a few seconds, it was ready for shooting. Eileen and I stuffed twigs, thorny roses, slushballs, icicles, and ice boulders into the launcher, and Alexandria yelled my name and signaled me to take over the battlefield.

Sure enough, Eric had collapsed, and I sprinted over to him to take his place. Dueling Zack was not as difficult as I had imagined since the cannon was doing most of the work. With a great effort, he managed to dodge my strikes, but not the ammunition. The cannon aimed perfectly and got him every single time. A glance at the exit told me that Eileen and Eric were sneaking turquoise fireballs and spiky flowers into the cannon.

Eric nodded at me, and I ran over to join him.

Zack, looking confused, came in pursuit of me, but then—*boom!* The cannon started chucking Eileen and Eric's ammunition at him. Zack waved his wand in a vain attempt to deflect the spiky flowers and turquoise fireballs, so he parried them with his shield instead.

Eileen, Eric and I watched, beaming.

"Now, for step D," whispered Eileen, her smile becoming rather mischievous. "Come on, Daphne!"

The two of us hurtled across the battlefield. Eileen pointed her scepter at the ground and muttered a few incomprehensible words. Small, thorny bushes popped out between the tufts of grass, growing at a rapid speed. I followed Eileen as she circled the battlefield, watering the tiny bushes with slushballs. The bushes grew bigger and bigger, kissing at the edges and trapping the two Elders. Zack blasted one to pieces and would probably have destroyed the rest, if Eileen's flesh-eating-Venus-flytrap had not chased him away.

"Alexandria!" I yelled, waving my arms to get her attention. "Assault number one accomplished!"

She nodded, just as a streak of lightning split the air.

Helen and Zack tried to break the cannon, which was still flinging ammunition at them. However, the flesh-eating flytrap was on their heels, so they had no choice but to run for dear life. The flytrap chased the two Elders all the way to the other side, giving Alexandria and Clarissa enough time to move the cannon onto their cloud.

I glanced back at the battlefield. Zack had put up a duel with the flytrap, and Helen was firing arrows at Alexandria and Clarissa, as predicted. Alexandria converted her arrows into fireballs and stuffed them into the cannon, allowing it to chuck them back at the Elders.

Clarissa gave Eileen, Eric and me a nod, and moments later, her cloud descended in front of us.

"Let the collaboration begin!" shouted Alexandria.

With the assistance of Clarissa, we got on the cloud, and the five of us gathered our ammunition.

"On my command," said Alexandria. "Full-scale attack waiting to be launched on ten, nine, eight...."

Two unibirds, one with a purple mane and the other a pink one, were resting on a cloud above us. I recognized them as our benefactors who had rescued us from the desert. I was the only one who noticed them, and I gave them a thumbs-up.

"Good luck, we'll be watching over you," the unibird with a purple mane neighed in an undertone.

"OPEN FIRE, EVERYONE!"

It was a spectacular sight as fireballs, lavabricks, icicles, slushballs, ice boulders, exploding leaves, and pointy foliage went soaring down from our cloud. Alexandria, Clarissa, Eileen, Eric, and I gloated over our victorious attack. Our ammunition rained on for a few minutes.

"Ah, I've never felt happier on a cloud," said Clarissa.

"Great, isn't it?" Alexandria grinned at us. "Well done."

The ammunition slowed down to a trickle and finally ran out. Smiling, Clarissa summoned a triumphant streak of lightning.

"IT'S TWO O'CLOCK, PLEASE!" poor Helen and Zack yelled from below. "WE SURRENDER!"

Clarissa lowered us to ground-level, and we dismounted, tumbling, giggling, and shouting.

"Excellent, you fought very well," said Helen. Perhaps I imagined it, but I was certain she had smiled.

"You did really well yourselves," I answered, for the two Elders seemed miraculously unscathed.

"That was the best fight I've ever seen," said Zack. "The attacks were meticulously planned and well-executed. Who's idea was it?"

"Mine," replied Alexandria, lifting her chin and beaming.

The two Elders regarded her with appreciation.

"Well done!" exclaimed Zack. "I knew from the beginning that you were a promising talent. I can't wait to see your performance in the final battle."

"Your parents would've been proud," agreed Helen.

"So, why not tell us everything? Some of your strategies would definitely come in handy during the final battle."

We explained everything, including the three assaults and steps A to H.

"Amazing," breathed Zack, while Helen recorded everything in her notebook.

"Let's take a break and have lunch, everyone," announced Helen. "We've got to be well-rested and prepared for the upcoming battle."

We looked around the war-torn clearing and unanimously agreed to find another place to settle down. After a quick stroll in the woods, Eileen spotted another huge clearing surrounded by trees and dotted with greenish white flowers. Everyone thought it was a lovely place to have lunch and recharge.

"Eileen, Daphne, and Zack go into the woods and pick some mushrooms for our lunch," Helen read from her chore list.

I groaned, but on the bright side, both Eileen and Zack were paired up with me.

Eileen and I had completely forgotten about the childish squabble we had had yesterday when first arriving at the Otherworld. The two of us talked and giggled like two sisters.

"All right, Zack," said Eileen as we delved further into the woods and came across a thicket. "Stop here."

The sunlight winked at us through the shade of leaves overhead. The trees, blanketed with moss, displayed a palette of turquoise, chartreuse, viridian, and innumerable shades of green that I was unable to name. "This is a great place to —"

"Shh," Eileen shushed me. She got out her scepter and pointed it at the ground, her expression solemn. "Rise," she said in a whispery voice.

I shuddered and edged closer to Zack. "Does she always have to do that to — ?"

Zack silenced me with a hard look. "Don't break the enchantment."

Eileen's charm worked. Thousands of colorful mushrooms bloomed everywhere like flowers, some nestled on the branches of the trees, others perched on the mossy ground.

"Let's get to work," said Eileen cheerfully.

My legs were sore and aching. "I'm so tired."

"The mushrooms in the Underworld are beautiful," gushed Eileen. "All in vibrant colors and different shapes. No two mushrooms are the same."

"Oh, can't you be quiet for just a moment?"

"Sorry, I—"

"Wait...hang on for a moment." A funny, glimmering mushroom the size of a chicken's egg piqued my curiosity. I scooted closer to it and picked it up.

It was not a mushroom. In fact, it was not even rooted to the ground. *It was an iridescent, crystalline rock shaped like a diamond.*

"Hey, nature master. Are there any mushrooms shaped like diamonds?"

"No."

"You sure?"

"Positive. Why are you asking?"

"Take a look at this."

Eileen stared at the diamond on my palm. "Whoa, what's this?"

"What?" Zack skirted closer to us. His expression melted into one of shock as I handed him the diamond.

Eileen glanced at me, her face wrought with confusion. I shrugged.

Zack examined it carefully. "No way...," he muttered, shaking his head in disbelief. "No...no, that doesn't explain...."

"What's the matter?"

Zack looked up at us. "*This* is the Gem of Hope."

"What?" Eileen and I gaped at each other.

"But...why would a stolen gem be lying about in the woods?" I asked.

"No idea. But...mission accomplished, everyone! No more fighting!"

"Yes!" Eileen and I cheered, giving each other a high-five.

I felt dazed at the abruptness of the end of our mission. Relief surged up in me as I realized that this was the end of all battles. A smile lifted the corners of my mouth, and a sense of accomplishment brimmed up within me.

Grinning, Zack looked from Eileen to me. "So, what are we waiting for?"

"Look at what we've got here!" I called out to the others as we reached our camp.

"It's a gem!" squealed Clarissa, clapping her hand to her mouth.

"What?"

A flicker of fear was visible in Helen's gaze. She paled as Zack showed her the gem. With great trepidation, she took it with her trembling fingers and gazed at it, horrified.

"The Gem of Hope?" asked Alexandria. "Where did you find it?"

"It was lying around in the woods, among the mushrooms," I replied, glad to know something she didn't.

"Oh, that's wonderful! We can leave the Underworld right away!"

"Wicked!" Eric roared with mirth. "Let's throw a party right here!"

"Shut it!" ordered Helen. Everyone fell silent at her words.

"What are you shouting about?" I frowned at her.

"There is *no* such thing as a free lunch. There must be a catch."

"Are you suggesting this artifact might be a counterfeit?" said Zack.

"No. See the translucent images of the four creatures glittering here? This is the *real* Gem of Hope."

"Then what's wrong with you?" I said, feeling slightly irritated.

Alexandria, Clarissa, Eileen, and Eric exchanged looks of perplexity.

"Like I said, there is no such thing as a free lunch. Nobody would leave a treasure lying around like that. So it must be a trap."

"A trap? But we got it without being attacked!" I protested, my temper rising.

"I would have guarded it safely if I were to hide a precious artifact," said Helen, raising her voice. "This is a trap, and we must leave the Underworld immediately. Now!"

"How many times have I told you, THERE'S NO TRAP!" I almost yelled at her. Waves of indignation flooded upon me. Why was she acting so paranoid instead of rewarding us for our hard work? Why was she deliberately spoiling our mood of celebration?

"For the first time in her life, that foolish Representative Elder is right. We have lulled you into a false sense of accomplishment."

Chapter Eleven

THE FINAL BATTLE
(HELEN)

We whirled around, only to find ourselves besieged by ten enemies, a peculiar assortment of creatures — two bearnixes, two unibirds, two kittenpillars, two dogfishes, and a strange-looking monster with two spiral horns, a pig-like snout, and hooves.

The last person, the one who had spoken, was a beefy, tattooed giant wearing a smirk and holding an axe. He had long, tangled hair, eyes with yellow pupils, and a dirty beard coated with grime. His skin was wrinkly and glowed faintly yellow. I recognized him as Ripper the Brutal, one of Alta's bodyguards. Zack and I had fought with him during our penultimate mission to the Underworld.

I glanced at the others, who had the sense to put their guards up. All of them were raising their weapons.

"So," I said, playing for time, "your master and mistress sent the ten of you here to do their dirty work, didn't they? Is it because they're cowards, or is it because they're incapable of fighting seven Otherworldians?"

Ripper, though, seemed to be deaf to my words.

"Ripper the Brutal, we meet again." Zack greeted him in a steely tone.

"Yes, Zachary, long time no see," said Ripper in a silky, dangerous voice. "Surely you realize that this may be the last time we meet?" His gaze drifted to the heiresses, and he drawled on, his voice brimming with contempt. "I see that the Otherworld has sent not only two Elders but also four...kids here this time." He spat on the ground.

It took the combined efforts of Clarissa and Eileen to keep Alexandria from charging against him. Daphne's hands balled into fists, and Eric made a rude hand gesture at Ripper.

Ripper smiled viciously. "Why, isn't this my young Master Eric? Tell me, how would your dear mother, my mistress, feel if she knew about your betrayal?"

"You think I give a...a.... I DON'T CARE WHAT MY MOTHER THINKS! MY LOYALTY LIES WITH THE OTHERWORLD!"

Eric's fierce declaration seemed to freeze everyone. Alexandria stopped trying to break free. Clarissa's mouth fell open slightly. Eileen gave Eric a look of strong reverence.

"Brainwashed, are you?"

Eric took a step forward, got out his wand, and directed it at Ripper's heart.

"I can, and I'm not afraid to use this. Keep threatening us, and I *will* kill you."

Surprisingly, Ripper took a step backward. "Whoa whoa whoa, young man. Please, no violence! Let's get down to business first. I don't want us swinging swords, hurling spears, or shouting incantations at each other. We come here in peace, all right? Here's a bargain. Give us the Gem of Hope, and we'll leave; give us the Gem of Hope, and nobody will get hurt; give us the Gem of Hope, and you can go back to the Otherworld. I heard that one of you Elders almost got killed on the last mission. You wouldn't want another serious injury to deal with, would you? Nobody will die or lose their memory this time if you relinquish the gem, I promise."

I opened my fist. The Gem of Hope twinkled under the sun, radiating beams of red, yellow, green, and blue light.

"Ah, yes, the gem," Ripper extended his hand, his palm facing up. "Give it to me."

"No!" Alexandria broke free and stepped between Ripper and me. She grabbed the gem and shoved it into her pocket. "Helen, listen to me, please! He's lying to you! I didn't understand before, but now I do. There's a hidden agenda behind the theft. This," she shook her finger accusingly at Ripper, "is all a scam. You foul Underworldians stole the Gem of Hope from our palace to trick us into coming here, to the Underworld. What you wanted was not the gem. You wanted a chance to get rid of us. It doesn't matter whether we give you the gem or not. You're going to kill us either way, aren't you?"

Deafening silence. I felt as if somebody had slapped me in the face. *How could I have been so foolish?* Now that Alexandria mentioned it, I reviewed everything that had happened since we arrived in the Underworld, and it all fit perfectly. The attacks were more frequent than my last few missions. Everything was designed against us. We could all have died anytime, from our encounter with the lion-cat to the suspension bridge, the Chirpy Bird, the trap desert, and the clones. And not to mention, Eileen, Daphne, and Zack stumbled across the Gem of Hope, which was lying about in the woods, as if it had been waiting for us to find it. Alexandria was right. It was a scheme. Somebody had planned and executed it well.

Ripper let out a sneer. "Well, since you already know everything, I'll play no more games with you. Yes, you were right. You Otherworldians think the Gem of Hope's some sort of treasure. Well, it was nothing but a pawn to us. You think King Alto and Queen Alta want to defeat the Otherworld by stealing a gem and making it fade away? No, no. That wouldn't be fun at all. What they really wanted was the triumph and glory of taking over the Otherworld by force, fighting and winning. Our goal was to kill all the foolish Otherworldians who showed up and then invade your pretty little realm after we've dealt with you. And—bingo! Our scheme worked magically!"

I nudged Zack, who was standing beside me.

"What?"

"On my command," I said, minimizing the movement of my lips. I felt in my pocket for my shrunken sword and shield, hid them behind my back, and enlarged them with my wand. "We have no choice but to fight our way out."

Zack nodded as Ripper kept talking. "Boy, the Gem of Hope was such a useful bait! Six fools from the Otherworld and a filthy traitor of a—"

"You've crossed the line." My voice quivered with anger or fear. I was not sure which. "Get them!" I dived at one of the bearnixes and put up a duel with it.

Zack charged at Ripper and hurled his sword at him like a javelin. The latter ducked effortlessly and laughed. "Pathetic! Is that really the best you can do?"

The bearnix I was dueling put up a sword fight with me. I was horrible at swordplay and kept looking for a chance to get out my bow and arrows, but I had to keep up with the pace of the duel. I swung my sword at the bearnix, and it intercepted my blade with its own. The potent force stung my hand. It was all I could do to hold on and concentrate on the battle, ignoring the tingling pain coursing through my arm. The bearnix slashed its fiery tail at me, and I barely leapt out of the way. It roared in frustration. Waves of fire spouted from its wide mouth, and I blocked them with my shield.

"Helen!" a voice shouted from behind me. "Bearnixes are afraid of water! Go to—AH!"

I looked back and saw Eric, who was dueling a dogfish while another chomped into his arm. However, I had no time to rescue him from his plight. The bearnix, who was no longer spouting fire, drew nearer and nearer towards me. I started to panic. Bearnixes were afraid of—water? Was that intended as a hint? I took another step backward cautiously. All of a sudden, my foot slipped on the wet grass, and I lost my balance. With a splash, I fell backward into a lake. I flailed my arms to get my head above water and paddled towards the bank. The furious bearnix roared again, upset that I survived the fall.

Suddenly, it hit me—bearnixes were afraid of water. All

I had to do was to trick it into jumping into the lake. I reviewed every spell and strategy I knew, and an idea fell into place.

"Why don't you come down here and get me?" I called out to the bearnix.

It snarled and made a snatch with its paws.

"What are you, a coward or a loser? Come on!"

The bearnix remained in its spot and growled through its teeth. I spotted some planks underwater, which resembled a shipwreck's ruins. Without a second thought, I dove and managed to retrieve three at once. They were soaking wet and had gone moldy. I tapped my wand on all three of them, and they formed a little bridge.

The bearnix looked at the bridge, then at me, but wasn't fooled. It glared fixedly into my eyes, ready to attack anytime. I sent a purple jet of light flying at its eye. The bearnix went ballistic and roared, snatching at the air wildly with its paws. It seized a handful of my hair, and I yelled for attention.

That was when Daphne came and jabbed the bearnix in the posterior with her trident. It lost its balance and tumbled headfirst into the water, bellowing as flames erupted from its mouth. My sleeve caught fire, and Daphne extinguished it with a wave of her trident.

"Helen, hurry and get out!" she shouted frantically, extending her hand.

I grabbed it without thinking, allowing her to hoist me up. "Thanks," I panted.

Daphne got to her feet, pointed her trident at the water, and drew a snowflake in the air. The lake, with the struggling bearnix trapped in it, froze over. The water became still, and chunks of ice began to form. In less than five seconds, the lake had become a glacier.

"Wow," I breathed.

Daphne shrugged. "My magic's become more powerful after all those battles."

"Have you thought of making another cannon?"

"No time," she answered, then ran in the opposite direction in pursuit of another monster.

"GRR!" another bearnix growled from behind.

I was too slow to duck, and a tuft of my hair got scorched. I shot an arrow at it, but my fingers were trembling so much that I missed. The bearnix roared, and flames scalded my arm, leaving a sticky, gooey spot on it. Pain exploded as if every inch of me was on fire. The coppery tang of blood filled my nostrils, and my stomach churned. I collapsed, swells of nausea and dizziness coursing through me as blood and dirt encountered my mouth. The wound on my arm was sapping away my stamina, yet I had no choice but to fight back. It was now or never. Summoning my remaining strength and energy, I tackled the bearnix and stabbed my sword into its eye, desperate to end this fight once and for all. It howled in agony before slumping to the ground.

A sharp stab of pain took over me, and I looked at my arm. The wound was more serious than I had expected. It throbbed and stung, blood oozing profusely from the gash and dyeing my sleeve scarlet. However, the battle was still raging on, which meant I had to keep fighting. I glanced at the battlefield and saw that there were only four monsters left.

Eileen had fully mastered the poison ivy trap and had caught a dogfish in it. It whined and struggled, trying to escape, but to no avail. Zack and Alexandria joined forces and managed to win a duel against two unibirds. I had killed two bearnixes with the help of Daphne, and one of Eric's turquoise fireballs had struck a kittenpillar. Just when I was counting the fallen enemies, I heard a battle cry coming from above.

I looked up and saw Clarissa steering a cloud. She yelled Daphne's name and summoned a powerful streak of lightning as a spray of water burst from Daphne's trident. Together, they wiped out another dogfish.

"Well done!" I called out, amazed by their attack.

Clarissa blushed, and Daphne tossed her head.

"Helen!" cried Eric. "Behind you!"

I turned around, just in time to see an enormous kittenpillar heading my way. A closer look told me it was no ordinary kittenpillar. A robot. Before I could react, it pounced on me, twisting and curling its body around my chest. I got out my sword and slashed at it, but the kittenpillar knocked it away with a swish of its metallic tail. The wound on my arm was not doing me any favors. It prickled madly, searing waves of pain engulfing me.

"Let her go!" A ball of turquoise fire sailed through the air, brushing past one of the robot's metallic ears.

The kittenpillar hissed angrily and obeyed. I looked towards the source of the voice, and what I saw almost gave me a heart attack. "No, Eric! You can't sacrifice yourself for me!"

I bolted towards the kittenpillar, but Eric beat me to it. His sword clanked against the kittenpillar's metallic head, and he hurled a turquoise fireball at its eye. Just when I thought he was going to make it, the kittenpillar pounced on him and wrapped itself around his chest, the same way it had with me. Eric tried to free his body with his arms, but the kittenpillar sprouted sticky vines from its mouth, trapping his hands.

I was about to free him when Zack appeared out of nowhere and fired a streak of purple light at the robot. It released Eric, who fell to the ground with a loud thump. He got up and backed away from the monster. However, the kittenpillar was not done with us. Not yet. Glaring at Zack, it let out a menacing hiss and curled its body into a spiral, like a cobra. The kittenpillar's tiny black feet dangled in the air, clutching a sword it had robbed from a fallen warrior.

"Zack, just leave!" I yelled. "Don't take your chances with it!"

"It's *my* fight. I've got to give it a shot."

I was impressed by Zack's courage, but at the same time, I couldn't help but dread the possibility of losing him, like I lost my dearest apprentice, Evonne. Torrents of what-ifs flooded upon me, like black clouds eclipsing the sky.

"Come and fight me," said Zack. "We'll see who dies today."

The kittenpillar hissed and remained still for a moment, but I was not fooled, and neither was Zack. It lunged at him, and he sidestepped the blade just in time. The kittenpillar snarled in fury. I had never heard a kittenpillar snarl in my whole life, but this one did. It brought its sword down at where Zack's head had been a second before, then almost sliced off his arm as its blade twirled and zigzagged in the air.

"Use your wand, Zack!" shouted Eric, waving his own wildly at him.

"Do you know the first thing about fighting?" Zack hollered back. "It's a robot—wands can do it no harm! The metallic armor it's wearing deflects all charms!"

The kittenpillar chomped at the air. Zack took aim at its stomach but missed, and with a flick of the kittenpillar's tail, he was slammed to the ground.

I clapped my hand to my mouth to suppress a scream, for Zack had sprained his ankle when he fell. Finally, however, he stood up, limping towards the kittenpillar robot.

"Nice try, but you haven't won," he announced. "Not yet."

The kittenpillar's body quivered with anger, its whiskers trembling furiously. It bit at Zack, who made a counterattack almost intuitively and bonked it on the head with his shield. The kittenpillar's eyes glowed green, and it chased him around the battlefield, brandishing its sword and slicing at him. Zack ducked and dodged while slamming his shield at his adversary in defense. The kittenpillar feinted with its legs. Zack dodged left and got struck. The blade left a deep scar on his forehead.

Horrified, I rushed over to Zack and aided him to his feet. "Are you all right?"

He winced in pain. "Don't worry. I have to do this alone."

"But—"

"Helen, do you have faith in me?"

"I do, but—"

"Good, that's all I need to hear."

"But surely—"

"I can handle it. I must finish it off."

"Oh, Zack!" I flung my arms around him. I was terrified, terrified that he would leave me like Evonne had. His hands tangled in my hair as he hugged me back.

"Helen...." Zack's voice broke. "See you on the other side, in case — in case anything happens."

"Don't!"

Zack patted me on the back rather awkwardly. "I'll...I'll do my best." He took a deep breath and gave me a meaningful look, as if wanting to say more, but then thought better of it.

I forced myself to turn away from the desire to give him a kiss, not only for the first but probably also the last time. The image of Zack blurred badly, obscured by my tears. I blinked them away, trying not to think about the chances of this as the last time to see him alive.

With one final glance at Eric and me, Zack turned around to face the kittenpillar. "Well, what are you waiting for?"

The kittenpillar growled and put up a duel with him. It tried to get Zack from above, but he was so slim and nimble that he managed to dodge every strike. The battle, if possible, was becoming even more intense. The silver blades, both stained with crimson, gleamed as the swords clinked and collided in midair again and again.

Zack was battered and exhausted from all that dodging and striking. Then he sank to the ground. The kittenpillar let out a scream of ecstasy as my heart gave a jolt.

No, how could he — ?

But before I realized what had happened, Zack stood up for the third time.

The kittenpillar glowered at him. Without another word, they started to fight once again, this time hand-to-hand. Both feverishly took offense, attempting to end the other's life, and at the same time dodging their opponent's strike. The robot feinted with its left hand, a blow that would have been fatal to anyone. But Zack, a prodigious dueler, did not fall for its trick. Meanwhile, almost everyone had called a temporary truce to witness this exciting duel.

Zack, while dodging and waving his sword, edged bit by bit, closer and closer to the kittenpillar, hoping for a good angle to strike. He finally succeeded by feinting with his right hand and thrusting his blade into its stomach. The kittenpillar yowled in anger and swung its sword at him, but I fired an arrow at its head. The robot's eyes snapped shut, and it slammed to the ground, moving no more.

"Zack!"

"Helen!"

We hugged and almost strangled each other to death, but neither of us cared.

"Hello? We've got a battle to fight!" Eric almost shouted. But even so, he could not wipe the big grin off his face. "That was some flawless swordplay, Zack," he said, beaming. "But still, we must keep going."

Eric's words did bring me back to reality. There were only two enemies left— Ripper and the snout monster. Alexandria and Eileen were fighting Ripper while the others were tackling the monster.

The monster got fed up with sidestepping Clarissa and Daphne's strikes and took vengeance by whacking its horns at Clarissa. It thumped her hard in the head and pinned her to the ground. Daphne tried to help her up, but the monster smacked her with one of its hooves. I dashed over to them and shot an arrow at the monster, piercing its snout. Injured, it howled and sprinted into the nearby forest, disappearing behind some trees.

"Clarissa!" shouted Eric. "Pull a cloud from the sky and leave! It's too dangerous down here!"

I watched her ascend into the clouds.

"Now what?" she cried from above.

"Stay there!"

"I want to fight! You think I'm going to watch you guys die down there? I can't!"

"Then do whatever you can to help us, but don't come down!"

I surveyed the battlefield and saw Zack join Alexandria and Daphne. They were dueling with Ripper three-on-one.

"Eric, where's Eileen?" I asked.

"I don't know! I think she went to fight the snout—"

Just then, Eileen herself emerged from behind a tree.

She ran over to the battlefield and slipped on the lichen-coated ground.

"Come on, get up and fight!" Eric extended his hand to her.

Astonishment etched upon Eileen's face as she took his hand. "Thanks," she said, blushing furiously.

Eric, too, went red in the face.

"I'm really sorry for yelling at you about the sticks," Eileen gained a sudden interest in her black sneakers. "It was plain stupid of me."

Eric shrugged. Then, without warning, he took Eileen in his arms, and she burst into tears.

"Oh, Eric!" sobbed Eileen. "What a big baby I was —"

"Hey, it's all right."

"What are you two doing?" I yelled. "For goodness's sake, the battle's not over yet!"

The two of them broke apart, their cheeks as red as strawberries.

"Well? Go and fight!"

They turned on their heels and sped towards the battlefield, holding hands as they ran.

The situation wasn't looking good for us. Alexandria, Daphne, and Zack were getting exhausted, as their stamina had been greatly reduced from the previous battles. Ripper slammed Daphne to the ground and made a lunge for Zack. He dived out of the way, but Ripper was too quick for him. The giant grabbed Zack by his wrist and got out his knife. Realizing what he was about to do, I fired an arrow at Ripper's arm. Bellowing, he dropped his knife and tossed Zack away. He soared through the air and got caught in the branches of a nearby tree. I cringed inwardly, praying Zack would be all right.

Ripper turned to face me.

"No, don't!" cried Eric.

"Leave, Eric! Get Alexandria, Eileen, and Daphne out of here! Don't you disobey me. This is an order!"

He obeyed, and I saw Alexandria kicking and screaming, trying to break free.

"Clarissa, go over to the tree where Zack landed and check on him! But, don't come near, no matter what!"

"Any last words you haven't said to your little friends?" Ripper spoke in a soft voice incongruous to his intimidating stature. He edged closer to me, taking one step at a time.

I stood my ground, refusing to back off. "No," I said through gritted teeth.

The next few seconds dragged by in loud silence. Ripper glowered at me, and I glared back into his eyes. The tension was palpable.

"Listen, I don't want to kill you," I said, and I meant it. "Don't make me. Please."

Ripper laughed. "Don't worry, I can take care of that."

All of a sudden, he attacked, stabbing his knife at the wound on my arm. Pain seized me, crawling from my arm to my shoulder, then invading every inch of my body. I tightened my grip on the hilt of my sword, resisting the temptation to thrust it into his heart. I could have killed him, but I didn't. Instead, I shot an arrow at his eye, but my hands were shaking so badly that I missed. Then, anger and agony flaring in me, I jabbed my sword at his shoulder, but he grabbed it by the blade and flung it at Eric, smacking him in the face.

I glanced in his direction to see if he was all right and saw Alexandria and Daphne darting towards me.

"DON'T! GO BACK!"

Ripper dived at his opportunity when I was distracted and made a snatch for my neck. I felt my chest tightening and my throat constricting. My lungs screamed with the need for air. I kicked my feet and flailed my arms, struggling in a fruitless attempt to break loose.

Alexandria chucked a fireball at Ripper, but he laughed and dodged it almost lazily. Daphne waved her trident, and an icicle zoomed at him, but he caught it with his free hand and threw it back at her.

"Ripper!" a cheerful voice shouted. "Look, up here!"

Ripper did, and he loosened his grip on my neck. I slid to

the ground just in time to see a powerful streak of lightning hit him. With a howl, he staggered backward and collapsed.

"Clarissa?" I said, looking up in disbelief.

"Yes, Helen! I did it!"

"Excellent timing!"

Clarissa descended and dismounted gracefully beside me. Alexandria, Eileen, Eric, and Daphne made their way towards us.

Alexandria slapped Clarissa on the back. "Brilliant!"

"You were wonderful." Eileen enfolded her in an embrace.

Eric beamed. "That was amazing!"

"Thanks," said Clarissa with a big smile.

"Is he dead?" I made my way over to Ripper's body and bent down to check on him.

"Passed out, more likely," said Daphne. "Like the Chirpy Bird when Clarissa zapped it."

My hands trembled with the urge to end Ripper's life. He was unconscious. All I had to do was to close my fingers around his neck and give it a squeeze. Or bury my sword into his chest. Or slit his throat with the blade. Then I could give him a taste of his own medicine and kill him like he had attempted to kill me. But I didn't. I couldn't bring myself to. I didn't want to stoop to his level and become a monster myself. So instead, I got to my feet and pointed my wand at him.

"Trap," I commanded. A transparent half-sphere burst from my wand and trapped Ripper, making him look like an ugly model in a snow globe. I turned to the others, who were still laughing and congratulating Clarissa on her successful attack.

Clarissa giggled. "You should've seen Zack's expression when —"

"Wait a moment, everyone," I said. "Where's Zack?"

Clarissa turned around to face her cloud, and her mouth dropped open. "He was — right there! On my cloud! I swear he was!"

Right at that moment, a dark shadow towered over us. I wheeled around and saw the snout monster, who revealed Zack's whereabouts. It was biting him by the arm, and there he was, dangling precariously from its mouth. He seemed to be in a coma.

Nobody dared to move a muscle except for Alexandria. She walked up to the monster, her spear clutched in one hand and her scepter in the other. Sparks of fire danced on her fingertips. "Come on! Let him down and fight me."

"Alexandria, whatever you're doing, stop doing it, okay?" Daphne hissed in her ear.

"What about a bargain?" Alexandria, deaf to her words, went on without the slightest trace of fear in her voice. "First, let Zack down. Then, we duel. If you lose, you'll have to let us go; if I lose, you get all of us."

I groaned at her foolishness. It was impossible for a fourteen-year-old to vanquish a fully-grown monster. However, it was too late. The monster laid Zack on the ground, picked up Ripper's axe, and inched closer to Alexandria, who tightened her grip on her spear and scepter.

Without another word, the two of them began their duel. Alexandria tossed a fireball at the monster's eye, but it leapt out of the way. The monster swung its axe at her, but she was too quick for it. Both fought and dodged their opponent's strikes with intense velocity.

"Shouldn't we help her?" asked Clarissa, looking apprehensive.

"She's handling it well," replied Eileen, though her voice shook slightly.

"Let's play it by ear." Eric shifted his weight from one foot to the other. "We'll wait and see."

Suddenly, the monster stabbed Alexandria in the back with its oversized horns, and blood splattered everywhere. Daphne screamed, and my stomach lurched. The monster let out triumphant "oink" and pranced around the battlefield. Alexandria, though seriously wounded, struggled to her feet.

"We have to help her, come on!" hollered Eric. "Helen, stay here and tend to Zack!"

"What? No! Come back!"

"She's my cousin, Helen Edmunds! And I'm not going

to stand aside and watch her die!" Eric streaked across the battlefield. Without hesitation, the heiresses got out their scepters and weapons and followed suit.

I did not know whether to be impressed by their valor or to be worried about their safety, but it occurred to me that they were all fourteen, old enough to make their own decisions, let alone Eric, who was fifteen. It was their choice, and I had to respect that. Plus, I could not leave Zack's side.

The snout monster against Alexandria, Clarissa, Eileen, Daphne, and Eric, was losing its mind. Alexandria pelted the monster with fireballs and lavabricks; Clarissa waved her scepter, zapping it with yellow sparks; Daphne had built a cannon, and with the assistance of Eileen and Eric, exploding leaves, twigs, ice boulders, and icicles zoomed at the monster.

"Look over here, lovely!" shouted Eileen.

The monster turned, and a stream of tiny red roses blossomed from the tip of Eileen's scepter. I took a closer look and realized that they were no ordinary roses. The petals were dotted with red thorns. The spiky roses invaded the monster's snout, and it screeched in agony. It charged towards Eileen to get revenge, and Alexandria, with a nimble leap, grabbed ahold of the monster's horns and crouched on top of its head. The monster shook its head wildly in a vain attempt to throw Alexandria off. I watched, horrified, as she swerved this way and that.

"What are you doing?" yelled Clarissa, pushing Eric out of harm's way as the monster aimed a kick at him.

"Want a snack, monster?" Alexandria taunted from above. The monster made the mistake of looking up, and she got out a carton of milk from the pouch of her sweater and dumped it on its head. The white liquid dribbled into its eyes as it oinked in pain.

Alexandria caught my eye and grinned. "My breakfast yesterday morning! A carton of sour milk! Never thought I'd use it in a battle, though!"

"Hey, catch this!" Eric called from below.

It was the big saucepan filled with the leftovers of yesterday's dinner. Alexandria caught it and emptied the contents right on the monster's head.

"Have a good lunch!" said Daphne. The five of them burst into hysterical peals of laughter.

The monster went berserk, oinking and shrieking. Alexandria hurled a fireball at its bleeding eye but missed. The monster waved its hooves wildly in the air, roaring in fury. I fired an arrow straight at its stomach in fear that someone would be injured. It pierced the target, and the monster slumped to the ground.

Torrents of relief blossomed in my chest, making me giddy and light-headed. It was over at last. The mission was coming to an end, and nobody had lost their lives or their memory. King Patrick and Queen Marianne would be reunited with their daughter, who had not only returned safe and sound from an important mission but also taken part in the most crucial battle. Clarissa, Eileen, and Daphne would all be regarded as heroes who had saved the Otherworld.

Last but not least, Eric, after escaping from his despicable mother, had found confidence and friendship in these two days. This mission turned out to be a huge success, and I could not help but smile at those wonderful thoughts. Finally, everything was over!

"Is that...the five of them over there?" said Zack, who had come around.

"Yes," I replied breathlessly. "They fought like true Otherworldians."

With my assistance, Zack got to his feet slowly. I saw Alexandria, Clarissa, Eileen, Daphne, and Eric dashing towards us, their faces radiating pure ecstasy.

"We won!" cheered Daphne.

"I knew you could do it!" Eric shouted at Alexandria.

"*We*, Eric, we," Alexandria corrected, beaming with delight as she gave her cousin a high-five. "Don't forget, there are seven of us. We accomplished our mission in the name of the Otherworld."

"Well done, very well done, indeed," I said, unable to

suppress a grin.

"Zack!" the five of them took turns giving him throttling hugs.

"Is the gem with you?" I asked Alexandria. She felt her pocket and nodded.

"You saved the Otherworld, every one of you," said Zack happily. "King Patrick and Queen Marianne will be so pleased!"

"Listen, I don't want to be a party pooper, but can we celebrate later?" said Daphne. "We have to focus on how to get—"

"I could not stop you from taking the Gem of Hope, but I can end…your…life," bellowed a weak voice that had not lost its menace.

I turned and saw the snout monster, sheer malice oozing from its baleful eyes. It was sprawled on the ground, yet undead. The monster's last words were actually a warning, but I was too careless to take it seriously. Before I knew it, the monster had immobilized me with a snap of its fingers.

Appalled and helpless, I watched the snout monster raise its axe with its trembling hooves.

"NO!" a voice screamed. The next second, a figure flung itself in front of me.

A blinding flash of silver came zooming at us. The blade. I squeezed my eyes shut, bracing myself for a painful death.

But nothing happened.

Chapter Twelve

UNEXPECTED ENDINGS
(ALEXANDRIA)

The last image I saw was an axe flying towards Helen. *No, not her.* She was more than just my friend. She was my partner, my comrade after we'd gone through so much. She was not going to die, or at least not in my presence.

Without hesitation, I ran as fast as my legs could carry me and flung myself in front of her. I was ready. I knew what I was getting into. As if in slow motion, the blade inched through the air for what seemed like an eternity.

A searing pain spread through my body as the cold metal encountered and sliced into my flesh at last. My consciousness dwindled; my vision blurred and receded and faded almost instantly.

My mind blacked out for several minutes, filled with a hollow emptiness. Then, I was jerked awake by an excruciating torrent of pain that seemed to penetrate my body. Every inch of me was burning in agony. With an enormous effort, I blinked. My eyelids felt heavy, as though laden with steel. Although my vision was fuzzy, I could make out the silhouettes of my six companions. Devastated and grief-stricken, their faces were wrought with misery.

"Alexandria, why?" Clarissa's cheeks were slick with tears.

Eileen buried her face in her palms as she sobbed. Eric's face was pale with shock. Daphne, overcome with woe, was in hysterics; Zack patted her heavily on the shoulder, tears pooling in his eyes and streaming down his cheeks.

Helen's face was a mask of utter consternation. She was the only one who wasn't crying. Her distress was beyond that. When she spoke, her voice was merely a whisper. "Alexandria...I'm...I'm terribly sorry."

"I...I knew...it...was...right...to...to...do...." I coughed, blood dribbling down my chin.

"Right?" Eileen cried out. "What are we going to do without you?"

"You've...still got each other, haven't you?"

Daphne shook her head. "Alexandria....I've been wrong all along. I didn't.... Should've treated you like a sister...." Sobs escaped her lips, deep, heaving sobs wrenched from her. "Oh, please — please don't leave me! Give me a chance to say sorry. Give us a chance to be friends."

"Shh, Daphne. I know, I know."

"Friends?" Daphne's hand was outstretched.

"Always and forever." I took her hand. "Fire and water may be born enemies, but together, we'll be an exception."

Daphne said nothing but clasped my hand tightly.

I coughed again and saw a lake of crimson beside my body. Realization swept over me, more powerfully than ever. I was going to leave this world. Yet, strangely enough, the thought of that filled me with inexplicable serenity. I had chosen to sacrifice my life for Helen, and I would leave without any regrets.

Knowing that my time would be up soon, I looked into the eyes of the person I owed the most to. "Eric...."

"Alexandria...."

"I'm sorry for hurting you just because you told me the truth about your mother. Having Alta as your mother is nothing to be ashamed of; on the contrary, you should be proud of yourself for turning out better than her. You were a hero right from the beginning, and you will always be. The Otherworld...will accept you as you are." My breathing seemed shallower than before. Time was running out.

"Helen...." My vision blurred so badly I could hardly see her face.

"Alexandria, how can I ever forgive myself?"

Although I could barely see, I could imagine her anguish and despair. "Helen, it's...not your...fault. Please don't...blame yourself. And...and tell...my parents....tell them...I'm...sorry...."

Darkness swallowed my vision. Finally, the end. Every last ounce of strength left me, and the icy fingers of death closed around my senses. A peculiar sensation engulfed me. Was dying painful? I had no idea. But at that moment, I felt calm, cool, and detached. I was rising, my body lighter than a feather as I hovered in the air.

Two unibirds with large, sad eyes stared at me as I drifted past them. Where was I going? I did not know. Up, up, and up I floated. Then, I stopped.

I glanced down from high above and saw six people mourning the death of a girl. Her body, sprawled motionless on the ground, was as still as a fallen statue. A shell. Hollow. Empty. Void of life. I recognized her body. I had seen the world from her eyes and felt the tender touch of fire from her skin.

The woman wrapped her arm around the man. She whispered words of comfort, partly for him and partly for herself. The three girls grasped each other's hands, reminiscing about the memories they had shared with the fallen girl, and at the same time, stubbornly refusing to believe those were bygones. The boy buried his head in his arms, unable to force himself to confront the body of his cousin.

Not having the heart to watch this tragic scene myself, I drifted up, and up, and up, and—

"Hello." A harsh, metallic voice greeted me coldly.

I looked up, only to meet the eyes of a strange, floating girl with a translucent body, who was hovering a few inches above me. Her gaze was cold, and an icy smile played on her lips. A pang of déjà vu struck me as I saw her. Red hair, asymmetrical eyes, a wide mouth—

I gasped. "Aren't you—?"

"I am."

I hovered closer and saw that she was not exactly Alexandria Richardson. Her lips, instead of being red, were as black as coal, her eyes seemed hollow and lifeless, and a deathly pallor reigned her bloodless skin. The ghost was clad in a black robe with tiny skeletons.

"What...what do you want with me?"

The ghost smirked. "Unimportant."

"Who...what are you?"

Her black lips formed a malicious smile. "I am *you*. Your past, your troubles, and your unhappiness. I, as you see, am not human. I'm made from the fragments of your failures, frustrations, traumas, and negative emotions in the past. I feast upon them. They make me stronger. I am Alexandria Matilda Richardson. The evil side of her."

She glued my lips together with a snap of her fingers before I could utter a reply. I struggled to move my lips but could only manage a few meaningless sounds. The ghost laughed maniacally at my plight. Her eyes glowed red, and the skeletons on her robe glittered and rattled their bones. I tried to glide away from her, but I couldn't move my body. I was rooted in the air, right on the spot.

"Now, now, now. I'll free your mouth for just a second. Answer me, do you want to go back to your crummy life? Or do you want to pass on?"

"I—Are you offering me a choice?"

"That is correct."

"Why? Am I not already dead? Why can I choose whether I want to pass on or not?"

"The woman down there, you see?"

"What woman?"

"The one with wavy hair." She pointed at the people below us.

I racked my brain to recall her name. "Helen?"

"Your life is bonded to hers. Your choice to live will preserve her life, and your choice of death will take her life as well. So now, you have to make a decision."

I blinked. "But how can it be? I've never heard my parents or even Helen herself mention this...link between us."

"That is because they are ignorant of it."

"But why?" I asked her, half-terrified, half-fascinated. "How did the link form?"

"The reason this mysterious link formed between you and Helen can be dated back to the ancient times when Ember, Zeru, Fern, and Walters were still alive. Alexandria, Ember had not selected you as her heiress in the first place. Instead, she had her mind set on a great woman who would grow to become the first Representative Elder of the Otherworld—Helen Wisteria Edmunds. However, the seer Delphia convinced Ember to pick you instead."

"Me? But why?"

"As your father told you, Delphia was a member of the Richardson family. Naturally, she wanted a descendant of hers to inherit Ember's exceptionally strong elemental powers. As a result, Ember, convinced by Delphia, chose *you* instead of Helen. Alexandria, since you and Helen were both selected or had been selected by Ember, your lives are forever intertwined with each other. You must make your big decision now. All you need to know is that if you pass on, Helen will die as well. But if you choose not to, you will also be saving her life."

"Let me get this straight. I can now choose whether to move on or go back to my life, right? And this is all because of a link between me and Helen. Is that so?"

The ghost's lip curled. "Yes."

"So if I choose to return, I'll get to be with the people I love again."

The ghost sneered in contempt. "Love? *You* loved them. But are you sure that *they* loved you?"

"What do you mean?"

"Tell me then. *Who* loves you?"

"My friends who came along with me on this quest—
Clarissa, Eileen, Daphne, Eric, Helen, and Zack. And my parents."

The ghost laughed, a bone-chilling laugh that could have
frozen the hottest desert in the world. "How pathetic. You really
are as gullible as you look. For starters, Clarissa Dawson was
never your friend. The only reason she agreed to take part in this
mission was because she wanted to test *her* limits and see how far
she could go. She, her, and herself, never you. Clarissa Dawson is
a narcissist of ambition and no feelings. You? You meant nothing
to her. Unlike Daphne Sinclair, she never—"

"Right, so Daphne—"

"Have you not forgotten how she smeared your reputation
and dishonored your parents in the orphanage? Daphne Sinclair
is a person of utmost evil. Plus, you are the heiress of Ember. She
is the heiress of Walters. Both are the two most powerful Creators
among the big four. You and Daphne weren't meant to get along,
understood? The two of you were *destined* to be enemies. So,
Alexandria, do not mess with fate, or you'll come to a sticky end.
Keep deceiving yourself and believing in your so-called friends,
and one day you'll regret it."

"What about—?"

"Eileen Spencer? She's nothing but a coward. She never
wanted to fight, let alone protect the Otherworld. The only reason
she didn't bail out in the middle of your quest is because she's in
love with your cousin, Eric Williams. Didn't you see them flirting
with each other in the middle of a battle? They only love each
other, not you—never you! You're too pathetic for anybody to
care for. Eileen doesn't give a toot about you or whether you live
or die; she only pretends to because Eric's your cousin. She has
been using you all along.

"As for Eric Williams, he's a cheat and a liar. He's been
scheming against you, all of you! He kept his parentage a secret
before the Elders admitted him because he wanted to trick you
into believing he's a vulnerable little boy so that you'll feel sorry
for him and take him back to the Otherworld. This way, he can
pry into the top secrets and tell his dear mother, Alta. Your
suspicions were right. He's a spy and a traitor, and his mother is

all behind it."

"How did you figure all that out?"

The ghost put on a mocking expression. "You are so naïve, so foolish. You think everything in this world is rosy and lovely? Wrong. There is no trust, no friendship, no love. Only betrayal, manipulation, and hatred. Humanity is a dark and evil thing, Alexandria. It is vulnerable, fragile, and weak, so very weak. People scheme for their own good, seemingly do favors for you when all they actually want is to obtain greater benefits for themselves. You think you know the people around you, but has it never occurred to you that all you are seeing is a mere illusion, a façade that hides the selfishness within?"

"But what about my parents? They couldn't have been scheming—"

"They gave birth to you, then sent you to the mortal world. Don't you remember the lonely days you spent alone? You loved nobody, and nobody loved you. And your parents were living in a splendid palace when you cried yourself to sleep every day. They could've at least checked on you once in a while and shown some support instead of having grand feasts and—"

"You're not wrong, but—"

"I know what's best for you, so stop contradicting me and listen. Helen and Zack are no better."

"But Zack—"

"Why don't you put it in this way? Zack wouldn't have stood aside and watched you die if he cared for you."

"But everything happened all of a sudden."

"That's no excuse. He would've had your back and sacrificed his life for you, the way you did for Helen. He could've at least stopped you from taking—"

"But—"

"You want to take Helen's side, don't you? Didn't you remember what happened on her last mission? Maybe you didn't know Evonne very well but now look at yourself. You are also a victim who suffered from Helen's incompetence. She deserved to die, but you didn't, so why did you not choose to save yourself?

Helen should've died last time, but Evonne saved her and lost her own memory. Helen ought to have died this time when the axe was meant to kill her. It was her fate, her destiny to be eliminated from this world. But twice, fate somehow failed. Evonne and you, two unfortunate people who were both incredibly loyal, took her place. Now, if you choose to pass on, you will have a full year of peace before reincarnating to a better life. No fighting, no secret identities, no truth or lies. As for Helen, she'll get punished for escaping death twice and involving two innocent people."

Seeing that I remained silent, she continued, "Alexandria Richardson, stop deceiving yourself. Face the truth, you have nobody to love. Nobody cares about you. So just go, leave this world. You will have an opportunity to be born in a family that cherishes you, but only if you reincarnate. Forget your so-called friends, forget your selfish parents, forget your life as a failure. Start again. It's not too late."

Her words got to me. What if she was right? What if my friends were just using me? What if I was born to be a joke? A failure? I could enjoy how it felt to be actually free if I chose to pass on. No fighting. No secret identities. No truth or lies. Only me, myself, and I, existing in harmony.

But what about Helen? Did she deserve to die?

No. At least I never thought so.

Helen was brave enough to face her mistakes and make amends for her last mission. She was the closest person I had to a family member when I was at school. She was the one who fought side-by-side with all of us during the final battle, doing everything she could to protect us. She was the one who offered an apology when I was about to die. Helen did nothing wrong.

No, I could not implicate her.

"I've made up my mind to return. Free me, please."

The ghost raised her eyebrows skeptically. "I wouldn't be so sure if I were you. Perhaps you'll change your mind after watching this." She took out her scepter and waved it, conjuring a thin sheet of mist. Then, she held it close to me as if it were a piece of paper and tapped her scepter on the mist three times.

I gazed into the magical mist and saw nothing but my

pale figure. Then, however, my reflection vanished and was soon replaced by another image.

A gloomy ten-story building loomed into sight. In one of the rooms sat an undernourished girl in shabby clothes. She was face-to-face with a tall man whose indifferent expression seemed colder than ice.

"Please, Mr. Jones," she said. "Are the rumors true? Did my parents really abandon me after I was born?" The girl's asymmetrical eyes were filled with fear and apprehension that did not fit her young age.

"How many times do I have to tell you, Richardson?" said the caretaker tersely, without the vaguest trace of acknowledgement that this was a sensitive subject to mention to an orphan. "Your parents abandoned you after you were born and sent you here. Then, three years later, they died from leukemia."

Alexandria's eyes welled with tears, but she bit her lip, determined not to betray any sign of emotion in front of the caretaker.

"Mr. Jones, Daphne Sinclair...she told the other kids that I was a bastard. She also said my father was a womanizer and my mother a slut. What did Daphne mean? Why did the others laugh at me when she said that? Was she right?"

Mr. Jones's expression hardened. "No more questions, Richardson. Leave." He pointed her out of his office.

"But—"

"What difference does it make if you really are a bastard? Listen, I've got better things to do than sit here all day and answer your silly questions!"

"I knew it!" wailed Alexandria. "Daphne was right, wasn't she?"

"Richardson, stop making a racket and get out of my office!"

Tears flowed down Alexandria's cheeks. She shot the caretaker a look of hatred before exiting his office. After closing the door, she wiped her tears away with the back of her hand and sat in the corridor. She wasn't crying anymore.

"Why?" she wondered aloud to herself. "What did I do wrong? Why is the whole world against me? Why can't I just—disappear?"

Dead silence. Who could answer her questions? And who would have the heart to?

The image dissolved into nothingness, and another took over.

"So Daphne Sinclair was right, wasn't she? Your dad was a womanizer and your mom a slut?" a boy said to Alexandria, obviously deriving immense pleasure from taunting her.

The two of them were in the courtyard of a school. An audience had gathered around them and was now howling with laughter.

"Boy, I'd die of shame if I were her!" said a pigtailed girl with a laugh.

"Have you heard the rumors?" a bystander joined in. "Her parents abandoned her and soon died. Daphne told everyone in the cafeteria yesterday."

"Now, what should I do with her? Punch her? Shove her into the fountain?"

"Punch her, Sandy!" a boy yelled. "Let's see how this loser can fight!"

The bystanders cheered in approval.

"Great idea," the pigtailed girl answered, grinning.

Alexandria glared at her, fury written on her face. Flames danced in her pupils.

"What, you angry?" said the first boy. "Wanna go find Mommy and Daddy and boohoo?"

But before anyone could react, sparks of fire emitted from Alexandria's fingers and zoomed towards them. Screams rent the air, and the crowd scattered like a pile of leaves.

"Haven't I warned you? She's a witch!" another bystander shouted, sprinting towards the adjacent staircase. "I told you before, but you just wouldn't listen! Alexandria Richardson is a monster!"

I recognized the bystander. It was Daphne.

Another scene started to take place. This time, Alexandria was walking through the locker hall at school, which was packed with students collecting their belongings and buzzing with conversation. They stopped in their tracks and stared at Alexandria as they caught sight of her. Again, murmurs erupted throughout the crowd.

"That's her, isn't it?"

"The kid who made the podium explode? Yeah, it's her."

"Mr. Carson said he saw flames burning in her eyes and sparks of fire dancing on her fingers. And then the next moment, the podium exploded!"

"Why hasn't she been expelled yet? She's a threat to all of us!"

The carrying whispers were audible to Alexandria, but she bit her lip and chose to ignore them. More insults were hurled at her as she left the locker hall.

"Freak!"

"Monster!"

"Witch!"

The scene faded away, and the mist became white again.

The ghost turned towards me. "You've just seen the awful memories of your childhood. Now, if you choose to go back, you'll live twice as miserably as that. But if you pass on...." She gave her scepter a flick, and the magical mist glowed.

A clear image began to form. It showed a smiling girl and her parents sitting at a table. It was dinnertime, and the three of them were laughing and chatting like a proper family. A joyful atmosphere pervaded the house. I scrutinized the girl in the vision and realized it was me—a happier, more cheerful version of me.

Without warning, the image blurred and disappeared.

"Well?" said the ghost. "Surely you don't want to reconsider? A loving family who would never abandon you, and a place where you call home. These are your rewards for making the right decision. Just go, Alexandria. Have you not craved loving parents? Have you not yearned for a true home? Listen to me. I know what's best for you."

I compared the two options. Me, living with a normal family and loving parents. But at the same time, Helen would die. But was saving her worth it? Worth giving up a whole new life of perfection?

Suddenly, an earlier memory flashed across my mind. King Patrick's foreseeing. He had told me that I would find happiness in front of a mirror. The ghost had a sheet of mist that resembled a mirror, in a metaphorical sense — it reflected my past and probably my future. Could this possibly be the mirror King Patrick was referring to? Was it a hint suggesting that I should make the decision to pass on?

Alexandria, a small voice scolded in my head. *You disgust me. How could you? Helen was by your side whenever you needed her. You cannot do that to her. You are no better than Alta and Alto if you choose to hurt her in exchange for your own happiness.*

"She's not worth saving," said the ghost, as if she could read my mind.

Then, it hit me. How had she introduced herself?

I am Alexandria Matilda Richardson. The evil side of her.

Comprehension dawned on me. If she was made from the fragments of my negative emotions, it was highly possible that she would tempt me to make the wrong decision.

"Trust me, Alexandria," said the ghost. "I am your *friend*. I'm nudging you into making the right decision." A creepy smile crept onto her lips.

Yes, I thought, my mind wandering out of control. But fortunately, my conscience took over.

"I'm…I'm staying, no matter what." I had no idea why my illusionary twin would know my deepest desires, but Helen had been innocent all along. I would never implicate her.

The ghost glared at me. Flames danced in her eyes, and a tiny ball of turquoise fire that I recognized as Underworldian magic was blazing on her palm.

"I stand by what I said, and if you're not taking no for an answer, you might as well blast me to ashes. Go on."

Surprisingly, the ball of fire vanished with a pop. "Then

take a look at this." The ghost snapped her fingers, and the sheet of mist shimmered and formed a scene. I could make out two people, Clarissa and Eileen.

The image of Clarissa laughed, her voice cold, clear, cruel. "Unpopular, ugly, unwanted...Alexandria Richardson, you were never our friend. We're better off without a nuisance like you."

The illusion-Eileen sneered. "It's your cousin, Eric, who I love, not you—never you! You're too pathetic for anyone to care for." She exchanged a wide, devilish grin with Clarissa, and they broke into a peal of mocking laughter.

Another figure appeared. It was Helen. "See? Nobody likes you. Nobody needs you. Nobody cares about you. Alexandria Richardson, you are nothing. Your existence is a disturbance to the world."

The ghost looked at me. "Don't you understand? This is what your so-called friends think of—"

"LIAR!"

Anger seized me. Without a second thought, I got out the Gem of Hope and smashed it at the ghost. The magical mist evaporated as it struck her, and she let out an unearthly, bloodcurdling scream as her airy figure shattered into a million pieces.

A peculiar sensation washed over me. I felt as if a magnet was pulling me downwards, and before I knew it, I was falling, falling through the air, slamming at the ground. Gravity caught me in an embrace, and—

I opened my eyes and blinked. I was myself again.

Everything around me seemed ten times clearer than before. I blinked a second time and flexed my fingers. "Miraculous" was the only word that came to my mind. "I'm back," I called out to the others softly.

They stopped weeping and stared at me, wide-eyed and slack-jawed.

Clarissa was the first to speak. "You...aren't you supposed to be—?"

"Aren't you happy to see me back?" I grinned.

Then, after what seemed like a whole minute, Clarissa laced her arms around me in a hug. "Oh, Alexandria…of course, I'm happy to see you! But what…? How…?"

Slowly and clearly, I told everyone the whole story without exaggerations, but I left out the part about why I made the decision to return because I cringed at the thought of letting everyone know how much Helen meant to me.

The six of them reacted differently while I was talking. Clarissa gripped my hand tightly, her nails digging into my palm. However, it did not hurt at all. On the contrary, I was so happy to see her again that I didn't mind. Tears of relief and happiness poured down Eileen's face. Eric had his arm around her. His mouth hung ajar, and his eyebrows went up and down as I clarified everything. Daphne grimaced when I mentioned the orphanage and how she had spread rumors about my parentage. Helen and Zack, who had both calmed down, were listening with rapt attentiveness. They exchanged looks of concern when I mentioned the scenes from my childhood.

"…and I got so frustrated that I threw the gem at her, and I woke up as if everything was just a dream." I ended my story.

Zack looked aghast, and Helen opened her mouth to speak. "You threw it? We came here only for—"

That was when something in my pocket gave a little jump. I reached in and took it out. It was the Gem of Hope. Somehow, the gem had magically found its way back to me. However, it remained intact, even after I had hurled it at the ghost.

Everyone looked at me as if I were insane.

"I…I don't know why it's here, but—but you must believe me! Everything I said was—"

"I believe you," Daphne piped up, her voice small yet firm. Clarissa, Eileen, and Eric echoed her sentiment. Helen and Zack exchanged another look.

"Who—or what—was that ghost girl?" I asked. "Will I see her again, sometime in the future?"

The two Elders got into a brief discussion. Then, a few moments later, Helen spoke. "You know who she is. Tell me."

Taken aback at her curt reply, I answered with great

caution. "She resembled me in appearance and shared my name."

"That is correct. *You* were the ghost."

I looked up, appalled. "What? No way! I'm nothing like her! She's — she's evil, twisted, cunning, and — "

"But she *is* you," Helen cut across me. "You see, there is no definite good or evil in this world. Everybody, including you, me, and every living being, has good and evil in their hearts. Yes, even the best person in the world may harbor a tiny sliver of evil in him or her, and vice versa. However, some people turn out to be good, and others don't. This is because they chose to let the good side of their hearts rule their minds instead of the evil one. The ghost you met is the evil side of you. In fact, this is not the first time you've encountered her."

"But I've never seen — "

"You will sense her presence every time you feel a strong torrent of negative emotion, and she will meddle with your mind and tempt you to make the wrong decision. But, of course, she is a spirit rather than a human, so you will only get to actually *see* her when you aren't one."

"I don't really — "

"Don't you understand? She is a reflection — a reflection of your tragic past. She serves as a reminder of your past insecurities, depression, and suffering. She is made from your dark notions and traumatic recollections."

"But I thought — "

"Alexandria, I know you suffered a lot in your childhood," said Helen gently. "There were times that you wished that you were...gone, right?"

A pause of hesitation. Finally, I nodded, and she went on.

"There must've been much hatred and darkness accumulated in your subconscious. This spirit is made from those negative thoughts of yours. In other words, she doesn't corporeally exist. She is a spirit of emotion, with an airy body and the ability to manipulate your mind. She can feed you false information, beguile you with lies, show you illusions that bring out the worst of others, and trick you into making terrible decisions."

"All right," I said. "So, correct me if I'm wrong. She's an evil force."

Helen nodded and opened her mouth to answer, but Zack chimed in before she could speak. "I noticed something very interesting. Helen is right about the evil, and mind you, a wicked spirit of negativity is the most powerful force of the unknown. It can cajole you into making dreadful decisions or even result in your failure or death. It's almost impossible to fight it. There is only one way to conquer it: a strong will — an unyielding belief in kindness and justice. Obviously, your belief in kindness was so strong that it helped you vanquish the ghost. So how exactly did you manage to overpower her?"

"You're asking me why I chose to return instead of passing on," I replied.

Zack nodded. Eileen stopped sobbing, and everyone fixed their gazes upon me.

"I couldn't implicate Helen. The ghost somehow knew how much I wanted a normal family, and I admit I was momentarily tempted. But how am I better than Alta and Alto if I did that?"

"But what about — ?" interrupted Clarissa.

"Yes, I know what you're thinking. Maybe I would get a chance to reincarnate and have a better next life with a proper family if the ghost was telling the truth. But Helen, I just…I couldn't stand the thought of losing you. I wanted to protect you. That was why I'd taken the blow for you in the first place, as well as the reason I decided to return. Perhaps I didn't have a real family before, but I had you, and that's more than enough. You were always there for me when I needed you the most. So I…." I grasped fleetingly for the right word, only to find myself at a loss. There just wasn't a proper word for affection this deep, devotion this unmatched. "I love you, Helen. Always have. And I want to tell you this while I can."

Silence loomed upon the seven of us until Zack finally ruptured it. "You are one of the most noble Otherworldians I've ever met, Alexandria. Yet, it is not your magic that makes you so great. Few, almost none, would have made a choice like you.

There aren't many people who can think selflessly and act for the good of others."

I nodded and glanced at Helen, who was gazing wistfully at a random tree in the distance. "Thanks, Alexandria. I...I owe you one."

"I'm just glad that you made it back," said Eileen in a quiet voice.

"I'm sorry for everything," Daphne said, reaching out to hold my hand. "Really, I am. Could you give me another chance to...?"

"Sure." I turned towards Eric, who had been silent all along. "I'm grateful to have a cousin like you, and I take back everything I said this morning. You are a wonderful person."

"I have nothing on you," he replied humbly, shaking his head.

"I hate to interrupt you all, but we must leave immediately," announced Helen, returning to her grim self. "What's the time?"

Eileen checked her watch. "It's three-thirty now."

"All right, so where's the nearest river or pond?" asked Zack. "We could take our chances and see if it's the aquaportal."

Gingerly, I stood up by degrees and winced as the wound on my back stung in protest. "Ouch...I don't think we should go looking for the aquaportal now."

"If only we had something to heal—" began Eric.

"To heal...." It was as if a lightbulb had blinked on in my mind. I withdrew from my pocket the red velvet pouch and unfastened the ribbon. In it was a little vial labeled *Healing Potion*. Carefully, I uncorked the bottle, dribbled the contents down my back, and felt the pain subside as the gash healed by itself.

"How are you feeling?" asked Clarissa anxiously.

"Good as new," I said, smiling as I got to my feet. "Now, any ponds or rivers nearby?"

"I saw a lake there before—" started Daphne, but the rest of her sentence was drowned out by a shrill voice that issued from nowhere.

"SEEMS LIKE I'VE RUN INTO THE SEVEN OF YOU

AGAIN!"

"It's the Chirpy Bird!" Eric was the first to recognize the voice. "Run!"

The seven of us took off running, with Eric and Daphne bringing up the lead. I glanced behind and saw the Chirpy Bird, who had joined forces with the gigantic lion-cat that had attacked us yesterday when we first arrived in the Underworld.

"HA!" the Chirpy Bird screeched. "You're not going to escape me this time!"

Clarissa, who had gotten on a cloud, pulled Eileen on and accelerated towards us.

"Oh my...no...not again...," I heard Daphne groaning from far ahead.

"Huh? Oh!" What I saw made my heart sink.

The road had terminated, and we found ourselves facing a suspension bridge that looked exactly like the one we had encountered yesterday. Only this one seemed wobblier and more dilapidated. Clarissa and Eileen arrived and exchanged gloomy looks at the sight.

"I'll go first," Helen volunteered. She made her way across the first few planks, clinging on to the ropes on either side with her trembling hands.

"ROAR!" the lion-cat was only thirty feet away from us.

"Helen, just run!" Clarissa screamed from above.

The lion-cat and the Chirpy Bird were getting closer and closer. Closer and closer they got —

"Come on!" yelled Helen, motioning for us to follow.

A deafening shriek split the air. Clarissa, who had lost her balance, tumbled off her cloud and went soaring down into the rapid creek.

"Clarissa, no!" Zack made an attempt to catch her, but to make matters worse, Zack also lost his balance and dropped from the bridge.

"We have to save them, now!" hollered Eileen, crouching on the cloud. But the next moment, her foot slipped, and she, too, plummeted from the cloud. Eric reached out to catch her, but Eileen's weight caused both of them to fall into the ravine. The rest of us watched, flabbergasted, as gravity took all of them.

"Alexandria, Daphne, stay here and don't move," ordered Helen. "I'm going down to save them." She raised her wand and pointed it at the ropes. Just then, the planks beneath her feet collapsed, and she lost her footing.

"No, Helen!"

We watched, horrified, as the creek below swallowed her.

Daphne was close to having a meltdown. "Why is this happening?" she howled in dismay.

It was a nightmare. We had lost almost everyone and worst of all —

"HA, TWO DELICIOUS GIRLS!" shouted the Chirpy Bird, clutching me in one hand and Daphne in the other. It jabbed Daphne in the face with one of its fingers, and she recoiled in disgust.

"LET — GO — OF — ME — YOU FREAK!" she spat at the Chirpy Bird, kicking and waving her arms.

I hurled a fireball at the Chirpy Bird's right eye while Daphne stabbed an icicle into its left. It screamed and lost its grip on both of us.

Cold, moist air invaded my senses; it brushed my cheeks and whooshed in my ears as the creek flew towards me. The waters gleamed wickedly under the sunshine as though mocking my misery.

Alexandria, do not mess with fate, or you'll come to a sticky end. The ghost's warning rang in my ears.

At least I'll be reunited with Clarissa, Eileen, Daphne, Eric, Helen, and Zack, was my final thought before I closed my eyes. I knew I was facing my end, and I welcomed death.

However, as my head touched the icy waters of the creek, I felt myself falling through a bottomless pit, through an endless darkness, as if being transported to an unknown world.

Chapter Thirteen

WORLD, SWEET WORLD
(ALEXANDRIA)

Splash!

I dived out of the water, my clothes soaking wet. Strangely enough, everything around us looked completely different from the Underworld.

Clarissa paddled towards me, then stopped in her tracks. "Good gracious. Is this...?"

We looked around in astonishment. The creek had brought us to the courtyard of the palace of the Otherworld. The fountain we were now swimming in was the exact same one where we had begun our adventure. However, the courtyard was nothing like what we had seen on our first arrival. Everywhere, flowers bloomed and leaves rustled.

I heard a few splashes behind me and saw Zack, Eileen, Eric, Helen, and Daphne.

"Can you believe this?" said Zack breathlessly, his eyes shining. "We're home! I never would've dreamed that the creek was actually the aquaportal. Turns out the Chirpy Bird did us a huge favor!"

"Oh my...the Otherworld!" exclaimed Eileen, her gaze traveling around the courtyard. "This is unbelievable."

"You can say that again," I agreed. I conjured a fireball and dried everyone's clothes. For some reason, King Patrick's prediction crossed my mind. It was beginning to make perfect sense. "Well...seems like we ended where we started," I remarked, smiling. "Same creek, same bridge, same fountain, same world."

"I wouldn't be so surprised if I were you," said Zack. "The aquaportals may be in different parts of the Underworld, but they all lead back to this one fountain in the Otherworld." He surveyed the courtyard and beamed. "World, sweet world."

"Can we explore the courtyard, please?" begged Eileen. "Just look how lovely it is! It must be the Gem of Hope's magic!"

"Sure. I think we all deserve a little break after that mission. Take your time, everyone."

The others wandered off in twos and threes while I lingered behind.

"The cunning Underworld," muttered Helen. "It knew we were clever at escaping bridges and would unlikely fall into the creek. So that was where it set the new portal. Right there in the creek. Another one of its dirty schemes."

"At least we're back in the Otherworld," I said reassuringly.

Helen put an arm around me. "Promise me something. Don't ever save me again. I thought you were dead when...." Her voice became softer and softer, then ended with a whisper.

However, I couldn't give her my word. "No, Helen. You're my priority. I'd do anything for you."

"But...." Her voice faltered.

I met Helen's gaze and was stunned to see her eyes flooding with tears. That was when I realized that beneath her usual steeliness, beneath her harsh exterior as the Representative Elder, there lay a caring, motherly woman. I wanted to comfort her, thank her, and tell her how much she meant to me, but I didn't know where to begin. It suddenly occurred to me that some feelings were so deep they were beyond articulation. So instead of saying anything, I enfolded Helen in an embrace, pouring all my unspoken feelings into the hug.

A warm breeze swept by, humming softly as it teased the

leaves on the trees.

"Ah, paradise...," breathed Eric. He closed his eyes, and a soft grin spread across his face.

"Eric," I said, walking up to him. "Welcome home."

"Thank you," he replied, gazing greedily at everything in the courtyard. Then, in a hushed voice, he said, "I can't believe I'm here at last. It's been my dream since I was a kid. The Otherworld's such a beautiful place, isn't it?"

I looked around, and for the first time, everything seemed alive with joy. Words failed to describe the beauty of the courtyard. The pond on the other end was as clear as crystal; the gazebo in the middle had regained its charm — the cascades of wisteria nestled on the canopy were now in full bloom, a brilliant sea of purple. The little bridge that led into the gazebo was now immaculately white. The glossy marble statues in the courtyard were completely mended. I inhaled lungfuls of the fresh air, which was sweet with the blended fragrance of flowers. Tiny lilac and yellow buds dotted the verdant lawn, and colorful butterflies crisscrossed through the lush green shrubs, bushes and trees. Arbors with vibrant pink and white roses were located at the four arches. Small crimson and amber toadstools with white dots squatted at the foot of the arbors. Elaborate statues of grinning bearnixes, unibirds, kittenpillars, and dogfishes surrounded the three-tier fountain. The water rippled as if someone had tossed a pebble in it. The shining surface shimmered under the sunlight as though millions of tiny dancing sapphires.

The enchanting sight of the fountain drew Daphne's attention. She swept her hand across the water and mouthed "wow" softly as she gazed into the depths of the fountain. I did the same, wondering what had piqued her interest. There, in the fountain, I saw an illusion of six people streaking across a plain, chased by a giant lion cat. Soon, with the assistance of one another, they successfully crossed a bridge. I realized the fountain was showing the highlights of our journey. With great interest, I watched a redheaded boy join the party. They fought some monsters and met a large canary. It was fascinating to see our whole adventure on mini-display.

"Cool, huh?" said Daphne. "I'm glad that we're friends now."

"Me too," I replied.

"Mew?" a timid meow sounded from behind us. Then, a furry snow-white head poked out from behind a yellow rose bush. Then, Ella, the kittenpillar, wriggled into sight.

"Ella!" cried Eileen. She almost strangled the kittenpillar with a hug. I thought Ella would suffocate, but amazingly, she curled herself around Eileen as if embracing her in return. Eileen planted a kiss on the kittenpillar's head as she meowed. "I missed you so much, my dear."

"Meow."

"I kept my word," Eileen went on with a laugh. "I came back and paid you a visit! I never thought I'd come back alive! And it's all thanks to my friends."

Ella purred meekly and nuzzled Eileen.

"Hey, don't underestimate yourself," said Eric, who emerged from behind a tree with golden oranges dangling from its branches. "We wouldn't have made it without your nature magic."

Ella let out an aggressive meow as he approached Eileen. Eric shot a puzzled look at the latter, and for a second, their eyes met.

Eileen blushed. "Oh, Ella, um...he's our new recruit and my...my good friend. Eric, this is Ella the kittenpillar."

Eric beamed a dazzling smile at Ella, who gazed back at him curiously with her large innocent eyes. I watched them from behind the fountain. It made me smile to see my cousin being accepted. Zack was right, Eric had a heart of gold, and we were doing the right thing—to embrace him and show him the radiance and beauty of the Otherworld.

"Wow, what a cutie pie!" said Eric. "Just look at those big eyes and little ears! Isn't she adorable?"

"Will Ella grow? I mean, will kittenpillars grow up and become butterflies?"

"Butterflies?" Eric laughed and laid a hand on Eileen's

shoulder. "Don't be silly. There's no such thing as a kitterfly!"

The two of them burst into peals of laughter.

Eileen stood on her tiptoes and gave Eric a little kiss. "You are so cute sometimes."

"Well, not as cute as you are," replied Eric, his cheeks scarlet.

I beamed at the two of them, thinking secretly that they would make a sweet couple.

A few moments later, Helen came up to me. "Alexandria, you still have the gem?"

I groped in my pocket and handed her the sparkling gem. It glowed red, yellow, green, and blue at the same time, and illusions of bearnixes, unibirds, kittenpillars, and dogfishes glistened on every side.

"Ready?" Helen whispered.

I gave her a decided nod as a response.

"It's time, everyone," announced Helen. "We have to report to the king and queen right away."

"Don't forget our dress code," reminded Zack, changing his shirt and jeans into a lavender tuxedo with his wand.

Helen got out hers and muttered some incantations. Violet mist wafted from the tip of her wand, enveloping her figure as her mortal clothes transformed into an extravagant purple ball gown, the exact one we had seen yesterday.

Eric gaped at Helen, who now looked like a ravishing peacock, but Eileen nudged him hard in the ribs and had him distracted.

"Ow! What did you do that for?"

We delved into the winding passage ablaze with purple torches. I recalled the first time I had set foot in this very same passage, which was only yesterday. Everything then seemed so far away by now. I thought of my parents, who were anxiously waiting for my return at this moment. What would they say? Would they congratulate me? Would they slap me on the back and tell me how proud they were? A mixture of feverish anticipation and excitement coursed through me as I pondered these questions.

We ascended the spiral staircase that twirled all the way up to the seventh floor. The bright, splendid hallway greeted us, and I heard Eric utter a gasp of pleasant surprise.

"Oh, this is…this is…it's brilliant!" he gushed, regarding the carvings on the marble pillars, the gilded candelabras, and the ice and fire sculptures with great fondness.

I, however, only had eyes for the enormous pair of double doors at the end of the hallway. "Helen, Zack…could I…may I have a talk with—?"

"You want to talk to your parents alone?" said Zack. "Sure. We'll be here, waiting for you."

Helen nodded in agreement.

Without another word, I sprinted towards the large doors of the Throne Room. The two guards gaped at me as I neared. Taking no notice of their reactions, I pressed my ear on the right door and heard screams and shouts coming from inside.

"Your Majesties, pardon me for my blunt words, but I have already done my best to warn you," I heard Jenkins's bossy, high-pitched voice. "Helen Edmunds is a failure! We lost Evonne last time, and now we've lost Alexandria! We must banish our Representative Elder and put an end to this!"

"Wait a second," another voice, unmistakably Benson's, cut in. "I think Zachary Valentino should also take responsibility for—"

"BANISH THEM!" chorused the Elders. "MAKE THEM LEAVE!"

"What are you all shouting about?" I demanded, pushing the doors open before realizing what I had done.

Silence, loud and ringing, pervaded the room. Everyone gaped at me, horrorstruck.

King Patrick stood up, his face shrouded with disbelief. "Alexandria? Is that…is that really you?"

"Yes, Your Majesty." I made my way along the aisle and approached him.

Relief worked its way across his features. "So you…you are not…dead?"

"I'm not dead, no. I was just...you see...." I sighed and retold the story of my resurrection. "...and after that, we made it back to the Otherworld."

Queen Marianne looked at me, her brow furrowed in anger. "Why would you do such a foolish thing? You should've deflected the axe with your magic, not taken it for her! Never! Have you ever thought of your father and I—?"

"Marianne." King Patrick laid his hand on hers, and she became quiet. "You did very well, Alexandria. I am proud of you, of your loyalty and devotion, of your strength and courage."

"You were right from the beginning, Your Majesty. I *was* indeed destined to be a warrior. But in fact, I think Eric fought better than—"

"I won't deny his brilliance, of course. However, you not only vanquished countless enemies but also conquered the darkness in your heart."

I glanced at Queen Marianne, whose anger seemed to have dissolved. "I'm just glad you're all right, Alexandria," she said quietly.

"Greetings, Your Majesties, please pardon us for interrupting," said Helen. She curtsied, and Zack bowed, and they approached the gigantic thrones, followed by Clarissa, Eileen, Daphne, and Eric.

"Rise," ordered Queen Marianne. I was worried that she would start blaming Helen for what had happened, but with a powerful surge of relief, I saw that she was smiling. "Now, time to celebrate the return of our seven heroes." She stood up and clapped her hands.

Noir, the dogfish, approached her, holding a silver tray with seven golden medallions.

"What's that?" Eric asked, standing on his tiptoes. A wide smile crossed his face. "You're giving out gold? Hell yeah!"

"Language!" whispered Helen, slanting him a stern look.

"What language?" he looked at her, scratching his head in bemusement.

"Don't you play dumb with me, Eric Williams! Slang words are not allowed in the palace!"

Eric shrugged and stuck out his tongue.

"These, Eric, are medallions," Queen Marianne corrected, taking no notice of his discourteous choice of words.

"Medallions?" echoed Eric.

"We present medallions to every participant after a successful mission. First, to our Representative Elder, Helen Wisteria Edmunds, for displaying wisdom in the face of challenges and keeping a clear mind when encountering adversity. Your outstanding logic and firm leadership guided everyone towards success. I feel greatly privileged to have you as our Representative Elder, and I honor you for your excellence."

"Thank you, Your Majesty, for your grace. However, it is in my belief that Zack showed greater wisdom than I." I could have sworn I saw subtle red patches appear on Helen's cheeks as she said that. "He was the one who persuaded me to accept Eric's pledge. We would never have made it back without Eric and his contributions. Also, the heiresses fought valiantly and with remarkable skills and strategies. I attribute our success to each and every one of them." Helen curtsied, and a few Elders clapped while the others gazed bitterly at her.

"Next, Zachary Louis Valentino. Your kindness and compassion have gained the Otherworld a powerful new member...."

"How did she know about Eric?" I muttered to Clarissa, who shrugged.

"Beats me. It's kind of eerie, you know? Queen Marianne keeps talking about our adventure as if she herself was with us all along."

"...and I am deeply impressed by your performance. You have done a wonderful job this time."

Zack bowed to Queen Marianne. "Thank you, Your Majesty. I have learned from this mission the importance of keeping an open mind and showing fairness to everyone. After all, we are the same, Otherworldian or Underworldian. Everyone deserves to be loved and accepted." A round of applause greeted Zack's words.

"Our new member, Eric Ethan Williams—my nephew," said Queen Marianne, a warm smile playing on her cherry-red lips. "I am more than thrilled to have you in the Otherworld. From what I have seen, your integrity and loyalty are your greatest assets."

"You saw?" said Eric, tilting his head. Then, he added hastily, "Your Majesty?"

"Precisely. Eric, you are yourself. Not your family, not your relatives, nor anyone else. It's not the blood running in your veins or the genes you've inherited that makes you you, but your inner mind, heart, and soul. It's you and your beliefs rather than who you are born to be and what people expect to see in you. I assure you that you will find love, friendship, a strong sense of belonging, and everything you have so desperately yearned for in the Otherworld."

"Thank you, Your Majesty," murmured Eric, bowing.

Queen Marianne laid a gloved hand on his shoulder. "Well done, young man. You may have suffered in the past, but I promise you'll be safe in the Otherworld. You are going to live in the palace with us from now on."

Eric's jaw dropped in astonishment, his face irradiated with euphoria. His joy was infectious, and an inexplicably tender yet powerful wave of happiness for him swept over me.

"Next, Eileen Flora Spencer," Queen Marianne went on.

Eileen looked up nervously, her gaze meeting the queen's. A flush of scarlet rose to her cheeks as they made eye contact.

"Do not fear, Eileen. You are a talented young heiress who would have made Fern proud."

Eileen muttered a quick thank you, and her gaze dropped to her feet.

"So, did you unmask the real you, like I had expected?"

Eileen glanced at the rest of us, apparently flustered. We nodded and gave her smiles of encouragement. Finally, she spoke in a timid voice, which later intensified in both confidence and volume. "Before.... Before I went on this mission, I spent every day buried in my textbooks. The only thing that mattered to me was getting good grades and—and meeting my parents' expectations. But now, I guess…life isn't always about books, grades, tests, and studying. Wisdom, kindness, courage, and love…these are twice as important. What textbooks have taught me is nothing compared to these. I learned, from Helen, leadership and wisdom. From Zack, the importance of having an open mind. From Eric," she blushed again, "the indomitable spirit to never stop holding on to one's beliefs. From Clarissa, that giving is receiving and that the people we help may provide assistance in return when we least expect it. From Daphne, it's never too late to change. From Alexandria, the strength of love and devotion. Your Majesty, this quest made me see things in a whole new light. Thank you for everything."

We heartily applauded Eileen, and Eric gave her hand a little squeeze. Then, Clarissa's name was called.

"Never underestimate the power of kindness. Clarissa Estrella Dawson, as the heiress of Zeru, you may not be as powerful as Alexandria or Daphne, but kindness itself is the most valuable brand of magic…."

As Queen Marianne droned on, Daphne and I, the only two left who hadn't been presented with our medallions, exchanged a wink.

"Who do you think will be next?" whispered Daphne.

"No idea. Oh, and a *friendly* little reminder to you: you still owe me one. That time when I saved you from the bridge when we first got to the Underworld."

"Hey, I saved you from the bearnix during that fight we had before running into the Chirpy Bird," said Daphne with a grin.

"And I pelted Helen with fireballs and saved your neck during our rehearsal bat—"

"All right, truce, truce!"

The two of us both saw the funny side of it, and we lapsed into silent laughter.

"…Zeru would've been proud of you, Clarissa. Well done, and keep striving."

After Clarissa had received her medallion, it was Daphne's

turn.

"Daphne Adeline Sinclair, you are one of the most important contributors to this mission. You, as the heiress of Walters, weren't destined to get along with the heiress of Ember. The two of you started off as enemies, practically loathing each other. However, I am very pleased to see that this has changed — that the two of you eventually found trust in one another. It's never too late to bridge a new friendship, Daphne. Fire and water may be enemies, but I'm certain the two of you will be an exception."

Daphne curtsied as she accepted her medallion, and finally, the moment I had been waiting for came at last.

"Alexandria Matilda Richardson."

Queen Marianne presented me with the shiny golden medallion. I ran my fingers over the uneven surface, feeling the words and the intricate patterns engraved upon it.

"Alexandria, my child."

My heart thumped in anticipation as I gazed up at Queen Marianne — no, at my mother.

"You have demonstrated loyalty and valor beyond measure in this mission. I am referring, of course, to the final battle, in which you selflessly chose to protect Helen when you could have kept yourself from harm. Also, you stayed true to your beliefs and values. Your mental fortitude and inner strength have made me proud. As the princess, you will play a crucial role in the future of the Otherworld. Is there anything you would like to say to the Otherworld after returning from your first mission?"

"I…well…I never had any knowledge of kings and queens and kingdoms and…things like that. My very limited information on those came from fairytales. You know," I shrugged, "short stories people — mortals, I mean — write to entertain little kids."

King Patrick nodded. "Did you like the stories?"

I shook my head. "I didn't think much of the stories when I first read them, but now, as a princess, I find them insulting. These fairytales — they deepen gender stereotypes. All the princesses in the stories were tortured by villains and rescued by brave princes. But why were *men* always the ones who did all the fighting? Were dressing up, falling in love, and revolving around their lovers the only things important for women?" I paused. "No. Not for me, at least. I'm not at all concerned about my appearance nor romance. The one and only thing I care about is the future of our realm. We don't have much, but we have the Otherworld, and we're not going to relinquish it no matter what. So I want all the Otherworldians to know that I, as their princess, will do my best to defend our kingdom and fight for the Otherworld. And so should every one of them."

"Well said, Alexandria," boomed King Patrick. "I have faith in you. You have proven yourself to me and to the Otherworld as well."

"Thank you, Your Majesty." Then, to Queen Marianne, I said, "You seem to know everything that happened during our mission. Is it possible that...you were actually with us all along?"

Queen Marianne said nothing, yet her eyes twinkled mysteriously, like two stars on a moonless night. "You like the medallion?"

"I love it," said Clarissa, her voice awed. "Why is it shaped like a unibird?"

I looked down at mine and noticed that she was right.

Queen Marianne's smile widened. "Piece the two questions together, and you get—"

Suddenly, I understood. "You went with us on the mission, disguised as two unibirds."

"Exactly!" said King Patrick, chuckling and clapping his hands. "But we left when we saw you dying because I.... We couldn't bear to—"

"I was the exact same unibird Clarissa zapped in the clouds," Queen Marianne cut in, steering the topic away.

"Wha—what? I zapped you? I...I'm sorry, Your Majesty! I didn't know—"

"It's not your fault, Clarissa. I also apologize for shooting you in the arm, but you were getting so carried away by the scenery then, so I had no choice but to act as a reminder of your quest without giving myself away. I hope it doesn't hurt anymore."

"And I was the unibird who begged for your help," added King Patrick. "The one with the purple mane."

"Oh, I remember him—I mean, you!" said Clarissa brightly. "You talked to me in the unibirds' language and—hang on...you can speak in their language?"

"Funnily enough, I can speak in both English and the unibirds' language when I'm a uni—"

"Your Majesty?" said Eric, his eyes posing a silent question. King Patrick gave him a nod of confirmation and a knowing wink, and Eric responded with a smile. I didn't know what their gestures implied, but I felt certain that King Patrick was willing to accept Eric, and that fact itself was more than enough.

Queen Marianne turned to Eileen. "Would you like your pouch back? It was intended as a gift for you in the first place," she said, handing her the green velvet pouch.

A sharp knock on the door interrupted our conversation.

"Roxanne Green, reporting for duty," a voice announced.

"Let her in, Bessie," King Patrick commanded.

The doors flew open, and in wriggled a kittenpillar. A hush erupted among the Elders, who had been conversing with each other in low voices when the king and queen were talking with us.

I glanced at Zack. "Who's that? Why's everyone so quiet?"

"That's Roxanne, the royal doctor," he answered, looking worried. "She never leaves the infirmary unless...."

The kittenpillar wriggled her way to the foot of King Patrick's throne and muttered something to him. Queen Marianne went over to them, and they exchanged a few urgent whispers. Then, looking rather stricken, the rulers gestured at Zack to join them and murmured in his ear. He stared at them, speechless with shock, and swallowed. Finally, he nodded at Roxanne, who bowed and made her way out of the Throne Room.

"Your Majesties, could Helen come along as well?" Zack asked. Helen shot him a questioning look as she heard her name mentioned.

Queen Marianne shook her head. "I'm afraid not. I have

something important to ask her later."

Zack nodded sadly. Then, before following Roxanne out, he mouthed to Helen, "Evonne's getting worse. She doesn't have much time left."

Helen's hand flew to her mouth. "Is there any way to...?"

The answer was clearly etched in Zack's somber expression.

Helen's gaze dropped to the floor, and her shoulders sagged. I wanted to comfort her, but the words I needed didn't come to me.

A murmur broke among the Elders, but nobody dared to question what had happened, for an unmistakable shade of gloom was etched upon both King Patrick and Queen Marianne's faces.

Daphne tugged at my sleeve. "What was that all about?"

"No idea," I answered, shrugging. "Bad news, I guess." I did want to tell her the truth, but not in front of Helen.

"Alexandria," said King Patrick suddenly, "there's an important decision you have to make."

I didn't quite register his words, for my mind was still occupied. "Sorry?"

Before he could answer, somebody thumped on the door again, this time rather rudely. "Dennis Adams and Gary Harper, reporting for duty. Your Majesties, we've brought them here, on your orders."

"Perfect timing. Enter!"

With a loud bang, the two large doors opened, and in came two stout-looking bearnixes, followed by a crowd of forty people. Their hands were tightly cuffed together, and they were so wet they were dripping water all over the carpet. They reeked of the smell of the moat, and it occurred to me that they had probably swam through it. At that thought, the corners of my mouth lifted slightly. Daphne and Eric seemed to get what was funny, and both giggled. However, my smile faded as I caught a glimpse of one of their faces.

It was Mrs. Wilson, my foster mother. What a pathetic sight she was. Her thick makeup was smudged. Her curls, now hanging in damp clumps, were draped around her head like a soggy brown curtain. Her clothes were torn and dirty. Mr. Wilson, who was standing beside her, looked twice as bedraggled as she did. Apart from my foster parents, I recognized many familiar faces—Mr. Jones and every single bully I had encountered in the orphanage and school. They, like Mr. and Mrs. Wilson, were dirty, soaking, and exhausted.

I glanced at King Patrick and Queen Marianne, wondering where all this was headed.

"Well, we leave their punishment to you," said Queen Marianne.

"Punishment?" I repeated blankly.

"That's right. The perpetrators from your past. We, Patrick and I, have agreed that they ought to have a lesson taught."

"You could lock them in the dungeons and feed them only on bread and water," one of the Elders suggested.

"Or you could throw them into the moat, which they've already been through," said another, shooting the forty a look of disgust.

"You could slice them into halves and feed them to the unibirds in the stables," the first one added, sniggering. "They love raw meat."

A few more Elders joined in, and they went on and on, joking and smirking at the crazy options the others came up with, which got more and more ridiculous. King Patrick chuckled at the absurdity of their suggestions.

"Elders," growled Queen Marianne, her stern gaze sweeping across the advisors. Silence fell upon them almost instantly.

Mr. Jones caught my eye and glanced down immediately as I met his gaze. Mr. Wilson shifted his weight from one foot to the other.

I noticed that apart from the fact that they were soaking wet, all forty of them had something in common, something in their eyes. Fear.

Slowly I walked up to the front, facing the forty people. Seeing their faces again reminded me of my past traumas, and it was not until then that I realized how powerful the lingering, negative impact they had on me was. However, did it make me feel superior, or even happier, wielding power and taking vengeance?

No.

Helen's words crossed my mind. *There must've been much hatred and darkness accumulated in your subconscious. This spirit is made from those negative thoughts of yours.*

I also remembered the words I had said to her yesterday night: *Only you can free yourself from your past; only your change of attitude can brighten your future.*

And now I had an opportunity to reconcile with my past.

I forced myself to look directly at the forty people. The arrogance and malice that had once blazed in their eyes were replaced by trepidation. Many were even wringing their hands in uneasiness. The iceberg of hatred in me began to thaw at that sight.

"Well?" demanded King Patrick.

"Your Majesty, please send them back to the mortal world."

Some of the forty people cast looks of astonishment at me, some heaved sighs of relief, while the others remained as motionless as statues. On the other hand, many of the Elders were tutting and shaking their heads in disapproval.

"What do you mean by that?" King Patrick looked puzzled.

"It means that I forgive them. I remember a potion you mentioned yesterday, something called the Forgetfulness Nectar. Dennis, Gary, feed all of them some nectar and make *me* disappear from their memories. I want them to forget about me and start a brand-new life instead of being plagued by guilt and sins from the past."

"Are you certain?" asked Queen Marianne.

I answered her with a firm nod. I forgave myself at the same time I forgave them. By doing so, I earned redemption and set myself free from the past.

King Patrick, Queen Marianne, and all the Elders were

silent. I suddenly acknowledged the fact that I was good at creating awkward situations.

"Fine, then," said King Patrick finally. "Dennis, Gary, take these forty to the infirmary. Ask Roxanne for some Forgetfulness Nectar, then escort them back to the mortal world."

"Yes, Your Majesty," they said in unison. Then, they saluted the rulers and turned, ready to leave.

"Hold on," I called out to them. "I want a quick word with Mr. Jones outside the Throne Room."

"Why?" said Queen Marianne, her eyebrows raised.

"I want to tell him something. Something important."

Dennis and Gary led the forty out, and I tagged along with them. As they filed into the hallway, I motioned for a terrified Mr. Jones to come with me.

"Here," I said to him, "behind this ice statue."

"Ms. Richardson...you are the most noble—"

I held up my hand to silence him. "Mr. Jones, just promise me something. Please. Take good care of the children in the orphanage. Promise me that they will receive a proper education instead of being forced to do chores day and night. Promise me that nobody will starve or freeze to death from now on. Promise me that there will be no more bullying. Last but not least, you must treat all the orphans as your own children. If you don't, I will reconsider—"

"But Ms. Richardson, I did...I wanted to, but we—the orphanage—we were too poor for—"

"That is no excuse for mistreating the orphans there."

"But—"

"Dennis," I said, "is there a vault somewhere in the palace?"

He nodded.

"Take Mr. Jones to the vault and give him some valuable items. He'll be able to sell those things in the mortal world for good money. Gary," I turned to the other bearnix, "ask King Patrick and Queen Marianne for permission. Tell them it's a...gift from me."

"Ms. Richardson," started Mr. Jones. "How should I

thank — ?"

"There's no need to," I replied tersely. "It's not a gift for you, anyway. It's for the orphans. Don't let what happened to me happen to the children there. Dennis, I order you to visit the orphanage from time to time and check if the situation there has improved at all and whether their caretaker has been squandering the money to feed his vanity." I gave Mr. Jones a hard look at that mention.

"Your Highness," said Gary, stepping out of the Throne Room. "His and Her Majesties have approved of your request."

"Very well. Mr. Jones, take care, and do not forget your word."

He had the grace to look mortified. "I won't. Thank you for your generosity, Ms. Richardson."

I watched the party wound their way down the spiral staircase. Then, I headed back into the Throne Room.

Queen Marianne looked up at me. "That was very noble of you, Alexandria."

I wasn't sure what to say, so I nodded. "Thank you for approving my decision, Your Majesty."

An awkward pause. The two of us looked at each other, neither knowing what to say next. King Patrick nudged her elbow gently as though prompting her, and Queen Marianne cleared her throat. "So…Patrick and I were just discussing who your new guardian should be."

"My new guardian?" I echoed in disbelief.

"Your foster family has failed to care for you and Daphne properly. Therefore, we have decided that henceforth, Daphne will be living with Lilith. As for you, Alexandria, since there is such an interesting bond between you and Helen…we have just talked this over with her; that is, she will be your godmother. And yes, this means you will be living with her from now on."

Pleasantly astonished, I cast a glance at Helen, who responded with a faint smile. What would I not give to be with her after we'd gone through so much together?

"I appreciate that, Your Majesty," I answered, unable to

wipe the big grin off my face.

"Excellent, we're all settled, then," said a beaming King Patrick. "Time for a banquet of celebration! Our five young guests are also invited. To ballroom 410! It's on the fourth floor, heiresses. Just follow the Elders downstairs, and you'll see it. All right, Elders, you're all dismissed. Enjoy the feast!"

The Elders rose, bowed and curtsied to the rulers and poured out of the Throne Room. Clarissa, Eileen, Daphne, and Eric turned to follow them.

"Alexandria." I heard King Patrick call my name.

"Eric, King Patrick wants to talk to me. See you guys later."

"Sure, we'll save you a seat."

After the last few Elders had trickled out, me and my parents were left alone.

"Yes, Your Majesty?" I asked.

"Um...are you happy with your new family?" King Patrick began rather shyly.

"Of course. I like Helen very much."

A pause.

"Alexandria," said Queen Marianne, "I would like you to arrange archery lessons with Helen, and in the meantime, learn swordplay from Zack. Both of them are incredibly talented. You must hone your skills every day, for we might call for you soon. Stay close to the Otherworldians in the mortal world, and heed the Elders' advice. Your friends are important and will play huge parts in your life. All right, I suppose you must be hungry. See you at the ballroom."

"Farewell," added King Patrick. Then, he turned to Queen Marianne, "I hope they serve golden oranges, don't you?"

Queen Marianne knit her eyebrows. "Patrick, you know I never eat golden oranges."

"Right, oh wait— Alexandria!"

"What are you doing? You're startling her!" scolded Queen Marianne. "Oh...we have a...a gift for you," she said to me.

"A gift?"

"We've prepared this." King Patrick handed me a purple box topped with a velvet bow.

Carefully, I opened the box. In it was a necklace with an amethyst pendant shaped like a bearnix. However, it was a note attached to the lid that piqued my interest even more. Eagerly, I pored over the curvy golden words, the first ever letter I had received from my parents.

To our dearest daughter:
We apologize for not being able to show moral support when you were abused in the orphanage or bullied at school. You were right yesterday. It was irresponsible of us to ignore our only daughter, even when we had countless battles to deal with. We do not know how to express our regret, but we do know that we love you with all our hearts, and we want you to know that. So, we hope you will like this necklace. Every time you see it, you know that we are with you, and so is our love.
From your parents,
Marianne Heather Williams and Patrick Sebastian Richardson

How foolish I had been, assuming that my parents had never loved me. They wouldn't have risked their lives and followed us to the Underworld if they didn't care for me. Instead, however, I was blind, blinded by my arrogance, self-pity, unhappiness, and dissatisfaction with my life.

"Your Majesties, please forgive me for my rudeness and ignorance yesterday." I stared at the carpet, my face boiling hot. Then, mustering up my courage, I forced myself to look them straight in the eyes. "Mother? Father? Thank you for everything. I...I love you."

Chapter Fourteen

MY FELICITOUS FUTURE
(ALEXANDRIA)

"Alexandria!"

My parents got to their feet and pulled me into a tight hug, and I draped my arms around them without hesitation.

It was as though time had slowed down and the whole world had melted away, leaving me with only my loving parents. Torrents of joy flooded upon the three of us, like waves lapping at a sandy beach on a warm summer day.

Finally, after bidding each other goodbye, again and again, I made my way to the ballroom downstairs. Everything that had happened since I left the mortal world replayed in my mind — how the four of us got whisked to the Otherworld, my shock when learning the truth of my parentage, and all the wondrous events along the way that made our adventure so colorful and memorable. Everything seemed so surreal, yet true.

As I savored those beautiful memories with utmost pleasure, a smile crept onto my lips. I knew deep down that I would miss the Otherworld dearly, and of course, getting into a battle with my friends, vanquishing monsters, and defending loved ones.

Suddenly, an eruption of laughter jerked me back to

reality.

The ballroom, a wide, opulent chamber with gilded walls, had arched window mirrors on all four walls and antique chandeliers with golden candles hanging from the vaulted ceiling. Flames in various colors danced enthusiastically on the tip of each candle, bathing the room in rosy hues. The polished floors were so shiny I could see my reflection in them. Elders, gossiping and eating, were sitting around small tables in little groups. A gay atmosphere pervaded the spacious ballroom.

Placed on the two long tables was a veritable cornucopia of food. Countless fancy dishes were served—roasted turkey, seasoned fish, baked potatoes, vegetable curry, sauteed mushrooms with garlic butter, stuffed peppers with cream cheese, and small portions of spicy beef casserole.

The second table had a myriad of beverages and refreshments—golden oranges, silver apples, tall glasses of fruit smoothies and fizzy champagne with tiny chocolate umbrellas and red cherries floating on top, miniature hamburgers and sandwiches shaped like the four creatures, and doughnuts and cupcakes coated with colorful sprinkles, marshmallows and frosting. At the end of the table, a huge chocolate fountain was perched beside dozens of whipped cream cakes topped with vibrant blooms of berries. Confections of all kinds—over ten different flavors of fudges and macarons—were piled on the plates like pyramids, having all the colors of a rainbow.

However, despite all the revelry, all I really cared about was finding my friends in the noisy ballroom. Everywhere, Elders were bustling around and making it impossible to move even an inch. Then, finally, I spotted Clarissa, Eileen, Daphne, and Eric sitting at a table in a corner.

"You're back!" said Clarissa. "Here, you must be starving! I've filled up a plate for you."

The five of us satisfied our stomachs with the food. The turkey was fine and flavorful, and the fish savory and scrumptious. I drenched a crispy baked potato in a golden tureen of vegetable curry, and that made it, if possible, even more delicious. Next, I took a sip of my strawberry smoothie. It was foamy and rich in flavor, and to my delight, little cubes of fresh strawberries found their way into my mouth. But still, my favorite was the macarons. Delicate and flaky, the powdered sugar and the sweet cream melted on my tongue as I bit into them.

"What are those?" asked Eric, regarding the mountain of macarons on my plate with a look of amusement. "They look like tiny colorful hamburgers."

"They're macarons," I corrected. "Here, try one. They taste awesome."

"Mmm, I never thought the food here would taste so nice," said Eileen, taking a nibble of the chocolate umbrella in her banana-and-pineapple smoothie.

"Of course," Daphne piped up. "Everything's perfect here in the Otherworld."

I looked up at Daphne, surprised at her positive remark. She was nothing like the Daphne I once knew, mean and sarcastic. She had changed, matured, somehow.

"I must say I like you better now, after this...suicide mission."

Daphne laughed. "Was it that dangerous?"

"Wasn't it? All those crazy battles. We could've died anytime."

"Well...you saved me quite a few times in our...adventure, if you could call it that," murmured Daphne, developing a sudden interest in the silk tablecloth.

"Yeah, don't mention it."

Daphne sighed. "I guess...we might have been born as enemies, but we have the Otherworld to believe in. So we must set our differences aside and focus on our common grounds." She extended her hand, and I shook it. "Eternal peace between the heiresses of fire and water."

"I thought we'd already reconciled?"

"Yeah, but we need to do it again formally, in front of our three witnesses." Daphne jerked her head at Clarissa, Eileen, and Eric, who stared at us with funny expressions on their faces.

"Are you sure you guys don't have a fever?" said Clarissa.

"Well, what do you think?" I grinned at her. "Anyway, Queen Marianne told me to stay close to the Otherworldians in the mortal world. So the four of us must stick with each other in school."

"Wait, you're all going back to the mortal world?" Eric asked, looking crestfallen.

"Unfortunately for us," said Daphne. "Lucky you, you get to actually live here and enjoy all this fancy stuff."

"Why can't you all just stay in the Otherworld? King Patrick and Queen Marianne will be more than happy to—"

"Our families are waiting for—oh no!" Eileen jumped up from her seat, knocking over her smoothie.

"What?" I said.

"My mom will be worried sick! Two entire days I've been gone!"

"Don't worry," said Lilith, who came over to our table. "No time has passed in the mortal world since your departure. It'll be nine in the morning on September thirteenth when you go back. Gee, you've got a whole day of school waiting for you!"

My jaw dropped. "What? That's impossible! We spent two days in the Otherworld and Underworld!"

"No, no," said Clarissa. "We were transported to the Otherworld at nine in the morning yesterday, and it's five in the afternoon now. So, we've been gone for thirty-two hours, which is one day and eight hours."

Lilith smiled and shook her head. "It will be the same time you left the mortal world when you return."

I blinked, trying to digest her words. All I knew was that abstract concepts like magic and time were extremely complicated.

"Heiresses, we'll be leaving at about seven," said Lilith. "Helen and I will be sending you home. Oh, and by the way, Helen's going to give you a quiz in her class today. So you'd better study for it," she added with a devious grin.

The four of us groaned. "Seriously?"

"Speaking of Helen, where is she?" asked Eric. "And

Zack?"

"They're both visiting Evonne in the infirmary," replied Lilith.

Dread stirred in my stomach. *Evonne is dying.*

"Yeah, yeah, never mind Helen and Zack, hope they're both okay," said Daphne, taking a bite of her blueberry cupcake. "Lilith, where shall we meet at seven?"

"At the fountain that first took you to the Otherworld. It's a two-mile walk from the palace. Sorry to cut it short, but I'm going to go refill my cup of coffee. See you guys at seven."

"I'm done eating," said Clarissa, slurping the last of her mango smoothie. Daphne crammed the rest of her cupcake into her mouth.

"Do you want to go and see the village?" Eileen said. "It would be nice to see it alive for the first time."

"Yeah, sure."

The five of us left the ballroom. Down the spiral staircase and into the courtyard we went. Ella, the kittenpillar, was curled up beside her favorite yellow rose bush, snoring peacefully. Eileen tiptoed up to her.

"What are you doing?" Eric asked.

"Shh, don't wake her up," said Eileen in an undertone. She placed her little green pouch by the sleeping kittenpillar. "A gift for her."

The corners of Clarissa's mouth twitched, and Daphne rolled her eyes dramatically.

"Bye, sweetheart. I'll see you around, I guess. Hope you'll think of me when you see it." With one last look at her beloved kittenpillar, Eileen walked back to us, biting her lip and trying not to cry.

"It's okay, Eileen," Eric patted her on the shoulder. "This isn't goodbye forever, is it?"

***

The reeking waters of the moat swished as we raced across the drawbridge. Two people were chatting animatedly on the other side.

"Zack?"

The two people turned around. One was indeed Zack. The other looked a little familiar—she was lanky in stature and was dressed in a pleated lilac gown with a billowing skirt adorned with lace appliqués.

I gasped. "Ms....Ms. Fitzgerald?"

Clarissa, who had also recognized our previous language arts teacher, Evonne Fitzgerald, gaped at her.

"You've heard all about my accident, haven't you?" said Evonne with a shy smile.

Eileen, Daphne and Eric looked at Evonne, then at me. "What accident? What's all this about?"

With the combined efforts of me and Clarissa, the story of Helen, Zack, Lilith, and Evonne's mission was once again retold.

Surprisingly, Evonne's smile widened at our words. "Thanks to you, the Gem of Hope is now restored. What's more, it healed me." Seeing the puzzled looks on our faces, she explained in detail. "The courage, wisdom, and kindness all of you have shown strengthened its magic. You see, the Gem of Hope is an extraordinary artifact. The gem's powers grow stronger whenever positive traits have been displayed in its presence. Because of your mission, it is now way more powerful than before."

"Well done, heiresses," Zack piped up. "And by the way, meet Helen and Lilith at the fountain portal by the village at seven. They'll take you back to school."

"Lilith's already told—"

"Where's Helen?" Eric cut in. "I haven't seen her since we left the Throne Room."

"Why do you keep asking about Helen?" said Clarissa. "Are you in love with her or what?"

Daphne and I snickered, but Eileen cast a sour look at Eric.

"She's in the Archive Room, recording everything that happened on our trip," said Zack. "That's part of her job, as the leader of our mission."

"Oh, cool," replied Eric.

"Great to see you again, Ms. Fitzgerald," said Clarissa.

"You can call me Evonne from now on if you don't mind.

Helen and Zack's told me everything about you, and I think you all are amazing. Most of the Otherworldians have heard about your heroic deeds as well and would like to congratulate you in person."

"Sure. We're heading to the village. See you!"

We waved goodbye to Zack and Evonne, and off we went.

The residential area was wide awake. Adults were bustling around, and children were playing hide and seek. In front of a cream-yellow house were two boys playing with their pet kittenpillar.

"Oh, look, it's them!" an adorable little boy in a red shirt cried out, pointing at us.

"Don't point your finger, Kent," said an older boy. "Mom said—"

"But it's them, the heroes!" the little boy called Kent exclaimed.

"Oh, um, hello," Kent's brother said, facing us. "Your Highness—"

"Alexandria will do. Nice to meet you."

"I'm Ian. This is my little brother, Kent." Looking slightly embarrassed, he added, "Kent's really young, and his manners—"

"Oh, no, no, it's all right," Clarissa chimed in. "He's really cute. I'm Clarissa, by the way, and this is Eileen, Daphne, and Eric."

"Is everything true? How you all fought the monsters and the stupid old bird in the Underworld? And the suspension bridge? And the colorful mushrooms? And the desert and the clones?"

"Kent, mind your manners!" said Ian.

"It's all right," answered Clarissa cheerfully. She turned to Kent. "Let me summarize everything: we went on a mission and brought back the Gem of Hope."

"Cool!" the little boy exclaimed, shaking his tiny fists and waving them in the air. "I want to be monster-fighters like you five when I grow up!"

"You could join the Elders," I suggested.

"I know! My mom is already one! I also want to take trips

to the Underworld and eat the colorful mushrooms!"

"You'll be glad you haven't," said Eric. "Trust me, they're disgusting."

"But I really, really want to fight for the Otherworld and —"

"Kent? Ian?" a man's voice sounded from inside the house. "Coming!"

The little boy raced to the porch and disappeared behind a door.

"Well, nice to meet you," said Ian with a smile. "You saved the Otherworld, every one of you."

"Any time," Eric answered. "Ian, we could be friends, and I can visit you and your brother someday. I'm staying in the Otherworld, and I'll be living in the palace."

"Good for you! Lord Zack told us that you're a great Otherworldian."

"It's all true," said Eileen proudly, slapping Eric on the back.

"Hang on, you know Zack?" I asked.

"Of course. He's one of the best Elders the Otherworld's got. Mom had been his apprentice before she became an Elder."

"Ian?" the man's voice shouted again. "Dinner's ready! Hurry up and come back before Kent gobbles up everything!"

"I've got to go. Thank you, thank you!" Ian shook all of our hands before leaving.

"That little boy Kent is so cute!" Clarissa gushed, a dreamy expression on her face.

"Ian's a nice guy," said Daphne, beaming. "I hope I'll get to know him better."

I rolled my eyes. "Oh, come on! Tell me, is teenage romance really that…?"

"Of course," answered Eileen. "You just never seem to get it. What a pity."

"Honestly, I can't picture myself in a relationship. I mean, I've got a whole life of endless possibilities lying ahead of me. I can't imagine having to settle down with a partner and devote my time and attention to him for the rest of my life. I want to be a maiden. Easier, happier, and less complicated for me. I might inherit the kingship in the future, and I'll spend every day doing something meaningful, like improving life for the Otherworldians."

"Oh, but Alexandria! How much you'll miss."

I shrugged. "Not that much."

"But if you don't get married, there won't be a king in the Other—"

"Doesn't matter. I'm not interested in romance. Anyway, we already have two lovebirds flying around us, don't we?"

It took a few seconds for everybody to register my words. Clarissa exchanged an amused look with Daphne. Eileen and Eric were trying not to make eye contact with each other.

"Eileen," began Clarissa, suppressing a grin. "Do you *like* Eric?"

Daphne burst into a fit of giggles while both Eileen and Eric's faces reddened, now the same color as the lovely horizon in the sky.

"Well...Eric's awesome and...and...."

"Let me be honest with all of you," said Eric, coming to her rescue. "Yes, I love Eileen. Everything about her." Then, without warning, he swept her up in an embrace, and they locked lips.

"Now, that's something!" yelled Daphne, clapping her hands. "A first kiss!"

"Wow, romance in our village!" a voice called out from behind us.

I turned around and saw a pretty girl who looked around ten. She had short silky hair the color of chocolate and a round face.

"Oh, um, good evening, Your—"

"Just call me Alexandria," I replied, shaking her hand.

"I'm Samantha, Your—oh, Alexandria, I mean. Was that your first mission?"

I nodded.

Samantha's gaze drifted to the others. "And you're the heiresses of the Creators!"

She took turns to shake hands with Clarissa, Eileen, and Daphne, but not Eric. "You're the son of that Alta, aren't you?"

"He's an Otherworldian now," Eileen retorted.

"Yeah, that's right," I said quickly. Then, deciding to change the topic, I asked her the first question that popped into my mind. "So, Samantha, do you have any brothers or sisters?"

"Oh, yes, I've got a brother, Jacob." Samantha pointed to a tree nearby. Perched on an exceptionally strong branch was an enormous treehouse with a rope ladder dangling from it. "I think he's up there."

"What's that for?" asked Clarissa.

"Jacob and I run a detective agency, and that's our headquarters."

At that moment, a tall boy climbed down the rope ladder.

"That's Jacob," said Samantha. "He just turned eighteen last week. He wants to be a detective, and he's studying at the local high school. I'm ten, and my dream is to join the Elders, like my mom and dad, and work for—"

"Samantha Richardson!" said Jacob with a laugh. "You'll be revealing our vault number and password to your friends at this rate!"

"But they are—"

"Oh, good evening." Jacob smiled at the five of us, and his gaze lingered on my face. "Alexandria, right? Good to see you."

I bowed my head. "What a lovely little sister you have!"

"You mean Sammy? Yeah, I've always enjoyed her company. Oh, by the way, Samantha and I...well, we're your cousins. On your father's side."

"Oh, all right." I grinned at him, "Nice to meet you, cousin."

The fact that a total stranger claimed to be my cousin did not surprise me that much after everything we'd gone through on that crazy mission.

"Jacob, this is Eric, another cousin of mine. On my mother's side."

"Yeah, the son of that witch!"

"Samantha!" Jacob raised his voice. "That's quite enough. Please, if you've got nothing good to say, be quiet."

Sulking, Samantha left, and up to the treehouse she went, the rope ladder swinging wildly beneath her.

"Excuse me. My sister...." Jacob sighed and shook his head. "I'll try to talk some sense into her. But Eric, I want you to know that personally, I think you're a hero."

"Really?" a big smile crossed Eric's face.

"Yes." Jacob gave him a pat on the back. "Just keep being yourself. You stood up to your mother and stayed true to your beliefs. You should be proud."

"Thanks," said Eric, blushing. "Samantha just told us that your parents are both Elders."

Jacob nodded.

"I'll be living in the palace from now on, and I'd like to get to know them."

"Sure. Their names are Sheldon and Juniper Richardson."

"How come you don't live in the palace with them? There are all sorts of fancy stuff in the palace, and I bet anyone would give anything to be allowed in there just for a day."

"Well, you're right, but I prefer living here." Seeing the confusion on our faces, Jacob explained in detail. "You see, life is much more complicated and formal in the palace. It's like being royalty, in a stressing way. For example, I have to mind my table manners every day while having meals in the Purple Room."

"What's the Purple Room?"

"It's sort of like the dining hall of the palace. All of the Elders sit at a long rectangular dining table and have the three meals there with the king and queen every day."

"A long rectangular table?" said Daphne. "But the five of us attended a banquet earlier, and we were free to sit wherever we wanted."

"Banquets are informal parties the king and queen hold from time to time, but it's breakfast, lunch, and dinner I'm talking about. When the food is served, we have to eat slowly, put napkins on our laps, avoid grabbing food with our hands or putting our elbows on the table, and behave like ladies and gentlemen." The more Jacob said, the more frustrated he sounded. "It's awful. What's the meaning of all these silly rules? What's more, I can't stand the vain, snobbish Elders." He started to talk in a hearty, unnatural voice, "Good morning, Lady Annette. Your new hairstyle looks gorgeous! Oh wow, who designed your ball gown? It's the most stylish dress I've ever seen!" Jacob let out a sigh, then continued, this time in his regular voice. "See what I mean? I've got no choice but to fawn on the Elders and pretend to be all respectful and complimentary about them."

"What happens if you don't?"

"They gossip about my parents' upbringing, which is twice as bad. I can't stand it when they do that. But what really irks me about the whole thing is that I have to shape myself into someone who isn't me. I hate pretentious people, and unfortunately, about ninety percent of the Elders are hypocrites. To make matters worse, they scheme against each other. Many of them did horrible things and pinned them on Lady Helen. They're all vying for her position as the Representative Elder, and they've done everything to bring her down. Poisoning the unibirds in the royal stables, fabricating rumors about her...you name it." Jacob shook his head in disgust.

"Poor Helen," said Eric. "No wonder she's always acting so grim and tough."

"Now I can totally understand why you chose not to join the Elders," Clarissa said.

"I'm not even done complaining. There's a dress code for wearing gowns and tuxedos, which I think is ridiculous. You now know why I hate life in the palace. I can't stand everything so decent and perfect, in a suffocating way." Jacob paused for a few seconds before continuing. "Why can't we just relax? Why torture ourselves with all those rules? Life is much simpler and happier here with my sister and grandparents. We don't have fancy meals, but the homey dishes Grandpa cooks taste twice as good as the food in the palace."

"*Homey,*" breathed Eileen. "I love that word. There's no place like home, is there?"

"Someone's getting nostalgic," said Daphne in a singsong voice.

"As much as I love it here, there's definitely no place like home," said Eileen truthfully.

Jacob smiled at her. "Exactly. Home is a place where we're all free to be ourselves. Plus, family members should support each other instead of plotting against them. So, this is why I'd never call the palace my home. Of course, I'm not saying Samantha and I never get into fights, but we get along pretty well in general. We call each other nicknames — I'm Jellycat, and she's Shorty."

"Hey!" Samantha protested from the treehouse. "It's Sammy, not Shorty! I'm going to get you, you moldy jelly!"

"See?" said Jacob. "You don't have to be rich to have a happy life. Simplicity is the key to pure felicity."

A scream of mirth split the air. "Ha! Got you!"

Before anyone realized what had happened, a red ball came flying at Jacob and bonked him on the head.

"You'll pay for that, Shorty!" Jacob hurled it back at the treehouse, narrowly missing the window. He laughed and shook his head. "Would you all like to join us for dinner?"

"Thanks, but we're going back to the mortal world soon," answered Clarissa. "Alexandria's starting a new life with Helen and Daphne with Lilith."

"That's wonderful, Alexandria! Helen's the wisest Elder in the Otherworld, and — "

"She's *already* in love with Helen," Clarissa quipped as Daphne made gagging noises. I rolled my eyes at their immaturity.

"Jellycat!" Samantha's voice shouted. "Have you forgotten about our meeting? Come up here right now!"

"I will if you say it in a nicer way," replied Jacob. "All right, I'm coming, anyway. Bye, heiresses. Eric, Sammy and I visit our parents in the palace every Saturday when the weekly evening banquets are held. So I guess I'll be seeing you there next time!"

"Sure," Eric winked at him. "If I'm lucky enough to get invited by the king and queen."

We waved goodbye to Jacob as he went up the creaky rope

ladder and vanished.

"Simplicity is the key to pure felicity…hmm, I like these words," said Daphne.

"You're just saying that because you're fond of him," giggled Clarissa.

Daphne shook her head. "No, but I think he's very wise."

"He sure is," I agreed. "I'm glad to have him as a cousin."

"Yeah, yeah," said Eileen. "Jacob's great, but I prefer you, Eric."

"Of course, baby. What are you looking at, Clarissa?"

"Some guy over there who's talking to a dogfish."

I looked in Clarissa's direction and saw a pink house with white-framed windows and a red roof. In front of it was a sweet garden that gave off a pleasant sense of tranquility. Neat rows of colorful hydrangeas were nestled in the flowerbeds.

The young man, who was talking with the dogfish, looked about twenty. Fair-haired and blue-eyed, he reminded me vaguely of someone, someone I knew but failed to recall at that moment. His mouth dropped open as he caught sight of us. "Aren't you… the five heroes who saved one billion Otherworldians?"

"Yeah, that's us," I said, grinning.

The man jumped up from his seat and shook our hands with great enthusiasm. "I'm Edward. I can't believe the five of you saved us all, and most importantly, my sister! Mom! Dad! Come quick! It's the heroes who saved her!"

"Your sister?" I said, wondering where all this was headed.

But before he could answer, an elderly couple appeared at the doorstep. "Welcome, welcome!" said the old woman. "Do come in, please! I'm Jenni."

We entered the house, and Jenni handed each of us a bouquet of flowers.

Eileen felt the soft petals with her fingers and planted a kiss on each of them. "Pink roses and purple hydrangeas! What a lovely surprise!"

The old man grinned a toothless smile. "I knew you'd love it."

"Those flowers," said Edward, pointing at our bouquets, "were planted by my sister herself. I knew she'd want the five of you to have them because you saved her life."

"Your sister?" I asked. "Who is she?"

"Evonne Fitzgerald. You've met her, haven't you? She wouldn't have been revived if the Gem of Hope had not been restored. We just got a letter from her."

"You're Evonne's brother?" Clarissa and Daphne exchanged looks of surprise. Eileen stopped examining her flowers and gazed wonderingly at Edward, her big eyes larger than usual.

Just then, the front door opened, and in came Evonne herself. The alluring fragrance of her perfume permeated the house. "I'm home, guys!"

"Evonne!" Jenni gave her a strangling hug. "Oh, Evonne, I never thought—I thought I would never see you again! I'm so glad you're back!"

"There, there, Mom." Evonne planted an affectionate kiss on her mother's cheek. She then greeted her father and brother with big hugs.

The five of us were completely forgotten until Clarissa cleared her throat.

"Clarissa? Oh, you're all here," Evonne suddenly noticed us. Her face went pink. "I thought you were going to meet up with Helen and Lilith at the fountain portal."

"We're meeting them there at seven," I said. "What's the time now?"

"I left the palace at six-forty, and...." Evonne glanced down at her watch. "Oh, it's already seven. You'd better get going. As for you, Eric, Helen told me to keep an eye on you since you're new to the Otherworld. What about staying with me and my family for a while? We could go back to the palace at eight if that's okay with you."

Eric nodded. "Sounds like a great plan."

"Then I'll see you four around," said Evonne. "Thank you so much for everything!"

Evonne and her family waved goodbye to the four of us.

Eric hugged us and kissed Eileen on both cheeks.

"Bye!"

A wave of heat engulfed us as Clarissa, Eileen, Daphne, and I left the house.

"Hey, race you guys to the fountain," said Clarissa, a mischievous grin on her face. "On my count, three...two...one...go!"

Eileen, Daphne, and I took off running, shooting across the street like rockets, but Clarissa got out her scepter lazily, drew a cloud from the sky, and clambered on. "Levitate and accelerate!"

"No fair, cheating!" I yelled.

"Whatever. You want a ride?"

"Why not?"

One by one, we shinnied onto the cloud, and together, we drifted towards our destination.

The blazing fireball high above us had begun its journey toward the horizon. The ombre sky, as if painted by an artist, was pink with purple clouds, orange with the golden sun that beamed jubilantly at us as though celebrating our success. We passed a few unibirds, who saluted us as they caught sight of Clarissa. Finally, our cloud descended as the fountain came into view. Helen and Lilith, both dressed as mortals, were waiting for us.

"That was a dramatic arrival," said Lilith in awe.

"You can say that again," replied Daphne with a smile. "So, what next? We jump into the fountain and wait for it to work its magic?"

"No," said Helen. "You see that big glittering tile over here? Good. All of us will have to climb into the fountain and stand on it. Then, wait for my signal, and shout our destination aloud—the mortal world."

We followed Helen's instructions and got in. She cued us with a nod, and we chorused the name of our destination.

The ground below our feet yawned and swallowed us. Darkness enveloped us in an embrace. I squeezed my eyes shut and held my breath as we fell down, down, down....

Splash!

"Welcome home," announced Lilith.

I clambered out of the fountain and dried everyone's clothes with a fireball. The school was exactly the same as it had been yesterday, moist with purple fog.

No time had gone by in the mortal world since our departure.

I glanced at the others and noticed their scars and wounds had all disappeared. Maybe it was because they had something to do with another world...a fascinating world full of magic. For some reason, I felt a little sad but overwhelmed with excitement at the same time.

"Listen up, everyone," began Helen. "Please come over to my house every day after school to practice fighting. Lilith, Zack, and some of the other Elders will also be there. Don't forget to bring your scepters and weapons along. Now, back to your classes. Alexandria, meet me at the school gates after the last period."

Joy brimmed up in me from head to toe. "Thanks."

"Daphne, come to my office after school, and we'll leave together," said Lilith.

Daphne gave her a thumbs up. "Roger that."

We collected our belongings, which were scattered haphazardly around the fountain, as they had been yesterday. Everything then seemed so far away, yet vivid in my mind.

"Goodbye!" Clarissa and Eileen, who had the same homeroom, headed up the stairs.

"We're leaving as well," said Daphne, her hand raised in farewell.

"Thanks for everything," I added.

Daphne turned to me. "Hey, let's walk to our classrooms together."

I nodded, indescribable happiness bubbling in my heart. Daphne was finally willing to be friends with me. Today was the end of our fourteen years of bitter enmity as well as the beginning of a new friendship.

***

It was a boring day filled with tedious assignments, but I felt enriched inside. During the morning assembly, I drew a timeline of our adventure in my notebook. Clarissa, Eileen, Daphne, and I kept shooting meaningful looks at each other in our English, geography, and language arts classes, which the four of us all had together. Coincidentally...or maybe not. Even my least favorite subject, science, had become more or less tolerable. I spent the whole period indulging in memories of our mission, trying to recall every little detail of it. What questions I had asked the Elders, and what their exact answers were. What my parents had said to me, and every word of response I had uttered.

By the end of the day, I left school with a smile on my face for the first time. The sun grinned at me, reflecting my cheerful mood. I beamed at the iridescent rays of light that showered over me, a sign of my bright, hopeful future.

Helen was standing at the gates. "Ready?"

Decidedly, I nodded. *Yes. I am ready for a new life, ready to accept my true identity, ready to be Alexandria Matilda Richardson.*

As the two of us left school, an earlier memory floated to the surface of my mind. "Helen, is the fountain in our school actually haunted? King Patrick said he charmed the fountain, and the two aquazombies were there on his orders."

"That is correct."

"But then what about the legend of the two lovers? Was it a true story?"

"Oh, that?" Helen barely concealed a grin. "I guess I've got a confession to make. I was the one who cooked up the whole story."

"You did? You had all of us totally fooled! No one would even go ten feet near that thing!"

"I told my students the story to keep them away from the fountain, the portal to the Otherworld. Of course, they passed it on to their friends, and soon, the 'legend' disseminated through the entire school."

"Really? But...but if the story wasn't true, why did the aquazombies say—"

"They were simply acting. You see, it was all a plan between us—the rulers, the aquazombies, and me. Pretty convincing actors, weren't they?"

"With an imagination like that," I said in awe, "you could publish a book."

"Come to think of it, I probably will, one day, after I retire from my position as the Representative Elder. Oh, here we are."

A lovely two-story house in a rosy shade of violet came into view. Pots of purple geraniums bloomed on the windowsills.

"What about my stuff? It's still at the Wilsons'."

"Queen Marianne's delivered them here by magic."

Sure enough, as we made our way through the front door, I spotted a purple suitcase waiting for us in the foyer. A note was attached to it:

From Marianne.

Helen tapped her wand twice on the handle, and it vanished. "I've just transported it to your new room, the first one on your left upstairs. You must be worn out from the mission and all those classes. I suppose you'd like some peace."

"Thanks," I said earnestly.

Helen smiled. "I'm glad to have a housemate. I'm lonely here most of the time."

"Really? You're...not married?" I blurted out without realizing what I'd said. "Oh, excuse me."

Helen shook her head. "It's fine to ask. We are now godmother and goddaughter, and I will hide no secrets from you."

"You know, Helen, I'm also glad that I have someone else to love, apart from my parents."

I mounted a flight of stairs and entered the first room on my left. Beside a bed sat the violet suitcase from Queen Marianne.

"Alexandria, you want some lemonade?" shouted Helen's voice.

"Sure!"

I turned, ready to head downstairs, but a full-length mirror that bore a striking resemblance to Daphne's caught my attention.

Was it all a dream? What if I open my eyes in a moment, only to discover that everything about the Otherworld was merely a dream?

Curious, I edged closer to the mirror and felt its cold, smooth surface. I gazed into it and saw my reflection: the same garishly red hair, the same asymmetrical eyes, the same wide mouth. But something was different — my newfound strength and courage.

Deep down in my heart, I knew I would forever fight in the name of the Otherworld. *Yes, in the name of the Otherworld, the place where I truly belong, where my loyalty lies. My roots, my origin, my pride.*

At that thought, I beamed at my reflection.

Only to see the teenager in the mirror flash a smile of confidence in return for the first time in my life.

Hermione Lee was born and raised in Taiwan, where everyone and everything in her life stimulated her rich imagination and inspired her to write. Although she prefers writing stories in her grandma's quaint, cozy home, she writes anytime and anywhere. To her, words are portals that whisk her to whimsical worlds of magic. When Hermione isn't writing, she indulges in epic tales of fantasy, horror, and adventure; but mostly, she dwells in her reverie.

Hermione's life motto says a lot about her stories: *Fight for what you believe in; believe in what you fight for.* This sentence best represents her journey of becoming a writer. She waged a constant war against invisible enemies— self-doubt, self-discrimination, and of course, countless rejections. However, these struggles only strengthened her will to succeed and pursue her ambition. Along the way, Hermione learned to stick to her goals, have humility and perseverance, and stay loyal to her own beliefs. As a result, her personality is strongly projected on the characters she created; firm, unyielding, and with a thirst to prove themselves.

When Hermione first started writing, she had eyes for only the fame and recognition accompanied by success; however, her opinions have matured greatly during the past few years. She continues to write stories nowadays, but out of sheer interest and passion rather than gaining profit.

CPSIA information can be obtained
at www.ICGtesting.com
Printed in the USA
LVHW090319080921
697225LV00003B/44